THIS TOWN IS DYING TO CELEBRATE

MURDER

at MARDI GRAS

To Sarah,
Hope you Enjoy this
Murder.

Doug Lamplugh

Doug Lamplugh

WILDBLUE
PRESS

WildBluePress.com

MURDER AT MARDI GRAS published by:
WILDBLUE PRESS
P.O. Box 102440
Denver, Colorado 80250

WILDBLUE PRESS is registered at the U.S. Patent and Trademark Offices.

ISBN 978-1-952225-90-1 Trade Paperback
ISBN 978-1-952225-89-5 eBook

Cover design © 2022 WildBlue Press. All rights reserved.

Interior Formatting by Elijah Toten
www.totencreative.com

Book Cover Design by Reata Strickland

MURDER
at MARDI GRAS

L'HISTOIRE DE MOBILE
MARDI GRAS ET LE
CARNAVAL SAISONNIER

For as long as Lent has been a part of Christianity there has been some form of pre-Lenten celebration. Much of the motivation for these celebrations was based upon practicality. Beginning centuries ago in Europe, the Catholic church had established days during Lent to abstain from eating meat. At the time there was no adequate way to preserve meat over an extended period, so there became a need to have a feast to use up stores. From a human behavior standpoint, the customs of fasting and giving up pleasures for forty days also seemed to necessitate a time before the beginning of Lent to gorge oneself and expel excesses. These feasts and celebrations generally took place on the Tuesday before Ash Wednesday, now commonly known as Fat Tuesday for obvious reasons. These excesses originally primarily included such things as large meals, music, and dancing, in more recent years they have grown to include drinking, acting upon sexual desires and even perpetrating crimes, though mostly of a petty nature. While a combination of practicality and the idea of cleansing oneself of desire before the abstinence of Lent may have been the inspiration behind the original celebrations, to outsiders it's the simple appeal of an immense party that has fueled the growth of what residents along the Gulf Coast refer to as Mardi Gras.

Mardi Gras comes to the New World

During the late 17th and early 18th centuries Europeans, particularly the French and Spanish, began to heavily colonize the northern Gulf Coast, bringing many of their traditions with them. No one can say where the first Mardi Gras celebration in the New World occurred, but the cities of Mobile, Alabama and New Orleans, Louisiana have shared the majority of the influence on the evolution of the event. Some believe the first celebration to have been held in 1699 by a French expedition along the mouth of the Mississippi River, south of present-day New Orleans. The expedition leader, Pierre Le Moyne Sieur d'Iberville, did make note of the day that was being celebrated back in France, and named the area Pointe du Mardi Gras in its honor. Some records indicate that the day was observed by a mass service and singing, but nothing like the "celebration" we think of today. D'Iberville would later be the founder of Mobile in 1702. His brother, Jean-Baptiste Le Moyne Sieur de Bienville, who was also on the expedition, would later found the city of New Orleans in 1718.

Mobile's Influence

The first organized celebrations in the New World appear to have begun in Mobile in 1703. At the time, Mobile was the capital of French Louisiana. In 1710, residents of the city used Fat Tuesday to celebrate Bœuf Gras, festival of the fatted ox. This was possibly the first Mardi Gras street procession held in North America.

In 1830, a group of Mobile men led by Michael Kraft took a New Year's Eve party to a whole new level. They stole rakes, hoes, and cowbells from a local store, then preceded to wake as many people in the city as possible, including the mayor. In honor of their first escapade, the group named themselves the Cowbellion de Rakin Society, forming the first masked mystic society in the country, and they continued their celebrations every New Year's Eve. Newspaper reports from 1835 indicate that the Cowbellions may have also thrown a celebration in New Orleans. In 1840, the Cowbellions began another tradition by holding a parade of themed, horse-drawn floats through the streets of Mobile. The concept of a themed parade was later applied to Mardi Gras day by the Krewe of Comus in New Orleans. What many don't know is that the Krewe of Comus, the oldest krewe in New Orleans, was founded in 1857 with help from six members of the Cowbellians who had moved from Mobile. Other Mobile natives have helped form several of New Orleans's other krewes, including the Twelfth Night Revelers, the city's second oldest krewe.

Soon after Comus's first Mardi Gras parades came the tragedy of the American Civil War. During the years of fighting, Carnival was not celebrated in Mobile or New Orleans. In 1866, a Mobile native named Joseph Stillwell Cain decided that the citizens of the city needed something to take their minds off the losses suffered during the Civil War. For Mardi Gras that year, Cain dressed as a Chickasaw chief named Slacabamorinico, a fictional character, and used a mule-drawn coal wagon to parade through the streets. The parade was not only meant to boost morale in the city, but also to insult the occupying Union troops, because the Chickasaw Indians had never surrendered to U.S. forces. Cain continued celebrating throughout the years and helped found many of Mobile's mystic societies, including the Order of Myths in 1867, the oldest continuous parading society in Mobile. He took part in each year's celebration until his death in 1904. Joe Cain Day is now celebrated every year on the Sunday before Fat Tuesday, when Mobile residents convene at Cain's gravesite at the Church Street Cemetery, behind the Mobile Public Library. They celebrate by dancing, singing, and drinking in an effort to wake his soul, thus the origin of the phrase "Raise Cain." The Joe Cain procession is also known as the "people's parade," as anyone is allowed to march, not just members of a mystic society.

Although Mobile may not be able to claim the first observance of Mardi Gras in the New World, the city can certainly lay claim to the first organized celebrations. Throughout the years, Mobile has made so many important contributions to the Carnival season, many of them firsts, that the city has earned the nickname "Mother of Mystics."

Mardi Gras Today

Mardi Gras is celebrated today throughout many cities and communities along the northern Gulf Coast and is fast spreading to other regions of the country. Carnival celebrations continue throughout the world from Europe to Rio de Janeiro. The parade season along the Gulf Coast generally begins in January and always culminates on Fat Tuesday. There are dozens of krewes and mystic societies in both Mobile and New Orleans, most of which present a ball and a parade in which lavish *papier-mâché* floats costing thousands of dollars will dispense thousands more dollars' worth of "throws." During the parade season, Mobile may welcome more than one million revelers, New Orleans more than twice that many, so if you want to visit make sure to plan ahead. There is only one rule during Carnival: do as the locals do and *"laissez les bons temps rouler."* However, as with any event involving large crowds, one should always be aware of one's surroundings. The celebration draws a unique cross section of the population, from priests and bluebloods to crack dealers and whores. In addition, the ingestion of large amounts of alcohol can always make a stable situation fall apart. Although Mardi Gras is a fun celebration that is generally safe, one must be careful and remember: you never know who you could be standing next to…

CHAPTER 1 – THE CRIME

"Members of the jury," Mobile County Circuit Judge William Wellborn began his charge to the panel, "in any jury trial there are, in effect, two judges. I am one of the judges; the other is the jury. It is my duty to preside over the trial and decide what evidence is proper for your consideration. It is also my duty at the end of the trial to explain to you the rules of law that you must follow and apply in arriving at your verdict.

"First, I will give you some general instructions which apply in every case. For example, instructions about burden of proof and how to judge the believability of witnesses. Then I will give you some specific rules of law about this particular case, and finally I will explain to you the procedures you should follow in your deliberations."

Detective William Robert Boyett looked over at the defendant. He wondered how the man sitting twenty feet away could possibly have committed the horrific crime he was being charged with, and no one figured it out. Obviously, the fragmented criminal justice system was not working—until now.

The defendant stared straight ahead at Judge Wellborn, his face an emotionless mask as the judge continued, "You, as jurors, are the judges of the facts. But in determining what actually happened—that is, in reaching your decision as to the facts—it is your sworn duty to follow all the rules of law as I explain them to you."

"You have no right to disregard or give special attention to any one instruction, or to question the wisdom or correctness of any rule I may state to you. You must not substitute or follow your own notion or opinion as to what the law is or ought to be. It is your duty to apply the law as I explain it to you, regardless of the consequences."

As Judge Wellborn continued, Detective Boyett's mind began to wander back over the investigation that had brought him to this point, into this courtroom today. He thought about how the investigation had begun, and the people he'd met during the two decades.

This investigation had also introduced him to people and places he'd never even heard of—towns and cities that ran the spectrum of size, economics, and friendliness: Blowing Rock, North Carolina; Youngstown, Ohio; Hattiesburg, Mississippi; and New Orleans, Louisiana. Boyett also thought about the differences in the police officers and public officials he'd met and the different criminal justice systems he'd dealt with. He was glad he worked in Mobile, Alabama. He wondered how he could have ever known what was coming into his life on February 28, 2006, and how it would consume him.

That was the night he got the fateful call that made him the lead investigator on this homicide, which would eventually become one of the most publicized investigations in Alabama history.

Boyett thought back again to that night and the events leading up to this day. February 28, 2006, was Mardi Gras day. Not just any Mardi Gras day, but the biggest Mardi Gras Mobile had ever had. The size of the 2006 Mobile Mardi Gras crowds were primarily the result of the devastation Hurricane Katrina had wreaked on New Orleans and the Mississippi Gulf Coast in August 2005. With the downsized Mardi Gras celebrations in New Orleans and cities along the Mississippi coast canceling Mardi Gras completely, Mobile had experienced a large influx of revelers who normally would have visited New Orleans or places like Gulfport or Biloxi. That influx of outsiders was the primary reason Mobile was in the news at the national level relating to this case.

Mardi Gras was a tradition in Mobile that went back to the reconstruction days after the Civil War. While under military occupation by the Union Army after the Civil War, a local citizen, Joe Cain, dressed up like an Indian and paraded down Government Street on horseback, throwing candy and treats to the children. Although the occupying Union Army disapproved, modern day Mardi Gras was born.

Thirty-six years old at the time of the murder, Boyett had spent fifteen years with the Mobile Police Department, yet although he'd been in the Mobile area his whole life, had never been invited to a Mardi Gras ball. The closest he'd ever come to attending a Mardi Gras ball was to work security for the police department, standing outside the Mobile Civic Center while one was occurring. During Mardi Gras season, most police officers in Mobile City and Mobile County were scheduled twelve to sixteen hours per day to handle the large crowds of people and frivolity that surrounded the celebration.

In Mobile, Mardi Gras was tame in comparison to New Orleans. Mobile billed itself as a "Family Mardi Gras," where drunks and nudity were not tolerated. The city still produced great parades, offering a minimum of one a night and sometimes more on weekends during the two weeks that led up to Mardi Gras day, also known as Fat Tuesday.

These parades brought anywhere from 10,000 to 100,000 people downtown to scream and wave their arms in an effort to attract the attention of the people on the Mardi Gras floats that disbursed "throws." "Throws" were the variety of beads, plastic coins, cups, candy, and "moon pies" that were flung from the many floats to the crowds. Kids and adults alike seemed to do stupid things in order to get a string of beads worth about two cents. It was not unusual to see people dressed in formal attire lining the parade route, or on the other end of the spectrum, men dressed as women or women in bikinis, all in an effort to attract the attention of the "throwers" on the floats.

Some parade watchers came carrying crab nets, large baskets, and even homemade basketball goals and similar homemade contraptions to attract more throws or make snagging the "throws" easier. Either way, Boyett and most of the Mobile Police Department thought it was a holiday they would just rather pass on.

During Mardi Gras in 2006, Boyett had been given a variety of "special duties," including working security for several of the Mardi Gras balls, working several parade routes and, on Mardi Gras day, handling security for King Felix and the Queen Athena during the day.

The coronation of the king was a tradition in Mobile that occurred on Fat Tuesday and the parade where King Felix and the court rode was an annual event. The coronation of the king and queen was a blue blood event, in which old money families worked for years to get a member of their family selected by the Mardi Gras Association as king or queen or even members of the court.

Back on February 28 of 2006, Boyett had worked the coronation and parade of the king and queen, starting the day at 8:00 a.m. and getting done with the Mardi Gras detail at about 6:00 p.m. After his Mardi Gras duties, Boyett went back to the station, where he assumed his normal investigative shift as the evening "duty" detective from 4:00 p.m. to 12 a.m.

About 11:00, Boyett was called and asked to report to a vacant lot at St. Louis and D'Iberville Streets, where a body had been found in a parking lot adjacent to a warehouse. The scene was about five blocks from the nearest point of the parade route and about seven blocks from Bienville

Square, which was the center point of Mobile's Mardi Gras festivities.

The initial call had come from Steve Brown, the owner of the parking lot, who utilized the lot as a daily parking lot for people who worked in the downtown area. On a normal day, drivers would park and leave coins in an honor box mounted on a pole. Brown came by every morning to ensure that users had deposited monies in the honor box and to collect the monies.

On Mardi Gras day, Brown had sold the spaces for ten dollars each and filled the lot by noon. He reported that he'd packed about a hundred cars in the lot and left after it was filled. At about 10:00 that evening, he'd returned to clean debris out of the lot, so that the normal daily customers would be able to park the next morning. Mardi Gras revelers often held tailgating type parties in the parking lots, setting up barbeque grills, picnic tables, and sometimes beer kegs. Usually by the end of the day, the lots were littered extensively.

Brown reported arriving about ten at night and picking up trash and litter. He reported seeing a rolled up carpet over on the side of the lot, but had concentrated on picking up bottles, cans, and other trash for almost an hour before going over and attempting to drag the carpet to his pickup truck. It was then that he'd noticed the weight of the carpet and a human foot protruding from the far end.

When Boyett responded to the scene, he noted that what appeared to be a woman's body was rolled up in a large piece of carpet and pretty well concealed. It was only visible if viewed from one end of the rolled carpet, where the foot could be seen. The first officers on the scene thought it might be a mannequin, but after touching the cold, stiff foot, they'd realized it was actually human.

Boyett's mind cleared. He rubbed a hand over his face and through his short brown hair and remembered he was sitting at the prosecution table next to Assistant District

Attorney Gloria Wood. Judge Wellborn was still charging the jury.

He knew that Judge Wellborn's jury charge was going to be long, even though the charge was a one-count, first-degree murder charge. The district attorney, Barry Mueller, had wanted to keep the charge simple and clean. Mueller, who had not been the district attorney when the crime occurred, hoped that would force the jury to convict the defendant of the appropriate charge and that there would be fewer arguments during the trial and on appeal. Mueller thought the evidence was so overwhelming that any jury would convict. Even if the defendant walked in Alabama, he still faced further charges in other states and jurisdictions.

As the judge's voice droned on, Boyett's mind returned to the crime scene.

***

When he arrived at the vacant parking lot, Boyett checked the foot and decided that the crime scene needed to be preserved, and a crime scene team was called. He had the patrol units rope off the area with crime scene tape, gloved up, and began taking photographs of the carpet and the parking lot. The body contained in the carpet is what was often referred to as a "packaged corpse," meaning that part of the crime scene was, in fact, the "package"—in this case, the carpet. In many cases, the "package" would yield more evidence than the body itself.

Boyett placed a call to the major in charge of investigations, followed by calls to the captain and lieutenant to inform them that the city had experienced its second homicide of the new year.

He assigned several of the patrolmen who were on the scene to canvass the area for witnesses, clues, and evidence. As these patrolmen began checking an area of about four blocks in each direction, several other detectives and the lieutenant arrived. The lieutenant of the detective squad, John Zumwalt, had recently been assigned to the detective bureau after the prior lieutenant retired at the end of December. Zumwalt had transferred over from the traffic unit in January. Many of the detectives in the bureau did not believe that Zumwalt was the best choice to run a squad, considering he'd never served in the detective bureau and the most complicated investigations he'd performed or overseen involved traffic accidents. Sensing this, Zumwalt was hesitant to second-guess his detectives, and he tried to utilize their expertise and experiences in making his command decisions. This homicide was the second to occur since his arrival in the detective division.

After the arrival of the crime scene team and the Alabama Department of Forensic Sciences (ADFS) team from the medical examiner's office, the team spent most of the night photographing, measuring, and recording every detail associated with where and how the body had been found. As the crime scene was unraveled, the victim was determined to be a white female, semi-nude, in her mid-twenties, with blond hair. It appeared she'd been dressed for Mardi Gras, wearing numerous strings of beads. There was no identification found with or near the body. A call was placed to police headquarters to determine if the description matched any recently reported missing persons, but it did not. There appeared to be some marks around the victim's neck, which indicated that she might have been strangled.

Detective Boyett and Lieutenant Zumwalt consulted with several of the other detectives who had arrived, as well as the Alabama Department of Forensic Sciences personnel. Boyett requested that the carpet be scanned for bodily fluids and vacuumed for the existence of any hair or human remains that might be used in a DNA test. The ADFS promised to begin the autopsy the next morning and to call as soon as the results were available.

The patrol units working the neighborhood canvass reported back to Boyett about 2:30 a.m. None of the patrolmen had found anyone with any information that was vital. One patrolman did mention that there were surveillance cameras about six blocks down the street on one of the federal buildings and that with any luck, the cameras might have picked up a vehicle or people walking in the area after the festivities had ended.

A huddle of the officers was held at about 4:30 a.m. It was agreed that everyone would head home and get a few hours' sleep before reporting in at the office at about 10:00 a.m. Boyett was past tired and drove home wondering where the next day would take him. He arrived home just after 5:00 a.m. and set the alarm on his wristwatch for 9:00 a.m. He left a note on the table for his wife, asking her not to wake him as he was heading back into work at 10:00 a.m. He then retired to the recliner in the den, so as not to wake his wife, who would be getting up in a little over an hour to get the kids off to school.

Boyett was awakened by the alarm on his wristwatch. After jumping up to do a quick shower and shave, he was dressed and grabbing a banana and cup of coffee on the way out the door by 9:22. The drive to downtown to the police department would take about thirty minutes in morning traffic. As Boyett was pulling out of his driveway, he reached for his cell phone and began making calls. His first call was to see if there had been any reports of missing persons filed since this morning or any way of further identifying the victim.

Boyett knew that in most homicides, the victim knew their killer, so associates were the first place he should look. As of 9:35 a.m., there still was not a report of any missing persons that might match the victim. His second call was to the Alabama Department of Forensic Sciences to see if the autopsy had been scheduled. He hated attending autopsies, but he thought it helped him understand specifics about the cause of death. He learned that the autopsy was scheduled for 2:00 p.m. He told the receptionist to leave a message that he would be there.

Upon arrival at police headquarters, Boyett went into the detective squad room where Lieutenant Zumwalt was already milling around with several other detectives from his squad, as well as Major Coachman, the commander of investigations. Coachman was telling Zumwalt that this homicide was going to be big news due to it occurring on Mardi Gras day, and that the victim was probably a visitor. Coachman said he'd already briefed the chief of police and that the department's public information officer was coming over to get information to try to downplay the event when the media called.

When Coachman left Zumwalt, Boyett informed Zumwalt of his telephone conversations during the ride into the station. He told Zumwalt that the autopsy was scheduled for 2:00

Zumwalt pulled Boyett aside. "Do you usually attend autopsies?" he asked Boyett.

"Boss, it makes it a lot easier to see the procedure and understand what happened, than to just read about it," replied Boyett. "Not everyone goes, but I find it allows me to ask questions in person, to clarify the details concerning the cause of death. That information usually helps me when I'm preparing affidavits for arrest and search warrants later in the case."

Lieutenant Zumwalt nodded. "I understand. Remember, I'm new to this game and just want to understand why we do certain things certain ways."

"Ever been to an autopsy, lieutenant? Wanna come? Might help you understand what we do during these cases."

Zumwalt replied, "Maybe I will. Let me check my schedule. I'll follow your lead on this case, Three B. You know a lot more about what you're doing and why than I do. If I have any questions, I'll ask. Other than that, you tell me what you need to solve this case, and I'll make sure you get it."

"Thanks, lieutenant," Boyett replied. "I'd better get some guys together and see what we can find out about who this girl was and why someone killed her."

"Let me know what you need. I'll let you know if I can make that autopsy," Lieutenant Zumwalt said.

With that, Boyett headed to the squad bay, where he called a huddle of available investigators.

The squad was made up of six detectives who primarily worked homicides but also shooting cases that were serious and could have resulted in death. The detective division was made up of numerous different units under the command of Major Coachman. Within the detective division were numerous other units including the narcotics squad, crimes against property, crimes against persons (such as rape, robbery, etc.) and the major crimes unit, which included homicides and shootings that could result in homicide. As Boyett called the huddle, all five investigators currently assigned to the squad, including Boyett, seated themselves around the squad table. The sixth position was currently vacant as the previous member had retired at the end of last December and had not yet been replaced. Replacements usually occurred twice a year, when promotions and transfers were announced, unless the position was considered critical.

Boyett started the briefing. "Well, we're no further along than when we left the scene this morning. The autopsy is set for 2:00 p.m. and I'm going to be there all afternoon into the evening. We still have no ID on the victim. Let's figure out what we can do, awaiting an ID on the victim."

Detective Bobby Moyer piped up, "How about I go back over and check out the crime scene area again in the daylight? See if there's anything we might have missed last night?"

"Sounds like a plan, Bobby," replied Boyett. He addressed Detective Mike Samson, a strapping African

American with several years' experience in the Mobile Police Department. "Mike, you used to be on the U.S. Marshal's fugitive task force. Go over to the courthouse and see if you can view or get copies of the surveillance tapes for yesterday, up till 10:00 last night."

Samson looked at Boyett with concern all over his face. "Sure, Three B, but I'm not sure it'll be the marshals who have them. It might be the General Services Administration. If it's the GSA, we may have to fight an uphill battle with the federal bureaucracy. Back when I was on the task force, it took eight months for me to get an entry card to get into the federal building garage. It was a nightmare."

Boyett thought for a minute before addressing J.T. Palmer. "J.T., you and I will go over and see Michael O'Brien right now to grease the wheels for any court orders or subpoenas that may be needed." He'd chosen Palmer because Palmer had been in the detective squad for almost ten years and had a great relationship with the district attorney. The relationship between Palmer and the D.A. spanned back almost ten years when Palmer often made cutting edge cases and Michael O'Brien, then an assistant district attorney, often prosecuted them.

Back in those days, O'Brien had often called Palmer to get ideas on how detectives in neighboring departments should be working cases and to get advice on strategy for prosecuting cases. Palmer had so much experience with the Mobile defense bar, he could often figure out what different lawyers in the area were going to hinge their defense on. From his many trials, he knew which ones would attack the technical evidence, which ones would go after the credibility of witnesses, and which ones would just stay late at the bar the night before trial days and wing it in the morning.

The advantage Palmer had over the many assistant district attorneys working for O'Brien was that he had longevity on the prosecution side. Most assistant district attorneys were with the office a few years before joining the *Dark Side* and beginning defense work.

"Jim, can you hang here and handle any calls that come in on this case?" Boyett asked Detective Jim Roberts.

"Sure, Three B," replied Roberts. Roberts was a thirty-one-year veteran of the Mobile Police Department. Known for being slow but adequate in his duties, Roberts was well liked, which made his slow speed bearable. He was now the most senior officer, by longevity, in the department. His assignment to this squad was based on his having been Major Coachman's training officer in 1979 and on Coachman's platoon for the first five years of Coachman's career. He and Coachman not only got along, but Roberts was the godfather of one of Coachman's children.

By 10:45 a.m., the detectives were out scouring the city, following up on their specific assignments. Boyett and Palmer drove over to the district attorney's office. At the reception area Mary, the receptionist, buzzed them in.

"Hi, J.T.," she said.

"Is Mike in?" J.T. asked.

"I know he's around the office somewhere," Mary replied. "If you head back to his office, I'll tell Nancy to find him for you."

Palmer and Boyett headed toward the back of the office. The Mobile County District Attorney's office was located on the twelfth floor of the county office tower in downtown Mobile. O'Brien's rear corner office had a great view of the Mobile River and waterfront.

Boyett nudged J.T. "I wish I had the juice you have around here. Sometimes I wait in the reception area for half an hour just to see an assistant D.A."

J.T. whispered, "Wait till this case is over. Do a good job and they'll know who you are too."

Walking back toward O'Brien's corner office, Palmer and Boyett passed several paralegals, each greeting Palmer with a smile and a good word.

"Hi, J.T."

"Good morning, J.T."

"How's it going, J.T.?"

Boyett began to feel like he was in the presence of a superstar—with his wavy blond hair and natural athletic build, Palmer certainly looked the part. He also remembered that's why he brought him. He knew Palmer could get access and ensure that O'Brien assigned the best assistant D.A. to the case and grease wheels that even Major Coachman couldn't.

Arriving at O'Brien's office, O'Brien's secretary, Nancy, greeted them. "He's on the way down from the County Commissioner's Office. He had to go fight some budgetary battles before next week's budget meetings."

"No problem, Nancy," said Palmer. "Is it OK if we go into his office and sit down?"

"Sure, J.T.," replied Nancy.

Palmer and Boyett went into the district attorney's office. Palmer motioned Boyett over to the east side window to take in the view. From the north side of the office, they could see the area of St. Louis and D'Iberville about fifteen blocks away.

The area held mostly one and two-story warehouses and vacant lots. But with redevelopment of downtown Mobile, the renaissance had not quite reached that area yet. Boyett believed that it would; it was only a matter of time.

A voice came from the doorway. "Morning, J.T."

Palmer and Boyett turned to see the district attorney entering the room.

"Hi, Mike," replied Palmer. "Mike, do you know Three B?"

"I've seen him around, although I don't think we've had the pleasure of actually meeting. "Hi, Three B," said O'Brien. They shook hands. "That's an interesting name, Three B," he commented. "How'd you get it?"

Boyett responded, "Well, my parents named me William Robert Boyett, which growing up became Billie Bob Boyett, which in this business got shortened to Three B."

"Makes perfect sense," said O'Brien, nodding. "Well, what can I do for you two today?"

"Mike," started Palmer, "we had our second homicide of the year last night. A female Mardi Gras reveler, found dead off St. Louis Street just before midnight."

"Think it was a robbery?" asked O'Brien.

"I doubt it. The victim was a twenty-something female. It appeared she'd been at the parades. From what we could see last night, I suspect a sexual assault. Not sure what we have yet or even any identification. We wanted to ask you to assign one of your more experienced assistants on it now, because we expect to need some subpoenas and court orders as part of the investigation. We also may need to move fast on some search warrants, depending on where the evidence takes us."

"Not a problem, J.T. Let me figure out who I have that has the time to devote to it. You know we have several major trials starting this week and next week. Can I call you on your cell when I assign it?" O'Brien asked Palmer.

"Well, actually Three B has the lead on this case. I'm in a support role, but I'll be working with him through it," Palmer replied.

"Sure, J.T.," said O'Brien; obviously disappointed that J.T. was not the lead investigator. "Three B, will you give Nancy your cell number, so she can call when I make the assignment?"

"Sure." said Boyett

"Thanks, Mike," said Palmer. "We'd better get out and beat the bushes and try to catch a perp."

"Go get 'em, guys," said O'Brien as Palmer and Boyett departed the office.

On the way out, Boyett stopped and gave Nancy his cell number. He was somewhat disappointed that had

Palmer been the lead investigator, O'Brien would have personally called him, but now that he (Boyett) was the lead investigator, the call would come from the secretary. It was obvious that much of what got done in the criminal justice system was based on who you knew, not what you knew.

During the drive back to the department, Boyett's cell phone rang. It was Lieutenant Zumwalt. Zumwalt confirmed he would be available to attend the autopsy. This was a first for the detective squad—a new lieutenant who recognized his inexperience and was willing to start at the beginning. Boyett told Zumwalt to meet him at the squad room by 1:30 p.m. in order to go to the autopsy.

"How about heading over to the crime scene to see if we notice anything different before grabbing lunch?" Palmer suggested after Boyett ended his call to Zumwalt.

"Good idea," agreed Boyett.

As they drove toward St. Louis Street, Palmer asked Boyett, "What are you thinking about our victim?"

Boyett replied, "Maybe she was just another reveler who met the wrong guy. What's confusing is why no one has reported her missing yet. Mardi Gras had been over since midnight last night, and most people not showing up at home or work would have been missed."

Over on St. Louis Street, they walked up and down for several blocks, looking along the parking lots and walking through alleys. This part of town was scattered with residences, but it was mostly made up of older warehouses and empty paved lots that were used as overflow lots for downtown parking. After forty-five minutes, the men agreed there wasn't anything noticeable that had not been found. It was time for lunch.

Lunch in Mobile can range from a business affair at places like the Magnolia Club for the bluebloods in the country club crowd, to a country-style buffet at places like the Back Porch for the worker type. Palmer and Boyett choose the Back Porch or "the Porch," as it was called by regulars. The Porch was an all you could eat buffet located in an old house a few blocks from downtown. Operated by Miss Angeline Windham, the Porch had been in operation for over fifty years and was a regular haunt for police and firemen and other government workers. The Porch consisted of the original dining room being converted to a buffet serving area, and the living room and parlor being converted to dining rooms. The kitchen had been improved and enlarged and performed its duty well. The rear porch, which had been expanded, also served as an outside dining area, thus the name.

Boyett and Palmer arrived just after noon and the place was already full. Today's menu consisted of fried chicken, jambalaya, and homemade seafood gumbo. Sides always included a variety of vegetables and corn bread. Desserts were usually home-made pies and cakes. While they were retrieving their first portions, Sam McKenna, a local newspaper reporter, spotted Palmer and Boyett.

"Hey, guys," exclaimed McKenna, "I hear there was a homicide last night. Anything you can tell me?"

Palmer frowned at McKenna and shook his head. "Sam, you know you'll have to contact the P.I.O. on that. We're not allowed to make comments concerning active investigations or anything like that."

"I know, fellas," said McKenna. "I was just hoping for a tidbit of info, because no one wants to call me back."

"Well, keep trying, Sam." Palmer gave McKenna a knowing look. "Something should be coming out soon."

Palmer and Boyett sat down at the only available table out on the rear porch. Both had gotten the seafood gumbo, corn bread, and sweet tea. Miss Windham's seafood gumbo usually contained most everything the sea had to offer— some variation of crab, scallops, shrimp, oysters, fish, and crawfish tails. Added to a spicy roux and served hot over rice, it made for a Gulf Coast delight.

Corn bread and seafood gumbo, thought Boyett as he munched. *The only thing better would be a cold beer to go along with it.*

As Boyett and Palmer were enjoying the gumbo, Boyett's cell phone went off again.

This time it was Samson. "Where you guys at?"

"Over at the Porch," replied Boyett. "What's up?"

Samson gave Boyett a synopsis of his meeting at the U.S. Marshal's office. "I went about the surveillance film. They confirmed that the cameras are on a timed loop that writes over itself every twenty-four hours. The problem is that the GSA controls it, and they're out of Atlanta. I have a name and number for the GSA supervisor, but the Marshals doubt the GSA will be very helpful as they're not *real cops.*"

Boyett responded, " Just see if you can get that tape. If it starts re-writing before we can get it, we might lose some valuable evidence."

"I know, that's why I'm letting you know. I'm on it 100 percent, Three B," Samson said.

"Thanks, let me know what happens. If you get to about 2:00 and can't get any cooperation, call J.T. He'll run and get a court order from the D.A.'s office. Just make sure we have someone to serve it on."

"Will do, Three B," replied Samson. With that the telephone conversation ended, and Boyett went back to eating gumbo.

Palmer looked at Boyett. "What have you got me doing this afternoon?"

"Not sure yet, J.T., but Samson may need a court order to get the surveillance tape from the federal building. He says the GSA is in charge of the security of the courthouse and he can't reach the guy in charge in Atlanta. I told him if he can't get cooperation by 2:00, to get with you and you can get a court order for the tape."

"That should be interesting, serving a court order on a federal police supervisor." Palmer laughed. Both went back to eating the seafood gumbo, then moved in for seconds.

Arriving back at the detective division, Detective Boyett looked at his watch. One-thirty, where was Zumwalt? He wanted to give the lieutenant the benefit of the doubt, but he also knew it was at least twenty minutes over to the morgue. Boyett debated whether to call the lieutenant on his cell phone or just take off without him. He decided to head for the garage and to call while enroute.

Zumwalt answered on the first ring. "Sorry, Three B, I'm on the way, I got called to the chief's office."

"I understand, Lieutenant. Meet me in the parking lot. We have to run, or the medical examiners people might get mad at us," replied Boyett.

They met at Boyett's car and took off for the medical examiner's office.

While driving, Boyett got another telephone call, this time from Jim Roberts, who was still minding the store back in the detective bureau. "Three B, I think we might have something on your victim."

"Really? What?"

"A patrol unit just arrived over at the Magnolia Hotel, over on Church Street. It seems there was a young female that checked in on Saturday, was due to check out this morning. Cleaning lady went to clean up the room and found most of the lady's belongings still there. No sign of her. The patrol unit thinks they have her car still in the lot too," Roberts explained. "What do you want me to do?"

"Can you go and hold down the fort?" asked Boyett. "Keep everything secure for the crime scene team, until we know whether this is our victim's room or not."

"OK. I'll head there and secure the scene right now," Roberts replied.

"What have we got, Three B?" asked Zumwalt.

"Possible victim from the Magnolia Hotel on Church Street. She was due to check out this morning and never did. Everything she owns is still in the room, but there's no sign of her. I'm betting this is our victim," Boyett explained. "Can you call over to crime scene and see if they can get copies of the victim's pictures over to Roberts to see if anyone there can identify this victim?"

"Sure," said Zumwalt, who got on his cell phone and started making calls.

Upon arrival at the morgue, Boyett and Zumwalt were taken from the reception area to the post examining room. The room was cold and sterile, somewhat like an operating room, but with more stainless steel. While awaiting the medical examiner, Dr. Robinson, and his technician, Boyett's cell phone rang.

It was Roberts again. He told Boyett that the desk clerk at the Magnolia Hotel had just identified a photo of the deceased as July Marcial from Blowing Rock, North Carolina.

Boyett decided that the autopsy would have to be done without Zumwalt and him. They needed to get over to the Magnolia Hotel and supervise the crime scene. He told Roberts to hold down the fort, that he was on the way. Just as he was explaining to the receptionist that he and Zumwalt had to leave, Dr. Robinson appeared. Boyett apologized for the hasty departure, and Dr. Robinson promised to contact him later in the day or early the next day to give him the cause of death and any other important data that was found during the autopsy.

During the drive over to the Magnolia Hotel, Boyett's telephone rang again. This time it was Mike Samson.

Samson informed Boyett that he'd finally gotten up with the GSA supervisor in Atlanta. The GSA supervisor had agreed to secure the original tape and copy it, but he'd said that he couldn't turn over the original tape without a court order. He said he'd made arrangements to get a copy of the tape from GSA. Samson said that the copy of the tape would arrive within two days and would be viewable by Friday.

Upon arrival at the Magnolia Hotel, Boyett and Zumwalt were met by Roberts and J.T. Palmer, who had come from the detective bureau. Roberts informed Boyett that the front desk clerk had identified the victim and that one of the housekeepers also related that she had information, although he had not taken a statement from either.

Boyett, with Zumwalt tagging along, began giving assignments. Several uniformed officers who were at the scene were assigned to guard the victim's room while awaiting the crime scene team. Palmer and Roberts were requested to interview all the guests to determine if anyone had observed the victim or any visitors to the victim's room. Boyett and Zumwalt headed for the office to interview the front desk clerk and housekeeping.

Boyett learned from the front desk that July Marcial had given an address on Tower Road in Blowing Rock, N.C. and that she'd booked her room through an internet travel service about a month before Mardi Gras. She listed herself as being the only guest staying in the room and no one at the desk knew of Marcial having friends staying at the hotel. Marcial had pre-paid for the room using a credit card. She'd also listed a 2004 Honda as her vehicle; this Honda was parked in the parking lot, a few spaces from the room. No one at the front desk remembered anything specific about Marcial, except at check in. There had been no complaints of loud noises or music or even contact with the front desk after she checked in.

Housekeeping reported that Marcial had not been in her room any of the days when housekeeping arrived. Maria Sanchez, the housekeeper on Mardi Gras day, reported that she'd seen Marcial leave the hotel as she was cleaning a room a couple doors down the corridor. Sanchez said that she saw Marcial walking into the parking lot, where she met a white male and walked toward downtown. Sanchez stated to the best of her recollection the white male was thirty-something and just appeared to be a normal-looking guy wearing beads and a Mardi Gras hat.

As Boyett finished the interview with Sanchez, the crime scene team was arriving at the Magnolia Hotel. He told them, "Right now, we have no evidence concerning the perpetrator of the murder. We've just identified the victim. I want you to go over this room and her car with a fine-toothed comb. We need to locate something that will lead us to the perp in this case. Make this search thorough."

Meanwhile, Palmer and Roberts were busy knocking on doors and interviewing guests. Unfortunately, they found that the majority of the guests had just checked in that day, and that most who had been at the hotel over Mardi Gras had already checked out. They headed to the front desk to request a list of all guests who had been at the hotel between Friday and Wednesday. By this time, the hotel was abuzz with activity and police vehicles. As Palmer and Roberts headed for the office, the first news van pulled up— Eyewitness News, Channel 21.

Charles Holland, the hotel's general manager who had arrived shortly after the police, was standing at the front of the office, expressing his concern about bad publicity. He complained that the police were attracting too much attention to his hotel and that it would result in losing business.

J.T. Palmer tried to explain that he would ensure that the media knew the Magnolia Hotel was not the scene of the murder, but that the victim had stayed there and that the crime scene technicians were looking for clues to further the investigation. Holland began making statements that maybe the police should vacate the premises immediately and take the media with them. By this time, the news reporters were descending on the hotel parking lot, cameras in hand. When Palmer broached the subject of obtaining the guest list from the Mardi Gras day from Holland, the middle-aged manager exploded.

"You're ruining my business!" he shouted, his face becoming redder with each word. "You don't have the right to obstruct my parking lot!" Holland continued yelling at Palmer, insisting that the guest list was private and that he wouldn't allow his guests to be harassed by the police.

Palmer backed away from Holland. He realized that getting the list voluntarily was not going to be an option.

Palmer stepped into the parking lot and placed a call to Michael O'Brien. "Mike, we're down at the Magnolia Hotel. We've identified the victim of last night's homicide. The crime scene team is here and working. Channel 21 just showed up. The manager is getting mad at us. He's concerned about bad publicity. We're going to need a court order to get a list of all the guests who were here over the weekend, so we can interview them. And if things deteriorate any further, we may need to get a search warrant to continue the crime scene search."

O'Brien thought for a minute. "Hang on, J.T., I'm going to send Gloria Wood to your scene. She's going to get the case. She's young, aggressive, and smart. She needs to chalk a big one up under her belt. I'd just decided to assign this to her about an hour ago. Let me get her in, brief her, and send her out to you."

"Thanks, Mike," was Palmer's reply. "Tell her I'll be waiting in the parking lot." He went to find Boyett, who was outside of Marcial's room. Palmer reported the incident with Holland and the subsequent telephone call with O'Brien.

"Do you know Wood?" asked Boyett.

"I know of her. Never worked with her. She's young, but she's smart, and she has a good reputation as a hard worker," replied Palmer. "I think she'll be for us, as opposed to the many that seem to be against us."

"Well, that's a plus. I only hope she's ready for a long, drawn-out investigation," said Boyett. He continued, "What standing does the manager have to kick us out?"

Palmer laughed. "He manages the place!"

Boyett rethought. "That's not what I mean, J.T. If we refuse to leave, he has no standing to file a motion to suppress any evidence we recover."

Palmer thought for a minute. "Well, that's technically true. He hasn't told us to stop processing the room yet. Although I think we could still introduce the evidence, it would only give the defense fodder in the case to muddy up the waters during trial. I think we'll leave it to Wood to work out."

Zumwalt, listening to this exchange, stepped up. "Let me go talk to the manager. Send Wood in when she gets here. Maybe I can soothe this guy down somewhat."

"Sure, Lieutenant," replied Boyett, as Zumwalt walked over toward the office. Once inside, Zumwalt asked to see Charles Holland.

The desk clerk gave a discerning look and said, "Just a minute." Several minutes passed before she returned. She informed Zumwalt that Holland was tied up on a telephone call and would be out in a few minutes.

Zumwalt waited about fifteen minutes, occasionally hearing Holland screaming on the telephone to someone. It was obvious to him that Holland was getting worked up about the situation and that he (Zumwalt) would have to use some significant tact in order to calm him down. The last thing Zumwalt wanted was to have an uncooperative witness.

After an additional five minutes, Holland came out of the office behind the reception area.

Zumwalt greeted him, "Mr. Holland, I'm Lieutenant Zumwalt from the detective squad. I'm hoping that I can help you and you can help me with this unfortunate situation. Can we talk?"

Holland look puzzled. "Yeah, come on back," he said, motioning for Zumwalt to come around the reception area to a rear door that led to the office.

Zumwalt entered the office and noticed numerous plaques from various civic organizations, including the local rotary club and optimists club. Zumwalt knew he needed to play on Holland's civic duty. "Mr. Holland, first I want to apologize for our intruding at your hotel. I realize how unsettling it can be to have detectives and crime scene people swarming the premises."

"It's very unsettling," agreed Holland.

"Well, you have to realize that we at the police department didn't ask for, nor do we want homicides. We're busy enough with the usual crimes, let alone people being killed. But we have to investigate what is thrown at us, so here we are," stated Zumwalt. "I'm hoping we can get your continued cooperation, as well as help you transform any bad publicity into good publicity, or at least put the hotel's management in the best light possible considering the situation. The last thing either of us needs is to be confrontational and to create an adversarial relationship. It doesn't help either of us."

"And how would good publicity happen?" enquired Holland, looking skeptical.

"Well, we haven't made much of a press statement concerning this homicide yet. It might be time for the department to issue its press release, emphasizing that the crime occurred several blocks away from the hotel and that the hotel management has been instrumental in helping identify the victim. And that because of the management here, we're one step closer to solving this murder," said Zumwalt.

Holland's skeptical frown deepened. "How will that help my business?"

"I'm not sure it will help your business, but it won't hurt it either. It will let the community know that you're doing your civic duty by cooperating. That you're assisting the police department in every way you can and that you don't take crime lightly. I can get the department's public information officer over here in a few minutes. We can do the press release from your parking lot, if you don't mind. I might even arrange for you to be interviewed by the local media to give your spin on it," Zumwalt continued.

"Well, my first inclination was to get the corporate lawyer down here and throw you off the property. He suggested that if we did that, you'd just get a search warrant or court order and do your business anyway," said Holland.

"He was right," replied Zumwalt. "An attorney from the district attorney's office is already on her way down to take whatever legal action is necessary."

"I guess you have me in checkmate then, Lieutenant."

"Mr. Holland, we're going to make the crime scene process we have to go through as painless as possible for you and your staff. We don't need to be uncooperative with each other, and hopefully the fact that the victim of a murder stayed at your hotel will not hurt your business in any manner," Zumwalt responded. "Let me get the PIO over here to prep the media."

"Yeah, OK," Holland agreed.

As Zumwalt walked out of Holland's office, back around the front desk, Holland followed.

"Heather," he said, addressing the desk clerk, "if the police need anything, make sure they get it ASAP."

"Thank you, Mr. Holland. I'll have the public information officer meet with you as soon as he arrives," said Zumwalt as he exited the building.

As Zumwalt walked across the parking lot, he could see Boyett, Palmer, and a taller-than-average African American woman wearing a navy blue skirt suit he believed was Gloria Wood talking on the walkway by the victim's room. Upon his arrival, Boyett spoke up.

"Lieutenant, this is Gloria Wood. We've just briefed her on the situation here. She said if necessary, she can have a search warrant for the room and car within a couple hours."

"It won't be necessary, Three B. I got with the manager, Charles Holland, and we came to an agreement. I'm going to get the PIO down to make the press release about the murder last night. He'll praise Holland for cooperating and we'll have whatever we want from the staff here," explained Zumwalt.

"Good job, Lieutenant!" exclaimed Boyett. "The last thing I wanted was to stop the processing and wait several hours to get a search warrant in order to start again."

Wood spoke up. "Are you sure Holland is really OK with this? The last thing we need is to have him flip flop later and give a defense attorney ammunition during a trial."

"I'm sure he's OK with it. We had a nice chat, talked about options, and he realized neither of us wanted this situation, but that we have to work through it. He's already told his desk clerk to ensure we get whatever we need," replied Zumwalt. "Now, how are we making out inside the room?"

"Well, Lieutenant, they've just finished photographing everything and now they're inventorying everything in the room. After we remove the victim's belongings, we'll process the room for prints and DNA. Her belongings can be processed over at the lab," said Boyett.

"What do we know about the victim as of now, Three B?" asked Zumwalt.

Boyett replied, "We have her purse and wallet with a few different pieces of ID and credit cards in the name of July Marcial with an address in a town called Blowing Rock. The hotel registration indicates she has a North Carolina driver's license, which we haven't found. A driver's check indicates she's twenty-eight years old. We also have student ID for the University of Southern Mississippi, so she probably lives there."

"Lieutenant, did Holland give you a copy of the guests that stayed over Mardi Gras?" asked Palmer.

"I didn't ask yet. Let's get through the crime scene and press bullshit, then we'll make the request," replied Zumwalt.

"Sure thing, Lieutenant," Palmer acknowledged.

"Let me call the chief's office and get the PIO over here to manufacture some type of press statement. Is there anything we do or don't want mentioned?" inquired Zumwalt.

"Lieutenant, what usually happens is that the PIO constructs the statement and then runs it by us to see if anything needs to be added or removed," Boyett explained.

"OK, Three B," replied Zumwalt. "That sounds great to me."

The crime scene would take several more hours. Boyett looked at his watch; it was now almost 6:00 p.m. and it looked like he was going to be getting home late again. He called home, but no one answered. His wife must be at baseball practice with his son. He left a message: "Hey honey, I'm going to be stuck late again tonight. Not sure what time I'll be home, don't wait up for me."

Boyett cleared the Magnolia Hotel about 8:00 p.m. He returned to the detective division after stopping at a fast-food place to grab a burger and fries. Dinner was over back at the house, and he wasn't sure what time he would arrive. Besides, he was getting pretty hungry since the gumbo from lunch had digested hours ago.

Back at the station, Boyett ran a "Data Finder" on the victim's name. "Data Finder" is a public records system that compiles data on people all over the country. Police agencies and some businesses subscribe to these information systems, which can assist in day-to-day operations such as locating people or finding out about them.

A July Marcial record of data was relatively short. It showed an address on Tower Road in Blowing Rock, North

Carolina. It also showed a North Carolina driver's license number as well as several other persons listed to the Tower Road address in Blowing Rock. There was an automobile registration in Hattiesburg, Mississippi with the address of an apartment there. Other data included a previous address in Knoxville, Tennessee that appeared to be several years old. Boyett decided to begin his quest into Marcial's life the next morning, since it was now past 9:00 p.m. in Mobile and would be an hour later in Blowing Rock.

CHAPTER 2 – THE VICTIM

Thursday, March 2, 2006, also began as another early day for Boyett. He was up about 6:00 a.m. in an effort to see his wife and two kids, Samantha and Chris, before they headed off to school. The kids caught a bus at about 6:50 a.m. and it might be the only time he got to spend with them during the day, the way this investigation was developing.

Boyett's wife, Millie, reminded him that Saturday was opening day of youth baseball, and that he needed to make arrangements to be there. Boyett told Millie he would do everything possible to be there, but he couldn't predict where this investigation may go. Boyett had been married to his high school sweetheart for twelve years. She worked part time as a bank teller. Because of Boyett's inconsistent schedule and being called out, Millie had to be available to handle family matters and was often the lone parent. He could never tell her enough how much he appreciated and loved her for everything she was for himself and the kids. By 7:30 a.m., he was on the way down his driveway for the drive into town.

On the way in, Boyett began his usual series of telephone calls to get a start on the day's work. He started with a call to the intelligence division at the police department. He reached Jane Bonham, an intelligence analyst who was a favorite among the detectives. Bonham was known for being thorough and resourceful in her quest for information.

"Jane, it's Three B. Last night I did a choice point on the victim in the homicide from the other night." He told her what he'd learned, adding, "Can you run her through whatever additional systems you have and see what you can find out about her? Also, if you can find me the name and telephone number of the police department in Blowing Rock, I'll need to make some calls up there and find out how I can contact the family."

"Sure, Three B, let me get on the computer and pull up some data," replied Bonham. "What time you going to be in?"

"I'll be there in twenty minutes."

"Come by when you get here, Three B. I should have the Blowing Rock info to get you started," Bonham said with her usual confidence.

Boyett continued the drive into the city while making a series of telephone calls. These included calls to the morgue, where he left a message requesting Dr. Robinson call with details of the autopsy. Upon Boyett's arrival at the police department, he went by the intelligence unit and retrieved the information from analyst Bonham. He went right to his desk and dialed the Blowing Rock Police Department.

Boyett's call was received by a dispatcher, who transferred him to the detective on duty—Detective Art Small. Boyett learned that Blowing Rock was a small but "well to do" town located in the mountains of North Carolina, not too far from Asheville and about ten miles from Boone, which was home to Appalachian State University.

He also learned that everyone who had been in Blowing Rock for any length of time knew everyone else. Detective Small explained that the Marcial family was a reputable family and that July's father, Milton Marcial, was a professor at Appalachian State. Small said that July's mother had died of cancer about ten years before, while July was still in high school. He said July had graduated from Blowing Rock High School in the late 1990s, a few years behind

Small himself. Detective Small said he personally knew July and that she'd left the area after high school and gone off to college. He said he'd heard she was working in the music business, but he was unsure of any specific details. He also noted that July had occasionally been seen in town, presumably visiting her father, although Small had not seen her in many months.

Detective Small offered to visit Milton Marcial to inform him of July's death and put him in touch with Boyett. Boyett thanked Small and asked if Small could ask around Blowing Rock to see if there might be any leads there that might relate to the homicide. Detective Small agreed he would be glad to do that. He said that homicides were a rare occurrence in Blowing Rock and that this would be a news event.

Boyett asked Small to let him know if he found out anything and to have Mr. Marcial call when he felt comfortable. He thanked Small for all his help and hung up.

Boyett began to write reports concerning the previous day's events. As he was doing so, several other detectives filtered into the detective bureau. At about 8:45 a.m., he received a call from the morgue. Doctor Robinson's assistant, George, told Boyett that the cause of death was asphyxiation by strangulation. George told Boyett the strangulation was manual and that it appeared July Marcial had been strangled from the front, most likely by the perpetrator's hands. He also related that it appeared Marcial had sexual intercourse not long before, if not right before her death. This determination had been made based on what appeared to be dried vaginal secretions in the pelvic region of Marcial's body. George also said that scrapings from beneath Marcial's fingernails appeared to contain some skin and blood and that it appeared she'd fought her attacker. Marcial's right foot had an abrasion on the middle toe. George said the abrasion appeared to have been made after Marcial died. He promised to have a written report to

Boyett as soon as the toxicology reports came back from the lab, probably within a week or two. He suggested that if Boyett needed any additional information before the arrival of the report, Boyett should contact the morgue and the information would be made readily available.

At about 9:30 a.m., Lieutenant Zumwalt came into the squad bay. He asked Boyett, "Did you see the 10:00 news last night?"

"No," replied Boyett, "I was on my way home. Did I miss something?"

"Not really," Zumwalt said. "The news covered the homicide and the press conference. When they interviewed Holland at the Magnolia Hotel, you'd have thunk he was working with us side by side. He did everything but offer a reward for catching the perp."

Boyett and Palmer started laughing.

"And I thought we were going to put the asshole in jail before the night was out," piped up Palmer.

"Well, it goes to show sometimes we can get more bees with sugar than with vinegar," replied Zumwalt. "So, what's on the agenda for today?"

"I called Blowing Rock P.D. and they're going to notify the family. I expect them to call here anytime to get info on releasing the body. I need to interview them about who she might have been here with," said Boyett.

"I've started an affidavit on my computer laying out all the details we know so far," added Palmer.

"Are we getting a warrant for someone? asked Zumwalt.

"No, Lieutenant, but in these complicated cases, we usually keep a running affidavit of the events that we can use to cut and paste in case we need a search warrant or an arrest warrant in a hurry. That way, we don't have to look up the information as we try to write it later," replied Palmer.

"Sounds reasonable," said Zumwalt, "but quite different than how we ran things back in the traffic squad. But whatever works." He shrugged.

"I spoke with the coroner's office this morning. Marcial was strangled, most likely from the front, she had sex with someone before her death, and there was some type of abrasion on one of her toes," Boyett told Zumwalt.

"Do you think she had sex with her killer?" asked Zumwalt.

"I dunno," replied Boyett. "She could've had sex with someone else and maybe the killer was jealous. Who knows at this point? All we can do is follow the evidence."

"Well, I trust you guys are going to get to the bottom of it soon," said Zumwalt. "So, where do we go from here?"

"Lieutenant, can we get the squad in for a roundtable in the next hour or so?" asked Boyett.

"Sure. How about we do a roundtable with lunch?" Zumwalt suggested.

"Perfect, we gonna order out?" asked Palmer.

"Yeah, I'll send an order sheet around and we'll call it in. I'll make sure everyone knows there's a roundtable at noon," said Zumwalt.

A "roundtable" was a term used by the detective squad to describe a meeting when all the detectives gathered around the circular conference table in the squad bay to discuss a particularly difficult case. A roundtable gave everyone a chance to hear everything that had developed and to weigh in with diverse opinions and possibilities of how a crime occurred and who might have committed it. It was also a time when assignments were usually given out to follow up leads in these same difficult cases.

Zumwalt called the various detectives on their cell phones, informing them of the roundtable at noon and asking if they wanted to bring lunch or have it delivered. Within ten minutes, everyone had been notified of the meeting and the lunch sheet was going around the office.

At 10:55 a.m., Boyett received a call from Milton Marcial in Blowing Rock, North Carolina. Boyett consoled Mr. Marcial and apologized for the way Marcial had been notified, but it had been late last night when Marcial's daughter was identified.

Marcial asked Boyett what Boyett could tell him about the murder, whether they had arrested anyone, and when the family could retrieve the body "for a proper funeral."

Boyett explained that they were early in the investigation, and he promised to keep Mr. Marcial informed of the status of the investigation. He asked Mr. Marcial about his daughter and if he knew who she might have been in Mobile with.

Marcial explained that July had been a graduate student working to get a master's degree in music at the University of Southern Mississippi. He said his daughter had graduated from the University of Tennessee with a bachelor's degree in music and had gone off into the music business, where she'd done well doing studio work, playing back-up, and traveling with various bands. He added that his daughter played a variety of instruments including piano, guitar, and some woodwinds, and that she had a variety of friends all over the United States and even in foreign countries. He said that July had some "weird" friends, but he doubted that any of them would do her any harm. He furthered explained that she'd been very outgoing, easy to make friends, and not afraid to have conversations with total strangers. He described her as the "ultimate extrovert."

Mr. Marcial also said that his daughter knew some people in New Orleans who promised her studio work whenever she needed it. Between studio work and playing some weekends in the bars along Bourbon Street, July had thought she would do fine financially.

He said that this idea was good only in theory, because Hurricane Katrina had come in and shut New Orleans down. He was afraid his daughter might have been getting tight with money. He knew she'd played a couple times in Mobile and had done some singing during a songwriter's festival at some Alabama beach just before Thanksgiving.

He and July never discussed money, but July had recently asked him if he could loan her enough to finish graduate school, if needed. He said he'd told her he could cover whatever she needed.

Boyett asked Marcial for his daughter's cell phone number and confirmed the address of her apartment in Hattiesburg. Marcial gave Boyett July's home and cell telephone numbers. Boyett asked Marcial if he would grant consent to a search of July's apartment. Mr. Marcial said he didn't understand what the police could find at her apartment that would lead them to a killer in Mobile, but he would sign whatever they needed to help them find the killer. Boyett thanked Mr. Marcial for the information and promised to fax him a consent form so police could search the apartment and also to keep him informed of any progress in the investigation. He promised that Mr. Marcial would get a call shortly from the coroner's office and that arrangements could be made for July to get a proper burial. He ended the conversation by supplying Mr. Marcial with his cell phone number and telling him to call if he remembered anything else or if Boyett could be of any assistance.

The noon roundtable started with Boyett giving all the vital details about the autopsy and his conversation with Mr. Marcial.

Palmer explained what he'd detailed in the affidavit thus far and each detective reported what information they'd gathered. He started the conversation with the notion that the killer was probably not from the area, and that this was a fairly unusual method of murder in Mobile. Most were either domestic-related or drug-related, usually in the "drive by" fashion.

Most of the detectives agreed that the unusual method might lead to other, similar cases. Samson suggested putting out a law enforcement message to other agencies throughout the southeast region detailing the homicide and requesting any information pertaining to similar homicides in the recent past.

Due to specifics about this crime, it was determined that the best avenue to pursue the follow-up was through the ROCIC, which was an acronym for the Regional Organized Crime Information Center. This organization assists police departments in making connections and gathering intelligence with member departments throughout the southeastern United States. Detective Jim Roberts was tasked with developing the criteria to provide to the ROCIC in order to survey other departments that may have had similar crimes.

Mike Samson reported that he'd had a follow-up telephone conversation with the supervisor at the GSA in Atlanta. GSA had assured Samson that a copy of the videotape had been made and was being sent to Samson via overnight mail. Samson was hopeful the video would arrive on Friday morning and could be reviewed before the weekend.

Lieutenant Zumwalt brought up the subject of requesting a profiler from the FBI to assist in the case. Zumwalt, a recent graduate of the FBI National Academy, was big on bringing up the FBI every time the opportunity availed itself. Most of the detectives who had experiences with the local FBI office reported that their experiences were negative. Although Zumwalt had been thoroughly indoctrinated by the FBI, most of the detectives were of the opinion that getting federal assistance was much more difficult than placing a telephone call. The consensus at the roundtable was that Zumwalt could work on requesting the profiler, but that it might be weeks before the FBI actually came through, if they ever did.

Boyett suggested that J.T. Palmer, Bobby Moyer, and himself should travel to Hattiesburg, Mississippi to take a look at July Marcial's apartment and talk to her neighbors or friends. Boyett asked Palmer to call the Hattiesburg

Police Department and see if they could get some help the next day. It was just over one hundred miles from Mobile to Hattiesburg and there may be some leads that come from her apartment, especially if she had company when she came to Mardi Gras.

Lieutenant Zumwalt suggested that they make the trip over and back in one day. If it extended to an overnight trip, he would have to complete "overnight travel" forms, which often took a week or more to get approved.

Boyett also explained that he'd gotten Marcial's cell phone number as well as her home telephone number from her father. He was going to meet with Gloria Wood and request a court order to obtain a complete set of telephone records, including text messages and a "dump" of her telephone calls. A telephone dump is a request for all incoming calls to the target telephone, as opposed to telephone toll records which only record outgoing calls. If Marcial had called the killer, or if the killer had called her, then the killer's telephone number should appear somewhere in her records.

Lastly, Boyett asked Lieutenant Zumwalt to request that Jane Bonham be assigned to this case. Boyett foresaw that there were going to be piles of data, including telephone records, which were going to need to be analyzed. Zumwalt, who had never utilized an analyst before, asked if it was truly necessary. Boyett explained that it was very conceivable that this case was going to generate several hundred reports as well as hundreds of pieces of evidence before it was over. He noted that it could be a full-time job going through the records and inputting them into a computer system spreadsheet, let alone actually following up leads in the case.

Zumwalt indicated that he understood and said he would request Bonham be assigned to the case immediately.

The meeting broke up with each of the detectives following up with their particular assignments. The consensus was that there would be another roundtable at 8:00 Friday morning. That would give Boyett, Palmer, and Moyer time to travel to Hattiesburg and back by Friday evening.

Later that afternoon, Boyett met with Gloria Wood to put together language for court orders to obtain the information from July Marcial's phone records. Boyett made a call to the local DEA office where he'd previously served on the DEA task force. He needed assistance getting the latest address and contact information for the two telephone companies that Marcial had service with, in order to address the court orders.

DEA was famous within law enforcement circles for sending out subpoenas on every investigation, and why not? Drug dealers utilized cell phones and other technology as their most reliable means of communications. DEA had also become an organization on the cutting edge of telephone wiretaps, or T-III intercepts, as they were called by the DEA.

With the constant mergers and bankruptcies of telecommunications companies, just trying to find out where a company's compliance department was located and who would accept a subpoena or court order could take hours or even days. Boyett knew the DEA's database was always up to date, due to the number of T-III wiretaps and telephone subpoenas they sent out. It would have the latest addresses and contacts for every telephone company in the country.

Boyett had enjoyed his two-year assignment to the DEA task force; he'd learned a lot of investigative techniques that were unheard of in local law enforcement. He'd also had the opportunity to travel extensively, although most of the travel seemed to be to south Texas, along the U.S./Mexican border, which was the weak link as far as drugs entering the country.

He remembered traveling to McAllen, Texas and learning that twenty thousand vehicles a day crossed just one bridge over the Rio Grande River into the United States.

He remembered seeing school-aged children wearing backpacks walking home to Mexico after attending schools in the US, within sight of the border. Boyett knew from that instant that any attempt to stop the flow of drugs at the border was a lost cause, at least under the current guidelines.

Boyett decided he'd had enough of the DEA when he realized it had become an ineffective bureaucracy. Additionally, DEA management was like musical chairs, with new resident agents in charge changing every three years and sometimes sooner. Part of his reluctance to stay at the DEA task force involved breaking in a new boss who was coming in from Washington, D.C. and probably had never been in Mobile before.

Also gone were the days when agents worked undercover and made drug buys, got search warrants, and locked up the dope dealers. By the time Boyett left, the local DEA office was consumed with doing T-III wiretap after T-III wiretap, often watching kilos of coke be distributed on the streets of south Alabama in order to keep the wiretaps secret. He was ready to go back to the streets and put crooks in jail.

From the DEA, Boyett was able to ascertain the telephone companies and contacts for Marcial's telephone numbers and to obtain both mailing and faxing information for the company's compliance department. He related this information to Gloria Wood, who would address the appropriate court orders to the proper companies for service.

Upon returning to the detective division, Boyett met with Lieutenant Zumwalt again.

"I called over to the FBI supervisor in charge of coordinating investigations with the local police," Zumwalt informed him. "And the FBI supervisor is going to contact the profiling section at their Quantico Academy to arrange for a consultation."

"Good," Boyett agreed. "That's a good step forward."

For an active homicide investigation, this was going to be a short day. It was only 4:00 and Boyett was able to leave and not have anything left to do, at least until tomorrow. Sometimes these investigations were hurry up and sometimes wait.

Friday, March 3 started out like most other days—early. Boyett was out of the house at 7:00 and enroute with the usual telephone calls during the drive in. These included a call to retired detective sergeant Bobby Hicks, whom Boyett had admired early in his career.

Hicks had been known as the best homicide detective in the South. He'd investigated over a hundred separate homicides and had close to 150 homicide convictions to his record. He'd retired from the police department several years before after being passed over for a promotion for the tenth time, in spite of having an excellent score on the promotional exam. Everyone in the police department knew that Hick's inability to be promoted was related to the fact that he wouldn't "bite his tongue" and often told the police department brass and politicians things they did not want to hear.

When Hicks retired, he went into the consulting business, offering his expertise to defense attorneys and sometimes consulting and appearing for news and talk shows. He'd done very well financially, and he was often seen as a commentator on the talking head news shows when homicides were discussed. Hicks had a contract with the Fox News network and was utilized as an expert by several prominent defense attorneys nationwide. During the telephone call with Hicks, Boyett ran the facts by him.

Hicks immediately told Boyett, "William, I'm sure your killer is from out of town. It also wouldn't surprise me at all if this wasn't his first murder. If it was his first, he was cool as a cucumber and must have gotten a thrill from it."

Boyett brought up Zumwalt's idea of the FBI profiling unit.

Hicks replied, "A profiler is a great idea, but getting the FBI on board might take a while. The few times I've utilized an FBI profiler, it took weeks and sometimes months to get the profiles completed." He suggested a retired FBI profiler, Nate Jamison, who had appeared on TV shows several times with Hicks. Hicks mentioned that Jamison lived in nearby Fairhope, Alabama and might be willing to help. He offered to contact Jamison, if needed.

Boyett thanked Hicks, who wished him luck and offered any assistance he could.

He closed with a short piece of advice to Boyett. "Of course, William, don't let the brass know you're talking to me. I'm still somewhat a leper with them."

"I'll only let them know after my career's over," replied Boyett. And with that, he concluded the call to Hicks.

Upon arrival at the office, Boyett met with Lieutenant Zumwalt, who reported that he'd spoken with the local FBI supervisor. Zumwalt learned that the profiling process through the FBI might take up to twelve weeks, due to the shortage of profilers. Boyett mentioned Nate Jamison and asked Zumwalt if he had any objection to utilizing him if he was available. He was careful not to mention that Bobby Hicks was the contact for Jamison.

Zumwalt told Boyett there was no objection, provided Jamison didn't charge for his services. Boyett agreed and said he would try to get in touch with the retired profiler to see if he would assist.

The day's roundtable began at 8:00. In addition to the usual detectives, Jane Bonham was in attendance. The briefings were short in comparison to the previous roundtables. Palmer reported that Hattiesburg detectives were on board with their arrival at about 11:00 a.m. Samson reported that the tape was due to arrive from GSA, and that he would view it over the weekend. Boyett asked Jane Bonham to begin putting together a data bank of information and a spreadsheet along with files containing the original information as it came in.

Boyett gave a quick overview of the evidence collected so far and mentioned the idea that it was very likely the killer was from outside the area. Most heads nodded in agreement.

Moyer brought up the idea of having subpoenas drawn up for every hotel in the Mobile area, requiring the guest lists for every guest who stayed the night before and the night after the murder. There was further discussion about how far out into the metro area they should subpoena records. It was agreed that Jane Bonham would begin compiling a record of every hotel and motel in the area, and the idea of the subpoenas would be continued on Monday.

At 8:45, Boyett, Palmer, and Moyer departed for Hattiesburg. The 100-mile drive took just over seventy-five minutes, as the Ford Crown Victoria was immune to most speed limit laws, and US Highway 98 was basically clear. With the exception of a few small towns like Wilmer, Alabama, the trip was without red lights or stop signs.

Upon approaching Hattiesburg, Palmer contacted the Hattiesburg detectives and requested they meet at Marcial's apartment, located at Camellia Square, a few blocks from the University of Southern Mississippi campus.

Boyett had already arranged for and had a signed "Consent to Search" from July Marcial's father. Milton Marcial had mentioned that he would have to travel down to Hattiesburg to empty July's apartment before the end of the month and that he dreaded that task. Boyett had thought he detected tears in the man's voice.

Upon arriving at Marcial's apartment and meeting with Hattiesburg detectives, the detectives went to the management office and spoke with the manager. The detectives already had July Marcial's keys, which had been found in the hotel room on March 1.

Camellia Square was an upper-middle class apartment complex, with amenities that included park-like grounds, a clubhouse, and a swimming pool. This was not the usual older, more dilapidated off-campus housing for students. Marcial, being a graduate student and having been gainfully employed, had rented a nice two-bedroom apartment with a balcony that overlooked the pool.

When the Hattiesburg detectives arrived, the Mobile and Hattiesburg detectives began their search of Marcial's apartment in a systematic manner, breaking down into teams and working one room at a time, with Moyer setting up to inventory the seized items at the dining room table. The apartment was very well furnished, with twelve-foot ceilings. Everything was orderly and well maintained and could have been designed by a decorator from *Southern Living* magazine. Marcial's taste in furniture leaned toward the Caribbean, with much of the furniture made of rattan, wicker, and dark woods. Bright, tropical colors made up much of the fabrics and several ceiling fans were present in the living and bedroom areas.

Boyett, who was working the master bedroom with a Hattiesburg detective, went through each bureau drawer, careful not to leave them in disarray. During his search, he located Marcial's laptop computer neatly packed in a computer bag. He also located several papers containing names and telephone numbers along with Marcial's PDA, which he expected would contain most of her contacts.

In the second bedroom, Palmer and another Hattiesburg detective were scouring through a whole lot of nothing. This room seemed to be used mostly for storage of memorabilia, musical instruments, and electronic gear. Besides the electric keyboards and guitars, there was an array of electronic amplifiers, input boxes, and microphones. The closets were full of memorabilia including posters of bands July Marcial had performed with and festivals and tours she'd been involved in.

Back in the master bedroom, Boyett came upon a medium-sized box under the king-sized bed, which contained an array of adult toys and DVDs. It was obvious that July Marcial had more than a usual sexual appetite and that her father's statement of her being an "extrovert" probably would fit her sexual desires as well.

At the dining room table, Moyer was listing the items they were taking. These included the numerous pieces of paper containing writings, an address book, and the laptop computer, and now Boyett brought out the box of adult toys.

"And we're seizing this... why?" asked Moyer.

"Well, I could argue that there might be some DNA on one of the toys that will match the killer's, but in reality, I just want to get them out of here so her father doesn't have to deal with it," replied Boyett.

"Are you sure you're not going to convert those things to personal use, Three B?" asked Palmer, laughing, as he entered the dining room.

"Come on guys, just write it up as miscellaneous items. Give her father a break. The poor man doesn't need to know his daughter was a sex freak," countered Boyett.

About 1:30, the detectives concluded the search of July Marcial's apartment and decided to interview neighbors to see if anyone could provide any information on friends or associates that Marcial may have had. Most of the neighbors were not at home, although the few the detectives could interview gave no substantive information. Most of the neighbors were aware of Marcial, but only knew her to see her. Several said they would see her hauling some musical equipment to her car every now and then. Others mentioned seeing her with male friends every once in a while. No one knew any of the friends' names or even had noticed descriptions. The Hattiesburg detectives promised to come back and interview additional neighbors on an evening or weekend to see if any additional leads could be developed.

Next, the detectives went to the University of Southern Mississippi, where they'd arranged to meet with several of Marcial's professors at 3:30 p.m. Again, most of the professors could tell them little of Marcial's personal life.

Several said she was an outstanding musician and that she was creative and willing to try anything musically. Several said she was one of the most outstanding students they'd ever had in all their years of teaching.

After the interviews were completed, the Mobile detectives thanked the Hattiesburg detectives for their help, packed up the seized items, and began the trek back to Mobile. On the way home, they stopped for a late lunch, having gone all day without any real food. By 6:30 p.m., they were back at the police station and walking into the detective bureau.

Boyett checked his in basket and found a list of sixty-two hotels and motels within the Mobile Metro Area. These ranged from Marriott's Grand Hotel in nearby Point Clear to little mom and pop motels located outside the city on Highway 90, west of Mobile. He thought about the task awaiting him, as they would begin screening the guests of all these hotels. He left the office about 7:00, hoping to enjoy the weekend that included the opening day of youth baseball with his son.

CHAPTER 3 – THE INVESTIGATION: FINDING LEADS

The weekend was pretty uneventful as far as work was concerned, with only a handful of telephone calls. That gave Boyett time to play catch up on family time and household chores.

Opening day of youth baseball went well, an all-day event that included lots of baseball games and large crowds. Opening day was always a major event with concession stands, baseball clinics, speeches, and a festival-like atmosphere. As always, it included the appearance of a couple retired major league ball players who lived in the Mobile area. One of the advantages of living in the south was that youth baseball started early and pros who lived in the area could give kids pep talks and hold clinics before going off to spring training. Retired major leaguers supplemented the active players by offering their wisdom after spring training started.

Boyett thought this was a good thing, despite his feelings that major league baseball had deteriorated over recent years with gambling, illegal drug use, and now, steroids. Although he'd always considered himself more of a baseball fan than a football fan and he'd played the game all through high school, he had not traveled to Atlanta to see the Braves play in several years.

He was out of the house about 7:20 a.m. Monday morning and did the usual drive into the city. Upon arrival at the detective division, he met with Palmer, who was the only other detective who had made it in. They began going through some of the evidence that had been seized at Marcial's apartment. The documents were copied, originals placed in evidence envelopes and marked with exhibit numbers, and evidence forms filled out.

Boyett and Palmer discussed the idea of issuing subpoenas to the local hotels in an effort to identify suspects. Palmer thought the idea might work, but he was worried about the number of man-hours involved in running choice points and criminal history checks. But considering there were no other major leads, Palmer thought it was the only real avenue to pursue at that point in time.

When they came to the laptop and PDA, Boyett called the Bureau of Immigration and Customs Enforcement. ICE, as it was referred to these days, included the old U.S. Customs Service that had been merged into the Department of Homeland Security after 9/11.

ICE now concentrated more on immigration issues than customs, but one duty they'd kept after the merger was the enforcement of child pornography. ICE had several special agents and computer technicians who were excellent with computer forensics, which they utilized in child porn cases on a regular basis. A forensic examination was just what Boyett wanted for Marcial's computer and PDA.

Boyett was hoping there might be some leads, like an email or Instant Message that referred to meeting someone at Mardi Gras. He really wanted a suspect to emerge in this investigation. He explained the investigation to an ICE special agent, who told Boyett that if he could get the laptop and PDA over to the ICE office today, there was a good chance they could have it done by the end of the week. The ICE special agent explained to Boyett that the forensics analysis could include making duplicate copies of each type of file such as emails, documents; and image files, and put them onto separate CD-ROMS. The ICE agents also said that keywords such as "Mobile" or "Mardi Gras" could be searched to try to limit the number of files that were reviewed. Boyett readied evidence forms to transfer the laptop and PDA to ICE.

As Boyett was completing the forms, Jane Bonham arrived in the detective squad room.

"Thanks for the hotel list, Jane," said Boyett. "What do you think of putting together a spreadsheet of guests so we can try and whittle down suspects?"

"The best method would be putting some extra columns on the spreadsheet so we can make notes as we find information. We also might want to start with the hotels closest to the victim's hotel and send the subpoenas out in waves. That way, the arrival and inputting of the information won't be overwhelming," said Bonham.

Boyett agreed.

Bonham also suggested that there be language added to the subpoenas requesting the information be provided on a CD ROM in addition to the printed forms, so that it could hopefully be converted over to a spreadsheet and not hand-entered.

Boyett asked Bonham how long it would take to get the spreadsheet going and she said they could be set up by noon. The real problem was going to be deciding what the important fields or columns would relate to and how the information would be entered. Bonham suggested that the evening and midnight dispatchers could be assigned to run vehicle inquires and criminal history information on subjects once they were identified. She suggested that this might save several hours a day.

Boyett agreed that it could save a lot of time, provided someone was checking the information and confirming it was done. He told Bonham he was going to meet with Lieutenant Zumwalt when he arrived.

When Zumwalt walked in at 8:30 a.m., Boyett met him at the door with a stack of evidence forms to sign and to talk about the idea of running the spreadsheets. He briefed Zumwalt on ICE taking the computers and Zumwalt agreed readily.

Zumwalt signed off on several of the evidence forms and then Boyett brought up the spreadsheets. Zumwalt asked if there was some shortcut they could take in order to identify suspects. Boyett told him there were none that he knew of.

Zumwalt suggested they make contact with the profiler first, in order for Zumwalt to be able to justify the numerous man-hours he was getting ready to expend. Boyett agreed, left his office, and put in a call to Bobby Hicks.

Hicks told Boyett he'd already mentioned the case to Nate Jamison, who had viewed the press conference at the Magnolia Hotel on the news. He told Boyett to keep his cell phone on and to expect a call from Jamison, most likely within hours.

After talking to Hicks, Boyett got back with Palmer and together they sealed the evidence envelopes and boxes and went to the evidence room to deposit the original evidence. Upon arrival, they found the evidence custodian was not there, so they deposited the boxes along with the forms into the "drop," a door in the wall of the evidence room that acted like a mailbox for times when the custodian was not present.

After dropping the evidence, Boyett and Palmer took the computer and PDA over to the ICE office and then drove to the district attorney's office to meet with Gloria Wood concerning the subpoena proposal.

Wood greeted them at the office reception area and took them back to her office.

Boyett explained the proposal of issuing subpoenas for guest lists of every hotel in the metro area.

Wood looked concerned. "You know, Three B, if the media ever gets a hold of this, they might blow it out of proportion and contend that we're illegally putting together files on innocent people."

"Gloria, we're not putting together files, we're preparing a spreadsheet of information that already exists. Things like driver's licenses, vehicle registrations, and criminal histories. The spreadsheet just allows us to compare the data in an easy manner," said Boyett.

"I'm just preparing you for what may be alleged," said Wood.

"I think we have to take that chance, if we want to catch this guy. If the public knew we weren't doing everything we could, I doubt if they would like that either," explained Boyett.

"Get me the list of hotels. I'll run this by Mike O'Brien, and although he'll probably approve it, I would keep it quiet. How many hotels do you want to start with?" asked Wood.

"I think about ten to fifteen, and hopefully we'll come up with some suspects. I'll be in touch later today."

With that, Boyett and Palmer left Gloria Wood's office and walked through the district attorney's office. Palmer suggested they go by O'Brien's office.

Boyett disagreed, explaining that he wanted to give Wood a chance to handle the subpoena issue on her own.

On their way out of the building, Boyett's cell phone rang. It was Nate Jamison, the retired FBI profiler. Boyett thanked him for calling and asked if he could assist.

"I'd be glad to give you an off the record opinion," Jamison said easily, "because it beats the hell out of regurgitating facts for the news media."

Boyett explained everything he knew about the case at this point to Jamison.

Jamison suggested that based on what Boyett was telling him, it was likely the suspect had committed a similar crime before and would do it again. He asked whether the carpet appeared to be in good shape or if it was something someone might have discarded and left out in the weather.

Boyett said it was definitely not something that had been discarded and left in the weather. He said the carpet appeared to be a remnant left over from a house being carpeted.

Jamison thought that if the killer had brought the carpet with him, he'd likely planned the murder. If this was the case, he also thought there was a good chance the suspect had left a trail of destroyed lives in the wake of his activities but, apparently, he'd slipped through the crack in the criminal justice system. He suggested that the suspect was a male, over thirty, and that he was some sort of loner or did not have a large social circle. Jamison thought it was unusual that the murder had occurred on Mardi Gras day and that it might be a factor in the killing, but since they did not know anything about the suspect's life or other crimes, it might or might not be crucial.

Boyett ran the idea of sending subpoenas to the various hotels.

"That's a good idea," Jamison agreed. "The things you might want to key in on are that the suspect most likely rented a room alone, probably within a reasonable distance to the crime scene and the victim's hotel. The suspect could drop the body anywhere, but being from out of town, he wouldn't want to risk driving up and down streets with a body in his vehicle, especially after a drunken Mardi Gras celebration. Because he most likely brought that carpet, his vehicle is likely to be an SUV or a van, which would make dragging the body out of the vehicle in a carpet easier."

"Wow," replied Boyett, impressed with the detailed information. "That all makes perfect sense when you look at it that way." He thanked Jamison for his time and offered to buy him a coffee or a beer next time he was over in Mobile.

Jamison agreed to the offer, wished Boyett luck, and told him to feel free to call if any additional information developed.

Boyett and Palmer returned to the detective bureau, where Boyett met with Lieutenant Zumwalt. He told Zumwalt about the conversation with Jamison and asked if he had a problem with starting the subpoena process.

Zumwalt approved the idea, but he suggested they proceed slowly in order to not inundate the other duties in the detective bureau.

After returning to his desk, Boyett began assembling a map of the hotels and where each one was located in reference to the crime scene. He realized that there were only fourteen hotels within a mile of the crime scene in the downtown area. Most of the others were located on the west side of the city, out toward the interstate highway and airport area or in neighboring Baldwin County, across Mobile Bay.

Boyett initially drew up language for the subpoenas to include guests' names, addresses, vehicles registered, and telephone calls made from the hotel. After a brief telephone discussion with Gloria Wood, the request for telephone records was dropped.

Wood argued that if a suspect looked good, they could always go back and retrieve the information. She thought this could be a hotbed of public relations problems, considering the federal government had just admitted to listening to telephone calls under the pretense of terrorist investigations.

Boyett thought this was a crazy analogy, since he was only seeking records of telephone numbers called from the guests' rooms as opposed to listening in on anyone, but he reluctantly agreed, realizing that the fight wasn't worth the potential problems they could cause later with Wood. He thought the added information of the telephone calls might be a red flag that might highlight one suspect and separate him from a host of others.

Upon drawing up the language, Boyett faxed it to Wood at the district attorney's office. The initial list of hotels only included seven hotels, but these included several of the largest in the city. The largest hotel had over 370 rooms; the smallest was a bed and breakfast with four guest rooms. Both of these were on the initial list based on their geographic location to the crime scene. Boyett estimated that information would begin arriving within a day, although some might take weeks.

Boyett called Jane Bonham and told her to ready the spreadsheet because the information would start coming in soon. They discussed the various columns and what they would include. They agreed that initially the information should include a column for the guest's name, number of occupants in the room, vehicle information, home address, criminal history, and telephone calls.

Bonham said the columns could be coded so that important information such as a criminal history that included a crime of violence or sex crime could be red flagged and stand out.

Boyett liked this idea. He told Bonham that the data would be brought to her daily as it arrived and that he was available to help her in any way necessary.

At about 11:30 that morning, Mike Samson called Boyett. Samson had been reviewing the federal building video from Mardi Gras day. He reported that the film was too busy to distinguish much until after about 7:30 p.m. as date stamped on the film. He stated that the film was shot from the federal building looking west on St. Louis Street, which was the direction toward the crime scene.

This covered the largest street leading to the crime scene, probably a good thing for police. Samson reported that the streets were fairly busy up until about 7:00 p.m., when the last parade ended. By 7:30, the streets were basically clear except for clean-up crews and some departing revelers. Since St. Louis Street was one way to the west, most revelers leaving the Mardi Gras by car wouldn't appear on the film, but would exit the area from the adjoining streets.

Samson told Boyett, "There were about thirty or forty vehicles on the surveillance video between 7:30 and 8:30 and only about twenty between 8:30 and 10:00, when Steve Brown got to the parking lot to clean it." He asked, "Do you know what type of vehicle Brown drove that night?'

Boyett replied, "It was a dark colored Ford Ranger pickup."

"OK. I'll go back and look at the tape to see if I can see Brown's vehicle on the tape. That'll indicate when the tape can be stopped."

"How clear is the video?"

Samson replied, "You can tell the makes and models of most of the cars, although exact colors are a problem because it was night and the only lights available were streetlights, which were sufficient, but not as good as daylight. Also, the camera was mounted to observe the side of the federal building for security purposes and was too far from normal traffic lanes to read license plates, although if it could be enhanced, there's a chance of reading them."

"Can you go through the video again and detail the time and makes and models of any vans or SUV's that might be observed?"

Samson agreed, and they ended the call.

By now it was lunchtime, so Boyett and Palmer headed out to West Mobile to eat at Smokey's BBQ. Smokey's was a hole in the wall place just north of Mobile near the border with the city of Prichard. Smokey's had been in the same location for close to fifty years and offered some of the best BBQ in the south. What it offered in culinary quality, however, it lacked in atmosphere. It was just a shack of a place on the border of a crime-ridden area, where you ordered and took your food out to a picnic table placed under tall live oak trees. Boyett went for a pulled pork sandwich and Palmer for a BBQ beef plate. Both came with fries and coleslaw.

After lunch, Boyett and Palmer returned to the detective bureau and began reviewing notes and files. They were given a message to meet Corporal Bruce McCrary down at the evidence room. Boyett and Palmer went to see McCrary, who confronted them with the box containing the adult toys and porn DVDs seized from July Marcial's apartment.

"Boyett, your description on this box, *Miscellaneous Personal Items*, isn't sufficient. I need to know exactly what's in the box," said McCrary.

"It's a sealed box containing several different personal items that may or may not be important to the investigation. Just log it in as a sealed box purported to contain those items. I'll take the blame if something's missing," insisted Boyett.

"Not a chance, Boyett! I'm sending it back to Zumwalt. If you and he want to re-submit it the proper way or get a memo signed by the captain, I'll take it."

"Thanks, asshole! Now I know why you're in evidence, instead of out on the street doing real police work," muttered Palmer as he and Boyett walked away from McCrary.

"What a dick!" grumbled Boyett.

"Don't worry, Three B. If this becomes an issue, I'll call in a favor and it'll be covered," said Palmer.

Back at the detective bureau, Boyett and Palmer went over their notes again to ensure that they had not missed anything that needed to be followed up. At about 2:00 p.m., Boyett got a call from Gloria Wood, saying the first batch of subpoenas were ready for delivery. He asked Palmer if he wanted to come along and deliver them.

Palmer declined.

Boyett left and drove over to the district attorney's office, where he found the subpoenas awaiting at the front desk. He picked them up and returned to his car. As he drove from hotel to hotel delivering them, he made sure to leave his business cards and cell phone number, in case anyone had questions or needed to call when they had the records ready.

Several of the smaller hotels said they couldn't provide the information on CD-ROM, but they did promise to have it the next day. By 4:30 p.m., Boyett was finished for the day and enroute home, hopefully to spend the evening with his Millie and the kids.

Tuesday, March 7 marked the one-week point in this investigation. Boyett knew that going a week without a viable suspect was not a good thing. Most homicide investigations were pretty much over within a week. It was not unusual for arrests not to be made till later because the district attorney's office wanted all the lab evidence and reports prior to indicting, but as far as investigative work was concerned, it was usually pretty well wrapped up in a week.

In this case, not a single name had emerged as a suspect. So far, they had the fact that July Marcial was a single woman who was friendly and an extrovert. She'd apparently come to Mobile's Mardi Gras alone and met someone, maybe not the killer, and had sex with him. She was last seen leaving the Magnolia Hotel the afternoon of Mardi Gras with a white male, average build, in his thirties, who was wearing Mardi gras beads and some type of hat.

That narrows it down to just several thousand men, Boyett thought in frustration.

As Boyett arrived at the detective bureau, his cell phone rang. It was the first call from a hotel concerning records being available to be picked up. He told the hotel that he would be over shortly. He went into the bureau and looked for Lieutenant Zumwalt, who had not checked in yet. He went to the coffee room to get coffee and wait for him.

When Zumwalt arrived at the detective bureau, Boyett approached him. They went into Zumwalt's office and closed the door.

Boyett began, "Lieutenant, we've been on this case for a week. We have no leads. We have subpoenas out, hoping for a good lead. We have no idea what happened, why, or who did it. I'm getting a little worried."

"I'm not sure we need to worry yet, Three B," said Zumwalt, "So far, it looks to me like we're doing all we can."

"What concerns me, Lieutenant, is that in this bureau, we usually solve crimes quickly or they get put on the back burner. This week, we'll have a whole new group of crimes to solve. I'm afraid this case will get pushed aside and everyone will get other assignments. The profiler, Jamison, believes there's a guy out there that has done this before and will do it again. I'm afraid the brass will get tired of seeing too many man hours in on this case, with no result to show for it," said Boyett.

"Three B, I know you're doing all you can on this, and I'm impressed so far. Let me handle the brass. You may be right on what they expect and all, but we'll keep them up on it as it goes along. I promise you that even if we have a crime wave, I'll try to give you all the time and resources you need to solve this one," Zumwalt replied.

He reached behind his desk. "By the way, evidence sent this back and said the description wasn't exact enough." He was holding the box containing the sex toys and porn DVDs. "What's in it?"

Boyett sighed. He should have known this would come back to bite him. "Lieutenant, while at Marcial's apartment, we found sex toys and porn DVDs. While it really isn't evidence we need, I didn't want to leave it for her father to find when he got there to clean out her apartment. I never thought a box of crap would cause such an issue with the evidence room."

"Don't worry, Three B, I'm sure you'll find a way to get it logged in," said Lieutenant Zumwalt, and with that he handed the box back to Boyett. He walked over and opened the door to the office to let Boyett out. "Go out and find this guy," he said.

As Boyett left, he didn't know that Zumwalt had already been summoned for a meeting with Major Coachman and the assistant chief of police concerning the status of the Marcial investigation. The major had questioned Zumwalt as to whether Boyett was the right detective for this investigation. It had already been a week and Boyett had not gotten anywhere. Zumwalt told Major Coachman that he was sure Boyett was the best detective he had to work the case.

When Boyett exited Zumwalt's office, he saw Mike Samson, who showed him the list of vehicles he'd made from the federal building video.

"There were a total of fifty-three cars from 7:30 p.m. until Brown's vehicle was observed driving past the federal building," Samson told him. "According to the video time/date stamp on the video, Brown passed the federal courthouse at 10:03 p.m." The list showed a total of sixteen vans, pickup trucks, and SUVs in the time frame that was under surveillance.

Boyett asked Samson to get the vehicle list to Jane Bonham.

***

For Boyett, the next several days consisted mainly of being a gopher. Go for this, and go for that. The subpoenas were yielding lots of records, which he insisted he personally retrieve in order to get the information to Jane Bonham as quickly as possible. Boyett also began running down leads on any additional information that was needed. As the hotel lists came in, he saw that many of the guest records did not list vehicles. He made lists of any omitted data and retrieved it to ensure that if the hotel guest owned a vehicle, the information made it to Bonham's spreadsheets.

Also, the telephone records arrived for Marcial's cell phone and her home telephone. These records were in both printed form and on a disc. The information on the disc was copied into a program called Pen-Link that Boyett borrowed from the DEA. Pen-Link is a computer spreadsheet utilized for telephone numbers and subscribers of those telephone numbers. Once the numbers were entered in the database, Boyett was able to look up the owners or subscribers of most of the telephone numbers through online databases. For those that were unlisted, not published, or otherwise unavailable, he started additional subpoenas to various telephone companies.

By Friday, March 10, several persons of interest began to emerge from the hotel lists. These included people who met Jamison's profile—all were males, most had rented hotel rooms and stayed alone, and many owned either pickup trucks, vans, or SUVs. Several had arrest records, and although none of the records included murder, several did include sexual offenses and assaults.

Boyett began wondering whether this course of investigation was going to yield any significant results. As Friday closed, records were still being entered into the spreadsheets, data and backgrounds still were being accumulated, and more potential suspects were being identified.

The weekend did not work well for Boyett. Although he attended Chris's baseball game, his mind was elsewhere. He spent the weekend going over the case, trying to get into the murderer's mind. No matter how hard he tried, he was unable to figure out the who and why. He just kept drifting off in thought, going over the crime scene and the evidence found at Marcial's apartment.

As the weekend ended, Boyett realized he was no closer to solving the puzzle. He wondered whether this was going to be one of those crimes that got put on the back burner because of reprioritization within the bureau, or because the investigator gave up on the investigation. He'd always believed that every crime could be solved, if the right investigator utilized the right investigative methods and had the time and resources necessary.

The week of March 13 started much the way the previous week had. Boyett arrived at the detective bureau and began looking over every bit of evidence again, hoping to see something he'd previously missed.

Jane Bonham was progressing well with the spreadsheets and Pen-Link programs. Most of what was lacking on the spreadsheets was follow-up material such as telephone subscriber records for some of the telephone numbers that Marcial had called and criminal history records for some of the guests who had stayed at the downtown hotels.

Boyett was still awaiting the telephone dumps, or the records of telephone numbers that had called Marcial, particularly the calls to and from Marcial's cell phone the day of the murder.

He also sensed that resources for the Marcial case were starting to thin out. Samson was now assigned to a series of rapes that had occurred in West Mobile. Palmer and Moyer had been assigned to a series of shootings that had not resulted in a homicide, but had been a major news story. The investigation indicated that the shootings were part of a turf war between rival drug organizations. These groups had committed a series of drive-by shootings, wounding several gang members and also throwing bullets throughout some neighborhoods and into innocent victims' homes.

This shooting case was the type of crime that resulted in television stations interviewing neighborhood people and filming bullet holes in the sides of houses, followed by news footage of kids getting off school buses, even though most of the shootings had occurred either in the daytime while the kids were in school, or late at night when the streets were relatively empty.

Many of the neighborhood people interviewed by the media in this series of events had not actually observed anything. They just had the opportunity to get on television and say that the neighborhood was going to hell, that they never saw the police in the neighborhood, and that they wanted something done.

This caused the local elected officials to call the chief of police and demand some type of action. This, in turn, caused the shit to roll downhill until Lieutenant Zumwalt assigned as many men to the crime as needed to solve it quickly. It also caused the patrol division grief when the captain of patrol was ordered to put double patrols in that neighborhood to appease the elected officials.

Boyett was concerned that if additional crimes occurred, the Marcial investigation would be put on hold, and he wouldn't be able to follow it up properly. He wished Marcial had some clout with the local politicians or news media. Her story had lasted a day and been eclipsed by other, more important stories.

About 2:00 p.m. on Monday, Jane Bonham called Boyett. She wanted him to come to the intelligence division and see the first draft of the spreadsheet she'd spent the previous week compiling.

Boyett met with Bonham and shared the two spreadsheets. The first one listed all the information from the hotels, including the hotel's name, room number, guest's name, address, and vehicle mentioned on their hotel registration. A total of 937 guests had stayed at the hotels. Many of the columns had been completed with additional data such as criminal histories. Several were showing red flags. Bonham told Boyett these red flags included subjects who had been arrested for violent crimes or sexual offenses and subjects who had registered vehicles that included pickup trucks, vans, and SUVs.

When Boyett reviewed the red flags, he was hoping to see a standout suspect. Instead, he saw eighteen subjects who had criminal histories for crimes like assault or statutory rape. He also saw over 150 red flags related to vehicles that matched the suspect category. He only found three who had serious criminal histories and suspect vehicle categories. Of course, this was just the beginning of the process. Boyett asked Bonham for a copy of the spreadsheet and went back to the detective bureau to begin his investigation of these suspects.

The first suspect to have both categories match was Larry Deese, who resided in Greenville, Alabama. According to Deese's criminal history, he'd been arrested several times for assaults in the mid-1990s and had served several years in prison. Greenville, located about 125 miles north of Mobile, was just off the interstate I-65, which started in the south in Mobile and went straight north to the Great Lakes.

Boyett's call to the Greenville Police Department went well, at least for Deese. Boyett talked to Detective Eric Blades and explained the investigation and how they'd gotten Deese's name. Blades related that Deese had been a resident of Greenville his whole life. He described Deese as a "born again Christian." Blades said he remembered when Deese had been in trouble ten years before and that the incidents were usually related to alcohol and often occurred in a local bar known as a "knife and gun" club. That term meant that if you arrived at the door without a knife or a gun, the bouncer would issue you one at the door.

Blades told Boyett that after Deese went to prison, he apparently found religion and now was a productive member of the Greenville community. He said that Deese even went to his church. He suggested that Deese was not a great suspect, but added that if Boyett wanted to come up to Greenville to interview him, Blades would be more than glad to assist in any manner.

The next call was to the police department in Stone Mountain, Georgia. Boyett was inquiring about James McNally, a local resident who had stayed at the Magnolia Hotel during some of the same days as Marcial. McNally had an arrest for rape in 1998, although there was no disposition on the arrest record. McNally also had registered a Toyota Scion xB, one of the new "box type" cars that had a hatchback.

Boyett spoke with Captain John Peters and related the facts concerning the Marcial investigation.

Peters told Boyett that he wasn't aware of McNally, but said that he would be glad to check into the prior investigation and get back to Boyett within a few days.

The last call Boyett made was to the Shelby County Sheriff's Office. Shelby County was a growing suburban county just south of Birmingham, Alabama. Boyett spoke with Captain Wilbur Jennings and explained the Marcial investigation. Boyett's interest was in a subject named Parker Davies, who had stayed at a hotel about a block from Marcial's, registered a Nissan Pathfinder at his hotel, and had a prior conviction for sexual abuse in the first degree in 1998.

Jennings told Boyett that he remembered the case involving Davies. He told Boyett that to the best of his recollection, Davies was a pedophile who had sexually molested the son of an ex-girlfriend. He said that as far as he knew, Davies had gone to prison, had been released, and was still on parole. He would pull and review the old case file and provide any information that could help Boyett.

As the last call terminated, Boyett felt like he wasn't moving forward. He'd been hoping to strike gold with one of those telephone calls but instead, he'd struck out. The day was over, and he needed to get away.

Boyett continued the week running down any and all leads he could find. He'd gotten calls back from Stone Mountain, Georgia, and learned that the charges had been dropped against McNally. The report detailed that the prosecution of the case had originally been pushed by the victim's father, and that during a subsequent investigation the rape turned out to be an affair that had gone bad.

In the follow-up to Parker Davies, Boyett found several important documents in the case file that made it unlikely

Davies was the killer. For one, he was a child molester of young boys and secondly, he'd agreed to a chemical castration as part of a plea bargain that reduced his sentence.

As each lead fizzled, Boyett was getting anxious. He continued reviewing each file, hoping to find some lead that he'd previously overlooked. He was anxious to get back more information from the subpoenas that had been served, especially those concerning the telephone dumps on Marcial's cell telephone. He also began preparing a second wave of subpoenas, targeting hotels in the one-to-three-mile radius of the crime scene.

On Thursday, Boyett got a call from George over at the morgue. The toxicology as well as some other tests had come back, and George wanted Boyett to have the information. The toxicology showed that July Marcial had been drinking the day of Mardi Gras, and she was legally drunk with a blood alcohol level just above .18%. The forensic examination also indicated that there was semen present, although DNA tests would take longer and wouldn't be available for several weeks and possibly months.

On Friday, March 17, the information from the dump on Marcial's cell telephone arrived. It included numbers from across the country that had called Marcial's telephone in the thirty-day period before February 28. Boyett immediately took the records to Bonham to be put into the Pen-Link spreadsheet system. During an initial review of the calls to Marcial's cell phone, Boyett noticed numerous calls during her stay in Mobile. One call that Boyett noticed was made on February 28 at 2:07 p.m. from a Mobile, Alabama telephone number. He immediately checked this number and found that it was registered to the Church Street Inn, one of the hotels he'd already subpoenaed the guest list for. Boyett immediately went over to the Church Street Inn to see the manager.

Upon his arrival, Boyett met the manager. He asked how the telephone system worked and who would have access to the particular number that had called Marcial's telephone. He learned that the number was connected to the hotel's telephone system and that any guest room could utilize the system and make calls. Because the hotel was utilizing a new free long-distance program, it was not possible to determine what room had called Marcial's telephone number. Boyett went back to the station to study the spreadsheets from guests who had stayed at the Church Street Inn.

There were sixty rooms at the inn, and all had been rented, which was not unusual for Mardi Gras. Most downtown hotels experienced 100 percent occupancy rates during the Mardi Gras season. As Boyett went through the list, he found several guests who were from outside the immediate area. None had been red-flagged based on criminal history, but several had been red-flagged based on vehicles.

Red flags based on vehicles was problematic in that between 20 and 30% of all guests who registered a vehicle, registered one of the three suspect classes of vehicles. Additionally, the idea that the killer had utilized one of those types of vehicles was just a hunch that Jamison had, although it made sense to Boyett.

Several names on the guest list at the Church Street Inn appeared to have some possibility. One guest was Jorge Rodriquez of McAllen, Texas. Another was James Pond of Pensacola, Florida, and another was Franco Russo from Steelton, Ohio. All three had listed vehicles which were vans, trucks, or SUVs. Boyett was familiar with McAllen from his trips to the border during his assignment to the DEA. He wondered how many Jorge Rodriquezes were in McAllen. He was also familiar with Pensacola, which was about a sixty-mile drive from Mobile. He did not know anything about Steelton, Ohio. Two of the flags next to Russo's name was the fact that he'd registered with a black Ford Econoline van and that he'd been staying alone. His initial criminal history from the FBI reported several minor scrapes with the law for offenses including disorderly conduct, menacing, and trespassing. These crimes appeared to have been committed in a variety of jurisdictions throughout Ohio.

Boyett got out his road atlas and looked up Steelton, Ohio. Steelton was a suburb of Youngstown, located midway between Pittsburgh, Pennsylvania and Cleveland, Ohio in the Rust Belt in northeastern Ohio. According to the map, Steelton had 12,500 residents and was located in Mahoning County. Boyett wondered whether a town the size of Steelton had its own police department or whether it would be covered by a county sheriff's office. He called telephone information to find out.

He got a telephone number for the Steelton Police Department and called, hoping to gain some background on Russo. The call was answered by a police dispatcher who listened to Boyett's introduction and then forwarded Boyett to "our detective." Boyett listened to the telephone ring about fifteen times in hopes that "the detective" would answer, but to no avail. He hung up and called back. This time, he told the dispatcher that no one had answered the detective's telephone. The dispatcher took Boyett's name and number and said she would relay the message to the detective to call him back.

Boyett continued studying the spreadsheets and running down missing information on potential suspects. He made a call to the Escambia County Sheriff's Office about James Pond. The detective there said that Pond had no criminal record.

He also placed a call to the McAllen Police Department in Texas and left a message requesting a call back. He waited through the afternoon, but he never got a return call from the Steelton police detective. He thought maybe the message had not been delivered or that some more pressing matter was being handled in Steelton. Boyett wanted to check out this guy in order to decide whether to expand the list of records to be subpoenaed.

As Friday afternoon wound down, Boyett made another call to Steelton, Ohio. He asked a dispatcher to take his cell phone number and forward it to the department's detective. After that last ditch effort, he headed home, hoping to get a telephone call from Ohio sometime over the weekend.

Boyett spent the weekend doing "honey do's" and attending his kids' events, including Chris's baseball game and Samantha's dance recital. Even though he was home and away from the office, he kept thinking about the Marcial investigation and where it might lead. So far, the investigation seemed to be spinning its wheels, going nowhere, although Boyett was hopeful that this lead in Ohio might pan out into something.

On Monday morning, March 20, Boyett was back in the office reviewing the latest copies of the spreadsheets that Jane Bonham had emailed to him. As these spreadsheets became full, the columns seemed to make some hotel guests look better as suspects and others not so good. Boyett was debating on asking Lieutenant Zumwalt if he could do a road trip. He wondered if it might be beneficial to go and at least interview the various suspects he'd identified so far.

In reviewing the latest spreadsheets, Boyett came upon another name: John Hundley. Hundley had been registered at the Holiday Inn not far from Marcial's hotel. He did not have a vehicle registered at the Holiday Inn, but a run of his criminal history showed a spousal abuse case in 2001 and domestic-related assault. Hundley had been arrested in West Chester, Pennsylvania and gave an address in Media, Pennsylvania on his hotel guest registration.

Boyett got out his map and looked up the towns in Pennsylvania. West Chester was located about twenty-five miles west of Philadelphia, not far from the Delaware border. Media was located about ten miles from Philadelphia, between West Chester and Philadelphia. Boyett decided to follow up.

His call to the West Chester Police Department was quick. While talking to a dispatcher, Boyett learned that Hundley actually had been arrested by neighboring West Goshen Township police and that he'd apparently been booked at the West Chester Police jail on a temporary basis. Boyett was given the telephone number of the West Goshen Police. He followed the West Chester call with a call to the West Goshen Police.

He talked to Detective Dave Snyder at the West Goshen Police Department and explained the Marcial investigation. Snyder said that Hundley and the case surrounding Hundley's arrest involved Hundley's former spouse, and that the two had a history of domestic calls dating over several years in the period 1999 through 2001. Snyder told Boyett that the domestics ended when the couple separated and got divorced. He said Hundley had moved from what had been the family residence and the ex-wife had stayed. He knew that Hundley worked at nearby West Chester University as a professor in the social sciences department. Snyder said that he personally knew Hundley, having taken his undergraduate degree at the university. He doubted Hundley was the type of guy who would commit such a crime. Besides, Hundley was in his fifties and looked his age, if not older, and probably wouldn't be confused with a guy in his thirties. Snyder told Boyett he would be more than glad to do whatever he could to assist Boyett on the investigation and that anything Boyett needed to just call.

Boyett thanked Snyder and hung up the telephone.

Another strike, he thought. It made him want more than ever to find a lead that seemed worth following.

When Lieutenant Zumwalt arrived, Boyett decided to discuss the case and get his input concerning whether he should travel to interview any of the potential suspects, or whether they should just expand the ring of hotels to the next grid and see what popped up on the spreadsheets.

He briefed Zumwalt on the status of the investigation and what each potential lead had uncovered.

Zumwalt said that Boyett should continue the lead in Ohio and that if he wasn't able to get anyone from the Steelton Police to return a call, that Boyett might try the Ohio State Police or some other agency such as the local sheriff's office. He added that it was probably time to expand the subpoena grid, since it would be days getting the records back.

Boyett thanked Zumwalt for understanding the difficulty he was having and went off to make the list of hotels for the next round of subpoenas. He decided to try his luck with another telephone call to Steelton. A dispatcher again answered this call.

When Boyett identified himself, the dispatcher asked, "He didn't call you yet? I gave him your name and number last week. Let me find him." With that, Boyett was placed on hold. After a few minutes, the dispatcher returned and told him she'd found Detective Pappas and would transfer him now.

Boyett heard the telephone ringing. After about twelve rings there was an answer.

A man identified himself as Detective Pappas and asked what Boyett needed.

Boyett explained the details about the Marcial murder and asked Detective Pappas if he could supply any background on Franco Russo or his prior arrests.

Pappas listened without saying a word. The only sign Boyett had that he was still there was the faint sound of breathing at the other end of the line.

After Boyett had finished relating all the details about the investigation, Pappas stated, "I don't know anything about the guy. Never even heard the name. I never arrested him."

Boyett countered, "Well, since he was arrested by your department on at least one occasion, and since he apparently lives in Steelton, I thought you might be able to assist me in running down some leads."

Pappas replied, "I think you need to find out which officers arrested this guy and maybe talk to them. I've got plenty of my own cases with their own leads that need to be run down. Sorry, I can't help." And with that, he hung up on Boyett.

Boyett was stunned! Never in his career had he encountered another cop who was so rude or uninterested in helping a fellow officer in a major case. Although he realized that sometimes officers were, in fact, very busy, in his past experiences even the busiest officers had referred him to others who could help. Policing was supposed to be a brotherhood.

He could only shake his head. *Pappas must be the family outcast.*

He sat for a few minutes and thought about what he could do next. He knew he could make cold calls to other agencies such as the local sheriff's office or even some state investigative agency, but he also knew that many of these agencies did not like to intrude on another's turf without being invited in. He decided to make a call out to the DEA office and talk to the new resident agent in charge to see if he could hook Boyett up with the nearest DEA office to Steelton. He knew that most DEA offices had state and local task forces and usually had great relationships with the state and local agencies. He figured that some type of introduction through DEA would probably help determine who would be a good agency to work with and who, besides the Steelton Police Department, had jurisdiction on Russo.

Boyett placed a call to the DEA office and asked for Detective Jim Patterson. Patterson was the Mobile Police Department officer who had succeeded Boyett at the DEA Task Force about four years before. Boyett told Patterson about the snafu he'd just encountered with the Steelton Police Department. He asked Patterson how the new DEA boss, Herman Mulberry, was. He'd briefly met Mulberry a few months earlier, but he did not feel friendly enough to approach him for help outside the DEA's jurisdiction.

Patterson told Boyett that Mulberry was somewhat aloof, probably because he'd spent his whole career in large cities on the east coast, but other than that, he seemed OK.

Boyett asked Patterson to approach Mulberry and brief him on the Marcial case. He was hoping that a call and introduction to the DEA resident agent in charge in northeast Ohio might result in an introduction to a good, solid cop in Ohio who had jurisdiction and whom Boyett could trust to assist.

Patterson told Boyett that Mulberry was out of the office, but that he would approach him as soon as he returned.

At 1:30 p.m., Patterson called Boyett back. Herman Mulberry was in and would be glad to meet with Boyett. Boyett made the ten-minute drive to the DEA office, located in a commercial executive center just west of Midtown, near Interstate 65.

Upon arriving at the DEA office, Boyett was greeted by several of the secretaries who worked out front. They were always the nicest people who always asked questions about how life was going, how was the family, and so on. Boyett had always felt at home with the office, although he realized that the women in the support staff were about the only stable thing in the DEA. Between DEA agents rotating about every five years, DEA bosses playing musical chairs, and task force agents coming and going to and from their departments, Boyett estimated that since he'd left, there had probably been a seventy-five percent turnover in the agent base.

Boyett met with Jim Patterson, who escorted him to the front office where Herman Mulberry had his office.

Upon entering Mulberry's office, Patterson made a brief introduction.

Boyett and Mulberry shook hands, and Patterson made an exit. Boyett sat down with Mulberry, and they exchanged pleasantries and brief introductions. Mulberry told Boyett that he'd started as a local cop in a small town in New Jersey before being hired by the DEA. They briefly discussed Boyett's career and his assignment to the DEA Task Force. Boyett was careful to only praise the DEA Task Force. When Mulberry asked him whether he would be interested in another assignment to the Task Force, Boyett danced around the real issues and told Mulberry that he realized that with the nature of the interstate drug trafficking DEA concentrated on, he probably was not in a position to perform that duty well, since he now had kids and his wife worked. The last thing he wanted at this point was another assignment to the DEA.

After this brief chit-chat, Boyett explained where the Marcial investigation was at. He asked Mulberry to make a call to the head of whatever DEA office covered Steelton, Ohio and make an introduction of Boyett to that office head. Boyett explained that he hoped the DEA boss in Ohio could further introduce him to a local officer in the area who had jurisdiction and was willing to work with him on the Marcial investigation.

At the end of Boyett's spiel, Mulberry asked Boyett if he'd considered contacting the FBI, as it appeared there was an interstate nature to the investigation. Boyett explained that Lieutenant Zumwalt had made the profiling request and that they hadn't gotten anywhere. Mulberry said he understood and that he would be glad to make a telephone call up to Ohio and see if the DEA office could help Boyett. He insisted there were no guarantees, but he took Boyett's cell phone number and said that as soon as he got a name and number from the Ohio DEA office, he would call.

Boyett left the DEA office with a positive feeling. Mulberry seemed genuine enough and really did seem interested in helping. He returned to the detective bureau and went back to reviewing the spreadsheets and running down missing data.

At 3:40 p.m., Boyett's cell phone rang. Upon answering, the caller introduced himself to Boyett as Special Agent Tim Miller of the DEA office in Youngstown, Ohio. Miller told Boyett that he was the acting resident agent in charge and that Mulberry had called and briefed him on Boyett's dilemma. He said that instead of trying to play telephone tag, Miller would just call Boyett directly. Miller said he was sure that Boyett could be hooked up with one or more great investigators in the area. The DEA Task Force in Youngstown was made up of twelve state and local cops and had some of the best investigators in the area. Like all DEA Task Forces, there were many investigators who had served on the DEA Task Force and had rotated back to their respective departments. Miller was sure that several of them had jurisdiction in Steelton.

Boyett gave Miller a brief synopsis of the case and the issues he'd had with the Steelton police.

Miller responded that officers from the Steelton Police Department were not known for being responsive or very interested in fighting crime. He said that on several occasions when the DEA was working the Steelton area, the DEA couldn't get assistance from the Steelton Police either. Miller described Steelton as a once thriving steel mill town and that the steel mill, which had closed many years ago, had provided most of the jobs in the area. Now Steelton was a shell of what it had once been.

Miller explained that crime was rising dramatically in Steelton and drugs were becoming a major problem. He said in spite of this, the cops seemed to go in to work, put in time, and never accomplish anything. Rumors and accusations had been rampant for years that the local mob made most of the decisions relating to the Steelton Police Department, including who got promoted. Several of these accusations were included in interviews and testimony relating to an organized crime investigation that had been the center of an on-going corruption probe in Mahoning County. That probe had produced a variety of indictments and convictions including judges, the former sheriff, the former county prosecutor, and a host of lower echelon political flunkies, as well as some cops.

Miller added that the police agencies in Mahoning Valley ran the gamut from excellent to very poor. Each little community had a chief of police and its own city leaders. The police departments in the area ranged in size from two part-time officers to 180 officers in the city of Youngstown. He promised Boyett he would make some calls and find a good investigator, hopefully a former task force agent, who had jurisdiction and was willing to work and help.

Boyett thanked Miller for being so responsive.

Miller replied, "If there's a murderer up here, we want him off the streets. We've had too many murders of our own to let a guy stay out on the street to do it again." With that, he and Boyett ended the conversation.

Boyett felt much better after the conversation with Miller. At least he seemed to be as interested in getting a killer off the streets as Boyett was. As he was cleaning up the paperwork for the day, his phone rang.

It was the D.A.'s office. Boyett was informed that a case he'd assisted on a year before was going to trial the next morning. Apparently, all plea negotiations had broken down that morning and the judge had set jury selection for Tuesday.

Boyett thought, *If anything can go wrong...*

He spent the next three days sitting at the courthouse with about half the detective squad, waiting to be called as a witness. His participation in the case had been working the initial crime scene, interviewing a few witnesses and later, sitting in for an interview of the defendant.

What should have been a fairly easy case, with lots of evidence and several eye-witnesses, turned into a theatrical production. Boyett finally got in to testify late Thursday morning and his testimony took less than an hour. As he finished, the courtroom adjourned for lunch. Boyett asked the assistant district attorney if he could be excused for the rest of the trial.

The A.D.A. told him to come back after lunch and if he wasn't needed for anything else, he would be excused.

During the breaks that whole week, Boyett had made runs to the security checkpoint down in the lobby to retrieve his phone and check messages. The Mobile County Courthouse had recently enacted a policy that no one (including police) was permitted to possess a cell phone on the floors where the courtrooms were. Apparently, cell phones ringing had bothered enough judges that they'd banned them.

After the lunch recess, Boyett was released from court and returned to the office to find his message box full and Jane's spreadsheets larger and full of more details. It appeared as the spreadsheet became larger, there were more suspects, as opposed to less. Zumwalt was not in and Boyett went to his desk to make some phone calls.

While Boyett was busy on the phone, Zumwalt walked through the squad bay and motioned that he wanted to see Boyett in his office when he was done.

When he finished his call, Boyett went to Zumwalt's office.

Zumwalt shut the door after him, immediately causing Boyett concern.

Zumwalt sat down with half a smile on his face and said, "I've got good news…and bad news."

Boyett frowned, perplexed, and waited for more.

"Well, let's start with the good news." Zumwalt handed Boyett an envelope with the return address as the chief of police. As Boyett opened it, Zumwalt said, "Congratulations."

The papers inside indicated that Boyett was being promoted to sergeant and that it would occur at the official "promotion ceremony" on April 10. As with most promotions within the department, those promoted were transferred to a new job, usually back to patrol, since about 80% of all police work was in patrol.

Zumwalt said that it wasn't for publication, but that Palmer, who was still at the courthouse, was also being promoted. He added that he, himself, had been hoping to get transferred back to patrol as he was more comfortable in that job than in investigations, but he had not been notified of any other transfers or promotions in or out of the unit. In the police department, there was usually a running list of scores for promotion by rank. There were two promotion tests and two promotional cycles per year. Boyett had taken the sergeant's exam several times, the last being in September of 2005. He'd done well, but the actual promotions depended on how many positions opened up.

If a captain retired, a lieutenant who had taken the captain's exam and was on or near the top of the list would be promoted. That, of course, meant that a sergeant would be promoted to fill the lieutenant's position and a corporal or a detective would be promoted to fill the sergeant's position. However, it was not always this simple. In addition to promotions, cops retired, cops quit, and some occasionally got fired. There were also always changes to the table of organization or organizational chart. One chief might create an office of community policing to be headed by a lieutenant, which would create another position and maybe a couple of sergeants' positions. Sometimes, a chief would merge two units such as the drug unit into the regular investigations squad and have one lieutenant over both units, thus eliminating a lieutenant position.

Where someone was transferred to was a decision that ultimately was made by the chief of police. However, it was widely known that after the promotional list had been determined, the three majors got together and had some sort of draft. They determined who would get whom. Since patrol was the largest division, the major over patrol had the most positions. It was believed by most officers that the majors would meet and choose their favorites for vacant positions and then the remainder would end up in patrol.

Not unlike the DEA, the Mobile Police Department (as with all police agencies) played its own version of musical chairs, the difference being that a promotion or transfer meant you were changing from one squad to another, while at federal agencies like the DEA, it usually meant moving to a new city and sometimes even to a new country.

Zumwalt said, "Let's not forget the bad news." He went on to say he'd been called to Major Coachman's office to meet with the captain and the major. Both men had serious questions about whether it was wise to spend so much time, money, and resources on the Marcial case. When Zumwalt said that Boyett, as well as other members of the detective squad and a retired FBI profiler thought there was a good chance that the killer had killed before and would again, the major asked what the odds were that the killer would commit another homicide in Mobile? Zumwalt said he had no way of knowing that. Major Coachman told him they wanted the case wrapped up and resources reallocated to crimes that could be solved.

Zumwalt looked at Boyett and said, "This one won't be your problem much longer," to which Boyett replied,

"I hope whoever gets this case follows the leads we've started."

As Boyett left Zumwalt's office, his head spun with mixed feelings. He wanted the promotion, which included a raise and some other perks, but he also wanted to finish this

Marcial case. He had the feeling it was much bigger than a single homicide.

Back at his desk, he called Millie to break the news.

"Oh, that's wonderful!" Millie exclaimed. "Now you'll be back on a more routine schedule, even if it is shift work."

Naturally, she was thrilled. Rarely did patrol get called at all hours of the night and rarely did they have to work much past the end of a shift. There were instances where some event occurred and they had to stay a few hours late or they had to go to court during a weekday when they were working the evening shift but generally, they had a set schedule for an entire year, and it stayed set 90% of the time.

As Boyett finished his day, he knew he was going to be leaving the Marcial case to someone—exactly who was yet to be determined—and that it was going to take someone dogged to follow the many leads.

Monday, April 3 came quickly. Boyett had spent the weekend attending his son's little league game and hosting a BBQ for some neighbors at the house. Between those events, he went through his closet and assembled his uniforms to see which ones still fit and which ones did not. With the exception of attending some official functions, he had not worn a uniform in almost seven years. Happily, Boyett found most of the uniforms shirts to be OK, but almost every pair of pants had to be let out in the waist by a couple inches. Still, it was not bad for a guy who was getting older and did not work out as often as he should. He'd assembled all his uniforms and put them into his car so he could take them to the department's tailor to have alternations performed and to have sergeant's stripes sewn onto the shirts.

Upon arrival at the squad room, Boyett did not know where to begin. Palmer came over and they congratulated each other. Palmer reminded Boyett to make sure that all the

Marcial reports were filed and evidence deposited before leaving Friday.

With that, Boyett remembered the box of personal items from July Marcial's apartment.

"You mentioned you could arrange for that to get into the evidence room," he said to Palmer.

Palmer looked back and said, "Not a problem, let me get on it."

Boyett spent the morning writing reports and ensuring that every piece of evidence was properly logged and documented in the reports. At about 2:00 p.m., Palmer called Boyett and told him to take that evidence back down to the evidence room and turn it in. He took the box and went down to find Cpl. Bruce McCrary sitting at his post.

McCrary looked at Boyett, his lips pursed. "Give it to me." He signed the evidence sheet, giving Boyett the copy that went into the case file.

When Boyett arrived back in the squad room, everyone was busy. Zumwalt was in his office with the door closed. Boyett went back to his desk and continued sifting through spreadsheets as well as reviewing lists of hotels, in hopes of sending out another batch of subpoenas before leaving the detective squad. As he was trying to clean up the piles of paperwork in the Marcial case, he continued to worry about who the case might be re-assigned to. When he finished for the day, Zumwalt was still in his office with the door closed.

Tuesday morning started with a telephone call while Boyett was still at home. It was Tim Miller at the DEA office in Youngstown, Ohio.

Miller told Boyett that he'd made contact with several former DEA Task Force agents who would have some form of jurisdiction in Steelton. He said his first choice for the job was a sheriff's deputy named Duckie Jones, but after discussing it with Duckie, Duckie didn't think the sheriff would allow it as it was an election year, and the sheriff wouldn't want to make any enemies in Steelton. Duckie said that if Steelton requested help, the sheriff would fall all over himself to oblige. He added that he went to another former task force agent named Jim Massarelli, who had been promoted to a supervisory agent's position at the Ohio Bureau of Investigation and Identification.

Massarelli was known for working long term paper cases and was currently in charge of a sex crimes team that worked everything from rapes to child porn cases. Miller said that Massarelli was interested in the case and actually mentioned that it would be good to go into Steelton. Under Ohio's BCI&I policy, the BCI couldn't go into a jurisdiction unless it was requested by an agency. In most cases, that meant towns like Steelton requesting assistance. However, if Mobile PD requested assistance, BCI could assist and go into Steelton without an invite from Steelton. BCI often went where they were unwanted when assisting the DEA, the FBI, or other federal agencies. Miller supplied Boyett with Massarelli's telephone number and said that Massarelli was expecting him to call.

Tuesday, April 4 was a sunny day that started with Boyett arriving at the office and getting a message to contact July Marcial's father in Blowing Rock. Upon calling Mr. Marcial, Mr. Marcial, started the phone conversation.

"Has there been any progress in the investigation?" he asked.

Boyett told Marcial, "We've made some progress but as of yet, there isn't one suspect that stands out."

"Has John Hood's name come up as a suspect? Has he been interviewed?"

Boyett, not knowing that name, replied, "No. Who's John Hood?"

Mr. Marcial explained, "Hood is a musician July had a close relationship with. I've met him on occasion and July even brought him to Blowing Rock once. He's a white guy, probably in his fifties. July said they were just friends, but there was some form of chemistry between them, and I suspect it was more than friendship. Hood lives in California, but he's still active in the music business and travels frequently. He didn't attend July's funeral, but he did call and express his condolences. Many of July's musical friends attended the funeral and several expressed bewilderment in Hood not attending."

Boyett asked Marcial if he had a contact number for Hood. Marcial retrieved the number and read off a 213 area code and number to Boyett, who wrote it down on his note pad. He thanked Marcial for calling and told him he would follow up with Hood as well as keeping him informed if anyone was arrested. The call ended with Boyett not mentioning his upcoming promotion or that the case was going to be re-assigned in the near future.

After completing the telephone call with July's father, Boyett went to Jane Bonham and supplied her with John Hood's name and telephone number and asked her to run him through all the systems available.

He then went back to writing reports and determining what the next batch of subpoenas would be sent to the expanded hotel grid.

As Boyett was sitting at his desk, Lieutenant Zumwalt came by and motioned him to come to the office. Once inside, Boyett saw that Palmer was already in the office.

Lieutenant Zumwalt closed the door and motioned for Boyett to sit down. He told Boyett and Palmer that he'd met with Major Holcomb, who headed the patrol division, the previous afternoon, and Holcomb had offered Zumwalt the opportunity to transfer back into patrol. Zumwalt said he was hesitant to do so since his tenure in investigations had only been a few months. But Holcomb told Zumwalt that if he agreed to the transfer, Zumwalt could choose three of the new sergeants for his squad. He'd accepted and asked Boyett and Palmer whether they would be willing to work on that squad.

Both looked at each other and nodded agreement. Boyett told Zumwalt that he would love to work for Zumwalt, because the one thing he'd learned in his short time working for him was that Zumwalt would take care of his people and was willing to learn things he did not know.

Zumwalt said he looked forward to having both of them on his squad, adding that the transfers of personnel would take place at the end of the week and would be effective after the promotion ceremony.

When Boyett got back to his desk, Jane Bonham had already dropped a copy of a public records printout on his desk. He observed that Hood's occupation was listed as "professional musician" and that he had one arrest back in the 1970s for marijuana possession. Other than that, his criminal history was clean. Jane had made some other notes, that Hood seemed to be a successful studio musician, having played in the back-up bands of numerous Grammy award winners as well as on several studio albums that had won Grammy awards. There were even some links to internet websites where photographs of Hood were located.

Boyett looked at his watch and saw it was just after 11:15 a.m. He decided to try calling John Hood, who presumably was on west coast time, which would be two hours earlier. As he made the call, he thought about how to approach Hood, who in theory could be a suspect as well as someone who might provide significant information about July Marcial. Hood's phone rang numerous times before going to his voice mail. Boyett decided to leave a message: "Mr. Hood, this is Detective Boyett with the Mobile, Alabama Police Department. I'm the lead investigator on the July Marcial investigation. Your name has come up as a close friend of July's and I'd like to talk to you and see if you can help us in the case. My number is (251)555-3399. I'd appreciate a call back. Thanks." With that, he wondered whether Hood might ever call back.

As Boyett continued to write reports, Palmer came over to his desk and asked if he wanted to go to lunch. Boyett said yes, and they agreed to leave right away in order to beat the lunch crowds. They chose "the Porch" as it was within walking distance and the food was always good.

As Boyett and Palmer sat in the outside eating area of "the Porch," they were approached by Billy Zindell, a twenty-something-year patrol veteran of the force. Zindell was considered by most to be a mediocre cop who did only what was necessary to get by. He was generally liked by the other cops because he had a great sense of humor and often was involved in practical jokes. It was just his approach to fighting crime that was an issue. Zindell had a plate full of food and asked if he could join Boyett and Palmer. Both motioned for him to sit down.

After taking his seat, Zindell asked if either of them was up for promotion. He told them that after taking the detective's test "too many" times, he'd just been notified that he was being promoted next week at the promotion ceremony and they all might be working together in the detective squad. He also said that he heard it from a reliable source that Lieutenant Stafford from Patrol Squad 3 was being transferred to detectives and that Lieutenant Zumwalt was going back to patrol, overseeing Squad 3.

It was obvious to Boyett that Zindell was getting pretty good, although incomplete, information. He told him, "Well, Billy, it looks like we're going to miss each other. John and I are being promoted and going back to patrol."

Zindell said, "That's great." He then explained that he wanted to get into investigations so he could "clean up" on all the overtime to boost his last years, so he could get a bigger pension. He further said that he owed a bit of his luck to Major Coachman, who had been one of his mentors over the years.

Boyett and Palmer both said that Zindell had better be ready to work long hours and be on call all hours of the day and night, because that's where the overtime came in.

Zindell said he thought he could handle anything after spending his entire career in patrol.

As lunch broke up, Boyett and Palmer bid Zindell good luck and said they would see him on Monday at the ceremony. On the way back to the office, Boyett asked Palmer what he thought of Zindell being promoted into the detective squad and Stafford replacing Zumwalt.

Palmer said, "Well, the detective squad is never going to be the same. Stafford has less knowledge about investigations than Zumwalt. At least Zumwalt's former assignment in traffic included actually investigating traffic accidents and deaths related to accidents. Stafford hasn't done much more than rope off a crime scene and call real detectives. As for Zindell, he won't make a pimple on a real detective's ass."

With that comment, Boyett let out a laugh.

Upon arrival back at the office, Boyett found a message from John Hood. He decided to call immediately.

Hood answered on the second ring.

Boyett introduced himself and said, "As I told you in my message, I'm hoping you can help with this investigation."

"I'd be happy to help," replied Hood, "but I'm hoping whoever did it is already in jail."

Boyett explained that they were still developing suspects and that since he understood Hood and July had been close, Boyett was hopeful that Hood could shed some light on July, her friends, and even her activities. He asked Hood when the last time was that he'd seen July.

Hood said he'd seen her over Christmas. That he wasn't working over the holidays and she was off from school, and that he flew into Mobile, got a rental car, and drove over to Hattiesburg. He said he spent the week from just before Christmas till about December 28 with July and then she drove to North Carolina to visit her father. He'd visited her father with her once, but the vibes he got from July's dad weren't good and he thought it best to avoid him. Boyett asked Hood when the last time was that he'd communicated with July and Hood said he wasn't sure if it was February 27 or 28, but he would be glad to check his phone bill.

As Boyett started to ask the next question, Hood stopped him. "July was someone very special in my life and no one took the news harder than I did. When I heard she'd been murdered, I started drinking and didn't stop for a week. I feel somewhat responsible for her death as I was her mentor."

Boyett started to ask another question and Hood stopped him again. "I'm in Miami finishing up some studio work, which should be done today or tomorrow morning. How about if I come up to meet you and you can ask me anything you want? Hopefully, I can shed some light on July and help you catch her killer."

Boyett readily agreed. They arranged for Hood to call Boyett with a time he would be in Mobile, but it was going to be in the next day or two. Boyett made sure to give Hood his cell number, which he rarely did, to make sure he could be reached. After the call, he felt he was going to make some progress on the case with Hood, as Hood seemed genuine and willing to tell whatever he knew. He went back to writing reports, including one that summarized the telephone call with Hood. He then went to Zumwalt and told him about the call. He said he would possibly accumulate some overtime doing the interview and writing reports, but he would try and keep it down to a minimum.

Zumwalt had no issue with the overtime and suggested that Boyett take one of the detectives who was going to continue his assignment in the squad to the interview too.

Boyett agreed that might be a good idea.

As he was finishing his paperwork for the day, a call came in that a shooting had just occurred at a Winn-Dixie supermarket located in the midtown area of Mobile. Boyett and Jim Roberts were the only ones in the detective squad bay when the call came out. Both rushed to their vehicles and responded. Upon arrival on the scene, they found numerous patrol cars already there and a young, black man seated on the ground, with what was obviously a bullet wound in his shoulder. Another young, black man was in the back seat of a patrol car, screaming obscenities at everyone who passed by.

As Boyett and Roberts tried to ascertain what had happened, other detectives began arriving.

Boyett spoke with some of the patrol officers and learned that the man sitting on the ground had exited the Winn-Dixie store and was walking through the parking lot when the man in the back of the police car approached him. This second man brandished a pistol and shot him, then fled to the streets behind the Winn-Dixie. A patrol car responding to the scene of the shooting observed the young man running down a street with a gun in his hand, pursued him, and took him into custody. The victim had identified the guy in the back of the car as the shooter. As Boyett waited on Lieutenant Zumwalt to assign the case, he knew it wouldn't be his.

Lieutenant Zumwalt arrived and while he was being briefed, Major Coachman arrived. Coachman was then included in the briefing. As this was happening, Officer Billy Zindell appeared as he'd been one of the first officers to respond. Coachman told Boyett to walk Zindell through the investigative process and told Zindell to report to investigations the next day, where Boyett could show him the paperwork and make sure he had a good first case.

Boyett agreed, thinking that Zindell was getting a ready-made case and that he was not going to learn much about being a detective from this, but then he reminded himself, *So what? It's not my problem.*

With Zindell in tow, Boyett started giving assignments. He had the arresting officer prepare a report of what he'd witnessed. He had Roberts respond to the University of

South Alabama hospital to get a statement from the victim as well as retrieve the bullet, so that it could be matched with the gun taken from the defendant. Boyett also got the names as well as summaries of a couple statements from witnesses who were in the parking lot of the Winn-Dixie and had observed the shooting. He then ordered a patrol unit to transport the defendant to the station, where he and Zindell would attempt an interview.

Boyett told Zindell to meet him at the detective unit and left in his car. Within ten minutes, he was back and awaiting Zindell before heading to the booking area to try to interview the defendant. He waited fifteen minutes for Zindell before calling dispatch and requesting they contact Zindell to ascertain his ETA. After several calls by dispatch, Boyett was told Zindell was enroute.

Another twenty minutes passed before Zindell arrived at the detective squad room.

Boyett, feeling disparaged, asked Zindell what had taken him so long.

Zindell replied that he'd met up with some fellow patrolmen who were asking about his promotion and new assignment. Then he added, "Don't worry Three B, it's just more overtime for us."

Boyett bit his tongue in order not to tell Zindell what he thought of this.

It was now 6:10 p.m. and Boyett and Zindell were just going to start the interview with the defendant. Boyett arranged for the defendant to be brought out of the processing area where he was being detained. Upon moving the defendant to an interview room, Boyett, with Zindell alongside, informed the defendant of his Miranda warnings and asked him his name so that he could detail his personal history. This was usually the moment when a detective could build a rapport with a defendant and induce them to confess to the crime for which they were charged.

In this case, the defendant looked at Boyett and said, "You arrested me. Damn, you don't even know who you arrested?"

Boyett replied, "I didn't arrest you. A patrolman arrested you when he saw you with a gun. My job is to figure out what led to all this. So, will you just give me your name?"

With more than a little attitude, the defendant replied, "My name is Jesse James... Ask me again and I'll tell you the same."

With that, Zindell shouted at the defendant, "Listen, asshole, you tell us your name, or I'll come across this table and beat it out of you!"

Boyett glared at Zindell and said under his breath, "Outside. Now."

Outside the room, he explained to Zindell that in investigations, you get more confessions by defendants liking you. "That the guy is already under arrest and a confession would just make the case easier to prove. We don't beat people to get confessions." He cautioned Zindell, "If you make those kinds of statements to defendants, it'll eventually catch up to you and you won't be a detective or maybe even a cop anymore. Now, when we go back in there, just listen and don't say anything. It's better that we get nothing rather than give some defense attorney fodder to argue for the defendant in court."

Zindell looked like he wanted to reply but in the end, he only shrugged and followed Boyett back into the interview room.

Boyett took his seat again and looked straight at the defendant. "OK, Jesse, where do you live?"

The defendant looked at Boyett and laughed. "You don't really think my name is Jesse James, do you?"

Boyett said, "It doesn't matter what you say your name is. Your fingerprints are going to tell us who you are, so it's just a matter of time till I know all about you. I'm asking because I want to know who you are and hear your side of the story."

With that, the defendant shook his head and said, "OK, my name is Frank Wright."

Boyett responded with, "Where do you live, Frank?"

"Here and there. I was staying down at the rescue mission, but I got in a fight a couple nights ago and they threw me out."

"So, what started the incident today?'

Wright gave Boyett a level look. "About thirty minutes before I shot that asshole, I was panhandling in the Winn-Dixie parking lot, asking for some money, just enough to get some food to eat for dinner. That asshole I shot? I asked him if he could spare some change and he called me a low life nigger and told me I needed to get my ass off the street and get a fucking job. That's exactly what he said. Then he went into the Winn-Dixie. Since I wasn't getting any money panhandling, I decided to see if I could steal from some cars that people left open. I probably got into maybe four or five of them cars and found some change, then in the last one I found that gun. I figured I could sell the gun for some cash. After I got outta that car, that asshole came walking across the parking lot again. I was still fuming from him calling me names earlier. When he said something to me this time, I pulled out the gun and shot him. I didn't mean to kill him, that's why I shot him in the shoulder."

Boyett shook his head. "What did he say to you right before you shot him?"

Wright replied, "I really don't know. I wasn't listening. I saw his mouth moving but I really didn't hear the words."

"OK. Do you need to make any phone calls? Let someone know you've been arrested?"

"Nah. I got no one to call." Wright then asked Boyett what was going to happen to him.

Boyett said he was going to be charged with assault with a weapon and probably theft from a vehicle. That he would be booked into jail and that he would have a hearing for bail, probably the next day.

The defendant looked at Boyett and said, "For the police, you're a real nice guy." Then he glowered at Zindell. "But you're an asshole."

After taking a written statement from Frank Wright, Boyett and Zindell went back to the squad room, arriving about 8:05. Roberts was there. He had the bullet that had been removed in the ER from the victim and a statement. The victim had told Roberts that he'd been harassed for money by the defendant prior to going into the Winn-Dixie. He said that after verbally abusing the defendant, he felt he'd overreacted. Upon exiting the store, the victim had observed the defendant again and attempted to apologize, when the defendant pulled out a gun and shot him in the shoulder. The victim had also told Roberts that he was confident the defendant did not mean to kill him, because when he first pulled the gun, the defendant had it pointed directly at his face from about three feet away. But before pulling the trigger, he moved the gun toward the victim's shoulder and fired, then fled.

As Boyett and Zindell were preparing to leave the squad room, Boyett told Zindell that work officially started at 8:30 a.m., but that detectives often showed up early, depending on what was on the agenda for that day. "I usually get here about 8:00 a.m.," he added, "so be here and we'll get the rest of the investigative paperwork together on this."

Zindell replied with a curt, "Roger," and the two parted ways.

***

The next morning, Boyett was out of the house at the usual time and making the usual phone calls while driving in. He arrived at the squad room about 7:50. Jim Roberts was already there, finishing the paperwork and packaging the bullet to be sent to the lab from the night before.

Boyett was hesitant to begin any paperwork since this was supposed to be a training case for Zindell, so he got a cup of coffee and went back to the Marcial case and checking his phone messages. One of his messages was from Ohio BCI supervisor Massarelli. He'd called in late the day before and had left a brief message for Boyett to call whenever he was free.

Boyett checked and determined that northeast Ohio was an hour ahead of Mobile. He called Massarelli.

Massarelli picked up on the first ring.

Boyett introduced himself and he and Massarelli started talking.

Massarelli said he understood that Boyett had been on the DEA Task Force in Mobile. Boyett replied that he was, but had been back in major crimes investigations for several years. Massarelli said he'd spent five years on the DEA Task Force in Youngstown, and it was the best job he ever had. He also said he had relatives in Tuscaloosa, Alabama and that he loved visiting there. Then he gave a "Roll Tide" yell.

Boyett just laughed.

Massarelli then said he loved working with the DEA, especially the big T-III wiretaps and traveling to cities all over the country for search warrants and round-ups. He said he loved every day of it, but that in order to get promoted at BCI, you had to rotate back to the main office, which he did.

Boyett replied that it was similar in Mobile, that most agencies wouldn't allow sergeants to be assigned to federal task forces, but that the experience had been very valuable.

"So," said Massarelli, getting to the subject at hand. "Tell me a little more about the case."

Boyett explained a bit and told Massarelli that one potential suspect was this guy, Franco Russo from Steelton. He then explained his little experience with Steelton and how he'd gone through the DEA to try and find some help.

Massarelli said, "The Steelton Police Department is worthless. Probably pretty corrupt, too, but for sure worthless. Steelton's full of drugs, gambling, and crime, and the police department rarely arrests anyone for anything more than a traffic ticket or public drunkenness."

He went on to say the only thing that might stop BCI from helping was that they needed a letter from the Mobile Police Chief requesting assistance. Then he would do whatever Mobile wanted. Massarelli suggested that he could fax down a copy of a letter that another department had used and that Boyett could change out the requesting agency, etc., and have the chief of police sign it and send it on. That because it involved Mahoning County, when approved in Columbus, Ohio, it would be sent to Massarelli. He suspected that process might take a week from the time the letter hit Columbus.

Boyett told Massarelli that he really appreciated the help, but also that he was being promoted and transferred. He said that if Massarelli would fax the "go by" letter, he would write the letter to the point that whoever got assigned the case could put in their name and send it to the chief for a signature and everything would be great.

The conversation ended with Massarelli saying the letter would be on the fax in ten minutes and wishing Boyett good luck with the promotion. When that call ended, it was 8:45 a.m. and Boyett still saw no sign of Zindell.

He went back to reviewing the Marcial case and writing reports. This continued until about 9:30 a.m., when Zindell finally appeared.

He apologized for being late, explaining that he'd stopped at the city garage to inquire about when he could pick put his new detective car.

Boyett asked him how that worked out, since it was common practice for the lieutenant in the unit to assign cars to detectives.

Zindell said that the people at the garage did not know how the cars were assigned and that he should inquire further up the chain of command.

Boyett decided to let him figure it out for himself.

He told Zindell that he needed to get the gun seized yesterday processed and sent to forensics along with the bullet to have it tested to determine that it did, in fact, come from the gun.

"Why is that even important if Wright confessed?" Zindell asked.

Boyett explained that if Wright recanted his confession or of the confession was suppressed, they would have to prove the case in court. This process ensured that if anything went wrong, the state would be ready to go to trial. He said that the reports also often were the things that made the defense lawyers want to plea a case, as they could see that all the Ts were crossed and Is dotted.

Zindell said, "OK. Just seems like a lot of work for a case that's already made."

Boyett and Zindell spent the next couple hours completing the required reports and transferring the weapon and bullet to the Alabama Forensics Lab. By the time they completed that task, it was lunchtime, and Boyett asked Zindell if he had a preference.

Zindell said he would prefer "the Porch" and they drove there.

After getting their meal and sitting down, Boyett's cell phone rang, and he answered.

It was John Hood, who informed Boyett that he'd just arrived in Mobile. He said he would have called earlier, but as the session broke up in Miami, he had the chance to hop on a private jet with one of the record producers who was flying to California, and they agreed to drop him off at the Mobile airport.

Hood told Boyett that he could meet him within thirty or forty-five minutes, but he preferred not to meet at the police station. He asked if there were any coffee shops around.

Boyett thought for a minute and said there was a Starbucks near the Belair Mall about five miles from the airport.

Hood said he would grab a rental car and meet Boyett there at 1:30 p.m.

After hanging up, Boyett told Zindell that after lunch they were going to a Starbucks to meet a guy who might have information on a major murder case.

Zindell looked perplexed. "Why are we meeting him at Starbucks? What's wrong with the police station?"

Boyett explained that the guy had flown in from Miami and requested to meet at a coffee shop instead of the police station, and sometimes it was more important to appease the person you needed information from, rather than get confrontational. "Zindell…in this job, you're going to learn you make cases based on information people share with you. You have to get them on your side, or they don't cooperate. You have a lot to learn."

Boyett and Zindell entered the Starbucks about an hour later and Boyett immediately spotted Hood. He was about six-foot-three, 220 pounds, and sported salt and pepper hair and a fu Manchu. He looked like a musician, right out of Central Casting.

Boyett introduced himself and Zindell and the three of them moved over to a table in a quiet corner.

Once seated, Hood said, "I presume you've done some background on me?"

Boyett admitted that he had.

Hood said that one of the reasons he did not like police stations was that back in the 1970s he was arrested with a half-ounce of weed. He said the arresting cops acted like it was 100 kilos of heroin.

"They wanted to know where I got it. I told them I'd bought it from a guy backstage that was working at the last concert and didn't know his name. They didn't believe me. They manhandled me, trying to force me to give up my source, as if I always got my weed from just one guy. Those cops left a real bad taste in my mouth. If my relationship with July wasn't important, I wouldn't be talking to you now."

Boyett asked Hood, "How did you meet July Marcial and what was your relationship?"

Hood began by explaining that he was on tour with a band back in 2000 when they played at the University of Tennessee. "After the concert, me and other band members went to a bar at the hotel we'd stayed at. I was approached by a very cute college coed who turned out to be July Marcial. It's not unusual for band members to be approached by groupies, but instead of stupid questions and asking for autographs, July asked intelligent questions about instruments and things like pay rates for touring and studio work. She said she was getting ready to graduate and that touring and seeing the country was what she wanted to do. I was impressed when she said she played seven different instruments. I noticed there was a piano in the corner of the bar and asked her to go play something. She walked over to the piano and began a great introduction to George Harrison's song "Something", then she played and sang wonderfully. Everyone in the bar took notice It was obvious from her first notes that she was a natural musician."

"Before the night was over, most of the band at the bar were crowded around the piano, singing while July played song after song from the 1960s and 1970s from memory. The night broke up when we got called that the tour bus was ready to depart. I gave July my phone number and email address and told her to get up with me when she graduated. I knew that night she was going to be successful in the music business."

Hood continued, "After that meeting, we began corresponding and calling each other. At first it was once every week or two, then more frequently. In addition to having music in common, we seemed to have some chemistry. In early 2001, when July was preparing to graduate from Tennessee, she asked me to try to arrange a position on a tour for her. I said that would be easy as I usually put together the back-up band members for tours. I arranged for her to begin touring with my group just after she graduated in May of 2001."

Boyett and Zindell listened, fascinated, as Hood explained how the tours often lasted for many weeks and sometimes many months. He said that while touring, July became a favorite of the band members because she had a bubbly personality and was good at what she did.

"She didn't cause any drama with the other musicians, which wasn't always the case," he said. "During the first tour, July began confiding in me about her personal life, everything from her financial situation to her sex life. She told me that sexually, she was confused. She'd been brought up in a very conservative household and was told not to have sex until she was married. She confided that she had a boyfriend in her junior year of college and that they'd indulged in regular sex, and that she loved it. She told me that it lasted for several months until one day the boyfriend just up and left school and refused her calls. I could tell that his rejection affected her pretty adversely. She also said that in her senior year she had a very short-term fling with another guy who degraded her after sex and called her names. She broke this relationship off.

"I was becoming a mentor to her in her personal life as well as her music career. I told her that there were people in life that would use her and that she needed to learn to judge people. I also told her I would be 100 percent honest with her, no matter what. July had no practical concept of money when I first met her. She had a credit card that was carrying a high balance at twenty-something percent interest, her credit score was in the dumps, and she had no concept of how to buy a car, which she desperately needed. I spent time with her, teaching her about credit and helping her whittle her credit card debt down to zero. I helped her get a credit card that paid her rewards and helped her start an investment account and an IRA. I coached her on buying the 2004 Honda and getting a good deal on it. She was an extremely fast learner, and she could easily have transferred that knowledge into the music business as she gained more experience.

"My relationship with July took a strange turn in late 2002, though. We were on tour in Palm Springs, California, staying overnight at a nice hotel. Every band member had their own room. About 2:00 a.m., July entered my room and climbed in bed with me. I don't know where she got the key. I didn't wake up until she was under the covers. She was naked. I woke up, and I knew it was July. I asked her if she was sure this was what she wanted… and she said, 'I've been waiting for this moment forever.' We made love all night.

"The next day, I decided we had to have a little heart-to-heart. I told July I loved her, but that the age difference was no good for her. But I'd always be there for her, no matter what. July just looked at me and said, 'That's all I can ask for… at least for right now. But I might want more sex later,' and she smiled.

"As the months and later years went by, we'd tour together for six to eight months a year, and we continued our relationship as well as our sexual affair. July would go back to North Carolina several times a year to visit her father, but she also had a key to my apartment in Los Angeles, where she'd spend several months a year, sometimes with me and sometimes without me. She became such an accomplished musician that she was often called to do studio work, and she became a better musician than me. I was proud to see her achieve great things and do so well. It wasn't unusual for either of us to go off and do sessions for weeks or go on separate tours for months, but we talked and texted almost daily, depending on where we were.

"Early in 2004, we were in Sarasota, Florida playing a music festival. After the festival, we stayed a few days longer, since neither of us had anything scheduled. We went to an art/jewelry/gem festival. Our relationship was going great, and I wanted to buy her a keepsake. July didn't want a ring for her hand as she already wore several, so we settled on a green turquoise toe ring. I had it engraved on the inside: JH-JM. When July put it on the middle toe on her right foot, she swore she'd never take it off. We joked that she didn't think our relationship was anything traditional, so where the norm is a ring on the third finger of the left hand, a toe ring on the middle toe of the right foot seemed perfect.

"Over Thanksgiving of 2004, July insisted I accompany her to North Carolina for the holiday. From the time I arrived and met her father, the chemistry wasn't good. In early 2005, July approached me and broached the idea of dropping out of touring and going back for her master's degree and possibly later to get a PhD. She really loved touring and studio work, but she was smart enough to see that the life could wear on her. She also confided that she might like to teach music at the college level and continue doing some studio work, but not so much of the touring in the future. I told her she'd make a great teacher and I'd support whatever decision she made. She began applying to various schools and settled on the University of Southern Mississippi.

"When we finished touring in early 2005, July went to Hattiesburg to get an apartment. I knew she had about twenty to thirty thousand dollars stashed away to keep her through her master's program. When Hurricane Katrina hit New Orleans, her idea of making extra money doing studio work there went down the drain. I helped her get some short-term and one-night gigs in the Mobile, Alabama and Pensacola, Florida areas."

Boyett asked Hood if he was aware whether July was dating or seeing other guys.

Hood said that their relationship surely was not exclusive. He was well aware of July's dating, and she sometimes asked his advice whether to date guys. Hood explained that July had developed a strong sexual appetite and that he and July had discussed sex on many occasions, and that he didn't have a problem with her dating or even having sex with others. He said that as a guy in his fifties, they both recognized that his sexual abilities were deteriorating while hers were increasing.

On that note, Hood said that during her stay in Mobile, July had mentioned meeting one guy at a parade, but she told Hood that she lost him in a crowd but hoped to see him again. She said she was thinking about posting an ad on Craigslist personal ads under "missed connections." Hood also said that he knew July had a profile on several internet dating websites including Plenty of Fish, but that she had not mentioned any particular men to him.

"Did you recover her cell phone?" he asked Boyett.

"No, we haven't," Boyett replied.

Hood said if he did recover it, he would find numerous texts and voice messages to July from him. He remembered texting July either late on Mardi Gras evening or early morning, the day after. He said he was in California the night of Mardi Gras and was not sure what time he texted July, but he thought it was close to midnight. He didn't get a response and didn't think much of it as July may have partied into the night or possibly gone to bed early after a hard day of partying. When he had not heard anything by Thursday, he began to worry and tried several texts and calls, leaving messages. He said by Friday, he was very concerned and texted and called a few more times, even calling a couple of local hospitals to see if she might have had an accident and been admitted.

Hood said he learned of July's death on Saturday, when a fellow musician who lived in the Mobile area called him and said that it had been on the news. He immediately called Mr. Marcial to ask if it was true. He said that right after that call, he was distraught and began drinking and stayed drunk for over a week.

Boyett then went back to the toe ring. He asked Hood whether July ever took it off. Hood laughed and said he didn't think so. He said that after she initially put it on, she tried to take it off and they had to use soap to remove it. When July put it back on, she said she was going to "wear it for life."

"Why'd you ask me about the toe ring?" Hood asked Boyett.

Boyett told him July did not have the toe ring on when she was found.

Hood said he didn't think July would have taken it off or that it couldn't have fallen off.

Boyett then asked if Hood might have a picture of the toe ring, and Hood said that he may have a picture of July wearing it, but was unsure whether it could be enlarged to get a good view. He asked that if Boyett found the ring, whether it could be returned to him, as he would like to keep it a memento.

Boyett said that legally it would be returned to her father, but that he intended to talk to Mr. Marcial and if it were found, he would let Mr. Marcial know about Hood's wishes.

The in-depth interview ended and Boyett thanked Hood for coming to meet him. He promised to be in touch if anything developed. After leaving, on the way back to the police station, Boyett asked Zindell what he thought of John Hood.

Zindell said, "That guy is a degenerate. He's having sex with a girl half his age. He ought to be in jail."

Boyett gazed at Zindell, trying not to frown. "And what law did he break?"

"That's part of the problem. These Democrats don't pass the laws we need in this country."

With that, Boyett ended the conversation.

Back at the station, Boyett went back over July Marcial's telephone records and saw the calls that Hood had described, starting the night of Mardi Gras and continuing until Friday. He decided to call Mr. Marcial.

He told Marcial he'd interviewed Hood and that the information Hood had supplied was very helpful. He also told Marcial that Hood was not a suspect. He then asked Mr. Marcial whether July's turquoise toe ring was among her possessions that Mr. Marcial had cleared out of July's apartment.

Mr. Marcial said that he had her jewelry box "right here" and would look. After about a minute, he said it was not in her jewelry box, but he remembered she had one.

"Is there something significant about the toe ring?" he asked Boyett.

"I don't know," Boyett admitted, "but Hood mentioned that she never took it off." With that, he told Marcial he would touch base if things developed.

He next made a call to Patterson at the DEA Task Force to ascertain whether the DEA had any information on where to send subpoenas for either Craigslist or Plenty of Fish.

Patterson said that to his knowledge no one in the Mobile office had ever subpoenaed either, but he would contact the DEA headquarters intelligence unit and see if they had what Boyett needed.

Boyett started the paperwork to request subpoenas for the text messages from July's cell phone while awaiting information back from Patterson over at the task force.

He pulled the photographs from the autopsy and noted that the abrasion to the toe that had been mentioned was on the right foot, middle toe, exactly where John Hood said July Marcial wore the toe ring. He went back to writing all the reports related to the Marcial case, including the interview with John Hood as well as a summary of the telephone call with Mr. Marcial concerning the missing toe ring. He believed there was a direct correlation with the toe ring. He decided to call Nate Jamison and discuss the case some more.

Upon reaching Jamison, Boyett updated him about the latest on the investigation. He continued, "I interviewed the victim's former boyfriend. They had a pretty non-traditional relationship—he's in his late fifties. But during the interview he said the victim was actively dating and had a high sex drive. The thing I wanted to run by you was he said he bought her a toe ring a couple years ago and that she never took it off. When her body was found, the toe ring wasn't on her foot and there was an abrasion on that toe. The coroner says the abrasion was made after death. Does this add anything to the profile of our perp?"

Jamison thought for a minute. "As to the relationship, you'd be surprised about the number of these age gap relationships that exist, although they often aren't very public. The age has little to do with it. The question is whether the evidence points to the boyfriend. As to the toe ring, that's an important piece of evidence. If the assailant took the time and effort to pry the toe ring off his victim's foot, he almost certainly wanted it for a souvenir or trophy. It would remind him of his exploitations and power, like a trophy would to most kids who play sports. The difference is the killer often utilizes the trophy as foreplay during his sexual fantasies. It tells me that he either planned the murder to some extent or had been in the position before and was of mind to take a trophy."

Boyett asked, "Is it OK to put that in a report? I'm being promoted and transferred back to patrol, and I think it might be important for the investigator who catches this case."

Jamison replied, "Not a problem. Put a note in the file with my name and number on it telling the new investigator to call me if he thinks I can help."

"Thanks, Nate. I appreciate all your help." And with that, Boyett hung up and went back to writing reports.

As the workday closed out, Boyett was almost finished updating the entire Marcial case file, including writing a letter for the chief of police's signature to the Ohio BCI. With the exception of the subpoenas to Craigslist and Plenty of Fish, he wanted to send them out.

At about 9:20 p.m., while he was at home, Boyett's pager went off and he called in immediately. He was informed that all detectives were to report to a crime scene with multiple gunshot victims and a least one death in the area of a housing project known affectionately as Happy Hills, on the north side of the city. Happy Hills was a decades old housing project that had been the hub of gang activity as well as "crack central" in Mobile for years. When cops received a call to go to Happy Hills, they routinely waited for back-up before driving into the area.

Boyett departed his house and headed to Happy Hills. Upon arriving on the scene, he found at least ten patrol units as well as three other detective units on the scene. He was informed that four people had been transported to the University of South Alabama Medical Center and that there was one dead at the scene. He was dispatched to the medical center to ascertain the names of the victims and take statements. He asked if Zindell had been contacted, since Boyett was acting as his training officer. He was told Zindell had been contacted and would be directed to USA Medical Center to assist Boyett.

Upon Boyett's arrival at the medical center, two of the victims were being treated for minor injuries and two were in surgery for more serious gunshot wounds. Boyett made contact with the emergency room chief and told him to ensure that the doctors performing the surgery followed protocol, keeping custody of the bullets and providing their personal information in case they were needed for future trials.

Boyett waited till the first victim in a treatment room was available for questioning.

The victim, a black man twenty-two years of age who identified himself as Tradavis Davis said that the four victims and a couple friends were standing in front of a house when a car came slowly down the street and someone in the back seat began shooting. Davis said he did not know who the shooter was or the motive behind it. He said when the first shot was fired, he ran for cover. He'd been grazed by a bullet on the arm, but the wound only required a few stitches and a bandage. Davis said the shooter fired at least eight shots and maybe as many as twelve.

Boyett gave Davis his card and asked him to call if he thought of anything else.

Wondering where the hell Zindell was, Boyett then went to the exam room where the other victim was being treated. He waited half an hour for the treatment to finish to interview victim number two.

Victim Two identified himself as Zachary Mullin, another black man twenty years of age. Mullin told Boyett he'd stopped to talk to the group of neighborhood friends when a car drove by, and someone started shooting at them. He said he ran as soon as the shooting started, and felt something strike his leg. He took cover behind a tree. He'd suffered a gunshot wound where the bullet struck his calf and passed right through the tissue, exiting out the front of his calf. Mullin couldn't identify the car nor the shooter.

Boyett checked back with the chief of the emergency department and learned that the surgeries of both victims in the operating rooms would probably last several hours and then the victims would be in recovery for several hours after that.

He called Lieutenant Zumwalt and asked whether he should stay overnight at USA or whether Zumwalt wanted to dispatch another detective to the hospital in the morning.

Zumwalt told Boyett to go ahead and depart USA Medical Center and to complete the interview reports on Davis and Mullins the next morning. He told Boyett to leave Zindell at USA in case anything happened overnight.

Boyett informed Lieutenant Zumwalt that he had not seen Zindell and that he did not think he'd ever arrived at the emergency room.

Zumwalt groaned and told Boyett to go ahead and depart the emergency room. He would find and deal with Zindell.

Boyett departed USA Medical Center and arrived home at about 1:15 a.m., slipping in so as not to disturb his wife and kids. He set his alarm for 6:00 a.m., so he would be able to get in early to write the interview reports and finish some more subpoenas on the Marcial case before his promotion on Monday.

On Friday morning, Boyett woke before the alarm even went off. He was up and was in the kitchen, brewing a pot of coffee, when Millie came out in her dressing gown, her curly blond hair still messy from bed.

She asked him what had kept him so late the prior night and he told her about the shooting in Happy Hills.

Millie gave Boyett a slow blink and asked the question of the century. "Isn't there some way Mobile could de-annex that shit hole?"

Boyett shook his head. "Everybody would love that, but if I had the answer, I could run for mayor and be mayor for life." He poured coffee into his travel cup, gave his wife a kiss, and was out before 7:00 a.m.

He was the first one to arrive at the office, and he immediately sat down to write the reports on the interviews of Mullin and Davis. As he was writing, the other detectives began arriving.

Boyett went to the Marcial file and found that Jane Bonham had deposited numerous documents that had been subpoenaed into the file, including some more telephone records, more guest lists from some hotels, and criminal history sheets and public records checks on different guests. Jane had a great grasp of the organization of the file, adding numbers to the spreadsheet and labeling every document that related to a particular person. Each person had a file with their name as well as their corresponding spreadsheet number. By this time, there were over a thousand sheets of paper in the case file and without these numbers and separate files, it would be very easy to lose them or mix them up.

At about 9:00 a.m., Boyett called out to Jim Patterson at the DEA office to see if Patterson had obtained any more information on where to send subpoenas to Craigslist and Plenty of Fish.

Patterson answered and told Boyett he'd just arrived. While waiting on his computer to upload, he asked Boyett whether he was looking forward to the promotion and going back to patrol.

Boyett said he was looking forward to both the promotion and being back in patrol, but this case was big and complex, and he was concerned over who might inherit it.

Patterson said that occurred almost monthly at the DEA. As agents came and went, cases were reassigned. Sometimes a fresh set of eyes were the best thing that could happen and other times, the investigations just seemed to fall apart. He then said he had an email from headquarters.

With that, he gave Boyett information on Plenty of Fish that included their address, which was in Vancouver, Canada and Craigslist, which was headquartered in San Francisco. Patterson told Boyett there was a note that Craigslist had been a little less cooperative with the DEA in the past, but that he should send the subpoena and then follow up with their legal department in a couple weeks.

Patterson said the DEA analyst noted that the DEA had never issued a subpoena to Plenty of Fish, but there may be some legal complications as it was a foreign company and may have no obligation to respond. He further told Boyett that if needed, there was a Royal Canadian Mounted Police officer assigned to the DEA office in Miami who covered the southeast U.S. for the RCMP. Patterson had met him a few months ago when he traveled to the states he covered. He said that if there were any issues, the RCMP guy might know how to overcome them as he dealt with international cases between the U.S. and Canada all the time.

Boyett said he would check with the D.A.'s office and see how they wanted to handle it. He thanked Patterson and hung up.

By this time, Lieutenant Zumwalt had arrived in his office. Boyett took his interview reports to Zumwalt's office for him to sign. Zumwalt was on the phone as Boyett dropped the reports into his IN box.

Zumwalt motioned for Boyett to hold a minute while he finished up the phone call. When he completed the call, he motioned for Boyett to shut the door. "Three B, what the fuck is going on with Zindell?"

Boyett looked at Zumwalt and asked, "What do you mean?"

"He never responded last night, even though he confirmed to dispatch that he was in route."

Boyett said he had not talked to Zindell the prior night, but he told Zumwalt about Zindell taking an hour to get back to the office after the shooting at Winn-Dixie and about his lack of interview skills.

Zumwalt swore under his breath. "When he gets here this morning, he and I are going to have a talk. If I thought it would do any good, I'd tell Coachman, but he's the reason

Zindell is being assigned here. I guess I'll just let him deal with his boy. As of Monday, you and I are out of here."

Boyett told Zumwalt he had to run over to the district attorney's office about issuing some more subpoenas before the day was over.

Zumwalt looked hard at Boyett. "Three B, for a guy who's being transferred, it's pretty obvious that you're going to work until your last minute here on this case."

"Yes, sir," said Boyett, and he turned and left.

Boyett went to the district attorney's office to see Gloria Wood about issuing subpoenas to Craigslist and Plenty of Fish.

Gloria told Boyett she didn't think she would have any trouble with Craigslist, since they were a U.S. company and did business in Alabama. She thought Plenty of Fish might be problematic, being located on foreign soil, but she said the best they could do was try and see whether the company did the right thing. She suggested including with each subpoena a letter explaining that it was pursuant to a murder investigation, that the victim was believed to have been a customer of their website, and that law enforcement was attempting to ascertain whether the victim had corresponded with anyone just before the murder.

She said, "Hopefully they'll do the right thing." She asked Boyett if the case had been reassigned and Boyett said it had not and probably wouldn't be until the next week, after the promotions and reassignments took place.

Boyett went back to the office and began cleaning his personal items out of his desk. These items included notes and papers that had accumulated over the years, ranging from business cards of people he'd met to phone messages that had been left on his desk months and even years ago. He found a lot of memorabilia and mementos from his years in the squad, even the plaque that the DEA had presented to him after he left. He'd placed it in the bottom drawer of his desk with the intent to hang it up, but had somehow forgotten. He spent the rest of the day packing file boxes and tossing stuff into his trash can, and trying not to feel nostalgic about leaving the detective squad.

CHAPTER 4 – A NEW ASSIGNMENT

The weekend was uneventful for Boyett. The squad had been called out to a couple minor calls, but since he and Palmer were on their way out, Coachman had said they were not to be utilized unless "all hell broke loose." Thankfully, it did not.

Monday morning was an exciting time. Boyett dressed in his fresh uniform and headed into headquarters about 8:30 a.m. The ceremony would be held at 10:00 a.m. in the police auditorium. The uniformed shift would have a skeleton crew answering calls while everyone else would be expected to attend the ceremony. The only people actually required to attend were those being promoted and the brass from each department, although most cops went to congratulate their friends and colleagues as well as to see how the transfers were going to affect them. The transfers would take effect that afternoon at 6:00 p.m. Boyett already knew he was assigned to Zumwalt's unit, which would begin its next shift at 6:00 a.m. on Wednesday morning.

Since Boyett had left patrol, the department had gone from three eight-hour shifts per day to two twelve-hour shifts. The shifts worked two days on, two days off, and then three days on and two days off, then two days on and three days off in a two-week period. This meant that the cops worked every other weekend, but they had a three-day weekend every other weekend too. Some guys liked it and some guys did not.

The ceremony started with speeches by the chief and the mayor. Each talked about how the department was one of the finest departments in the country.

Listening, Boyett thought, *If this department is so great, why are we one of the lowest paid departments in the country?* He, himself, had thought about jumping to another department, but he hesitated because he did not want to start at the bottom of the ladder again as well as learn a whole new set of policies and procedures. But he had numerous friends who had left Mobile city to go to Mobile County, Baldwin County, numerous federal agencies, and even the small town of Fairhope, Alabama, which had one of the highest salaries in southern Alabama.

As the ceremony wore on, the names of the officers being promoted were called out along with their new assignments, and these officers went to the stage to receive a handshake from members of the police hierarchy and stand in a line so the attendees could clap at the end of the promotions. In total, thirty-seven officers were promoted. Then the names of the officers being re-assigned were called and they were assembled onstage. When this was done, there were closing remarks about how the department expected good things from both the officers being promoted and the ones being transferred to new positions.

Boyett couldn't help but think, *I bet you're going to regret making Zindell a detective.*

After the ceremony, he went to a little alcohol-free reception that was being held in a conference room down the hall from the auditorium. There, he received congratulations from several officers with whom he'd worked over the years. He eventually ended up talking to Palmer and Zumwalt over in a corner.

Zumwalt said the squad they were going to had some problems and that he was depending on Palmer and Boyett to help fix them. They all agreed this was going to be a switch from what they'd been doing, but they were looking forward to the challenge.

***

The first day of shift was pretty unexciting compared to the detective squad. Calls ranged from people who had locked themselves out of their homes to minor auto accidents. About once per shift, there would be a felony such as burglary to armed robbery in progress somewhere in the city. In most cases, by the time a patrol car arrived the perpetrator had fled, and it became a case of getting a description and putting out a BOLO (Be On the Look Out) in case the perpetrator was observed by a patrol unit in the area. In most felony cases, patrol notified the appropriate detective unit and they arrived and followed up.

Most patrol arrests centered around instances such as minor thefts like shoplifting, domestic assaults, where the police arrived and one of the spouses accused the other of hitting them and there was some type of evidence to support that claim. There were also the usual calls about vandalism and car break-ins. But all in all, patrol was much less intense than investigations and rarely were patrolmen required to be called out. The schedules were so regimented that many of the cops took second jobs working security for businesses or apartment complexes. During the first several months of patrol, Boyett occasionally called over to the detective squad only to learn that the Marcial case had not been re-assigned. Finally in June, he learned it had been re-assigned to Billy Zindell.

Boyett thought, *I'm sure it's not going anywhere*, as he didn't think Zindell was capable of handling the case. *It's a damn shame.*

***

Over the next six years, Boyett earned a reputation as a very competent supervisor. He was fair with his troops, but he also didn't allow them to waste time and screw off when there was work to be done.

In 2012, J.T. Palmer was promoted to lieutenant and moved back to the detective division. By this time, the detective division had been completely reorganized after Coachman had retired. Palmer was assigned to the crimes against persons unit, which included all crimes against people (as opposed to property), but not homicides. After Palmer departed, Boyett became the senior sergeant in Zumwalt's squad, and he often filled in as acting lieutenant when Zumwalt was off.

In December 2014, Zumwalt retired and Boyett became the acting lieutenant pending the promotional announcements for the spring. He'd taken the lieutenant's exam several times and on the most recent exam had scored very well. He knew that meant little, depending on who was in charge of a division and who else was on the promotional list.

In March 2015, Boyett was informed that he was not getting Zumwalt's position or a promotion.

Palmer approached him after hearing the same news and asked if he wanted to come back into investigations. By this time, Boyett's son was in high school, had just gotten his driver's license, and didn't need his dad as much as before.

Boyett told Palmer, "Make it happen," and with a few memos and requests, he was transferred back to investigations at the spring promotional and transfer ceremony. He was assigned to Palmer's investigative squad that was responsible for crimes against persons, not including homicides or serious shooting situations. Those crimes were still handled by the major crimes unit. Still, Boyett relished being back in the investigative field and chasing down criminals. The detective unit still worked the two eight-hour shifts of 8 a.m. to 4 p.m. and 4 p.m.

to midnight, with the evening shift catching the calls that occurred after midnight.

Palmer's squad worked both shifts, but three quarters of the detectives were assigned to dayshift as that was when the investigations actually occurred. Things like interviews, grand jury, consulting with the district attorney's office and crime labs were only available during the daytime. Of course, many of the actual crimes occurred in the evenings, so when a detective caught a case while on evenings, he would begin the investigation and follow it up the next week when he rotated back to dayshift. Boyett was happy working with Palmer and the two made a great team, just as they had for the last decade.

In the spring of 2018, Palmer was notified that he was being promoted to captain of investigations. As captain of investigations, he would oversee all investigations, with the exception of the drug unit, special task forces such as street crimes, and officers assigned to the various federal task forces such as the DEA Task Force, FBI Task Force, ICE, and the child pornography task force.

Not long after Palmer assumed his new position, he called Boyett and invited him out for a beer.

Boyett agreed, and they met after work at one of the local joints not usually frequented by cops.

At the bar, Palmer asked Boyett if he would consider taking over a new unit he wanted to set up. The unit would start with a sergeant as the squad leader, but Palmer hoped it would be eventually organized as a squad headed by a lieutenant and Palmer wanted Boyett to be that guy.

Boyett asked for more information on what the squad would be.

Palmer replied, "Cold cases." Then he explained that there were dozens of half-worked cases sitting in the file room, ready for real investigators to come in and open them back up and get arrests and convictions.

Boyett asked, "Why me, J.T.?"

Palmer replied, "Three B, remember the July Marcial case?"

"Sure I do. I've thought about it several times over the years, but I guess it didn't work out."

Palmer studied Boyett for a moment and said, "You would've had that case solved if you had another month. But the bureaucracy caught us, and it was given to Zindell by a major who only wanted to worry about currying favor to his friends and keeping resources to a minimum. There are a lot of those cases that we can clear with good detective work. You're a bulldog. I want you to head the squad and if I can get you promoted along with it, I will."

Grinning, Boyett raised his glass to toast, "To the new cold case squad! May we clear up the unsolved murders and put some long overdue assholes in jail."

They raised their beers and toasted.

In April 2018, Palmer officially received the promotion to captain and within a month, he was re-drawing the table of organization of the investigative division under his command to include a "cold case squad" with a sergeant as a squad leader situated under the lieutenant of the major crimes squad. He managed to get three additional personnel slots assigned to the major crimes squad, so that the cold case squad wouldn't pull from the major crimes squad, which was now at nine people.

Three months later, Boyett was re-assigned from the crimes against persons unit to the cold case squad, reporting to a new office space on July 30. Additional personnel would be assigned after the fall promotion and transfer ceremony that would occur in October. Until then, Boyett was the lone ranger in the squad, working what he wanted and working mostly alone.

CHAPTER 5 - THE COLD CASE

In his first week in his new position, Boyett went to the file room and to his amazement, he found over 100 unsolved homicides from the proceeding decades. Many of these cases would never be solved, but some were boxes filled with what seemed to be enough evidence to have already charged someone. It was obvious that the department lacked "quality control" of its cases. Some sloppy detectives had done the very minimum on some cases that should have been easily solved, while other detectives may have just had too many cases to handle. But either way, some supervisors did not oversee what was going on, simply signing off on reports requesting to put the case in a pending status.

When Boyett got to the Marcial case, he found that many of the subpoenas he'd issued had come back with information, but that the records had been dumped into the file and reports not even written concerning the information. He also found that Zindell had apparently written the case off as unsolvable within a month of Boyett transferring back to patrol. Zindell had not requested a single subpoena or written a single report, with the exception of placing the file in a pending status, which meant it couldn't be solved at that time.

Boyett began sifting through the papers, trying to get them organized and reading his own reports in order to jog his memory about the things that had happened so long ago.

He called over to Palmer's office. "J.T., since I'm the lone ranger over here, and I've got limited people, would you care if I reopen the Marcial case, since from what I'm seeing in the file, it's pretty solvable?"

Palmer replied, "I brought you over to solve cold cases, Three B. I think you know that case better than anyone, so as they say, go for the low-hanging fruit first."

Boyett told Palmer, "You can expect this one to be solved in a matter of months, maybe weeks."

As he went through the file, Boyett began to match up information that had been returned with subpoenas he'd sent out back in 2006. As he looked at the information concerning July Marcial's texts, it became obvious that everything John Hood had said was spot on. There were messages from Hood to July Marcial almost every day up to Mardi Gras, then more messages beginning at just before midnight Mobile time and continuing until Friday, March 3.

In addition to Hood's text messages, there appeared to be several calls and one text that seemed interesting. The number was a 330 area code, and the phone records indicated that was Youngstown, Ohio. Boyett recalled the conversations with the DEA in Youngstown as well as the state agent in Ohio, and he began going through the old reports in an attempt to remember their names. As he continued going through the file, he found a copy of a DNA report that had been sent after his departure from the detective squad. The report indicated there had been semen found on July Marcial's body as well as on the carpet remnant in which she'd been wrapped. The DNA sample had been classified. In addition, several hairs had been found on the carpet and when analyzed had matched the DNA found in the semen.

Boyett continued reading through his old reports for two days in an effort to remember exactly what he had and what he could prove. He decided to go visit Jane Bonham, who was now an analyst supervisor in the intelligence unit.

When Boyett walked in, Bonham smiled at him and said, "I bet I know why you're here."

Boyett just looked at her.

Bonham said she'd heard Boyett was being put in charge of the cold case unit and she knew where he was going to start. She said after his transfer, she'd continued doing spreadsheets on the Marcial case, but no one in the squad had been interested, especially Zindell. She said she was completely ready to clear this case, even if it was about twelve years too late.

Upon hearing this, Boyett felt he was going to have a much easier time. He told Bonham he wanted to sit down with her and go over some stuff when she had time and they agreed she would make the next afternoon available.

Over the rest of that day and the next morning, Boyett emptied the file boxes and made stacks of papers on tables to make sure he was reading everything methodically. From his review of everything, the evidence seemed to point to Franco Russo, the potential suspect from Steelton, Ohio, whom Boyett had had zero luck getting the Steelton Police Department to assist with.

There were the original calls between the hotels, and the calls to and from the Ohio phone, and the text message on Mardi Gras day. The actual text message was short, just "meet me in the parking lot of my hotel" and it was dated at 2:07 p.m. Mardi Gras day. The last subpoenas to Craigslist and Plenty of Fish had not developed into anything. Craigslist had replied that July Marcial had posted a message on February 27, but their system had no record of a reply. Plenty of Fish acknowledged that July Marcial had an account, but in order to protect the privacy of their customers they needed more information as to what the police were seeking. Apparently, no one from the Mobile Police Department had ever responded to Plenty of Fish.

The next day, when Boyett and Bonham met, Boyett spread the information on the table and asked Bonham what she thought they should do next.

Bonham said that since 2006, more websites and other places had popped up where she could retrieve information. She first said she would run a new criminal history on Russo as he may have committed further crimes in the last twelve years. She also said she would run the DNA through some data banks that the federal government ran. These were used to match unknown DNA with potential suspects. Finally, she suggested they run a public records check that could provide history on Russo and that may include something they were unaware of.

"Thanks, Jane," Boyett said, encouraged. "Get on it, please. I'm going to try and recontact the Ohio BCI and see if I can enlist their help again."

When Boyett got back to his office, he pulled the reports he'd written back in 2006 and found the name of the Ohio agent he'd spoken to, which was Jim Massarelli. He even found a copy of the letter that the chief of police had signed and sent to Ohio BCI requesting assistance and his notes that had Massarelli's telephone number on it.

He called the number, which was answered by a female receptionist. He asked to speak to Massarelli and was informed that he'd contacted the wrong BCI office. Boyett explained who he was and why he was calling.

The receptionist told Boyett that Massarelli had been promoted to the special agent in charge of the BCI office in Cleveland. She provided a phone number and told Boyett to ask for Karen, who was Massarelli's executive assistant.

Boyett hung up from the Youngstown BCI call and immediately dialed the new number and asked for Karen.

When Karen answered the phone, Boyett explained who he was and asked if it was possible to speak to Massarelli.

Karen placed him on hold.

Within about thirty seconds, he heard Massarelli's voice. "Detective Boyett? Good heavens, what happened to you?" asked Massarelli.

Boyett replied, "I got transferred. And I have to apologize because the detective unit just dropped the entire investigation after I was gone."

Massarelli replied, "It's not the first time that has happened. So, are you back on the case?"

Boyett told Massarelli that he'd spent the last decade mostly in patrol but had recently been put back into investigations and was now going to supervise a cold case squad.

"Then it would appear you'll be solving a murder that has haunted you for a while. I know, I've been there." He went on to say that after he received the letter from Mobile, he'd pulled that assignment and called down to Mobile for Boyett. After numerous attempts, he'd been directed to another detective who seemed totally disinterested in the case. "If I recall, he basically said thanks for the call, but don't call us, we'll call you if and when we need something."

He went on to say that he'd done some background on Russo and thought Russo could fit the profile of someone involved in the murder.

Boyett told Massarelli he'd been reviewing the file that now included DNA and text messages, toll records, and that each day, "I'm more convinced that Franco Russo needs to be looked at thoroughly, although it's far from enough to arrest him or even get a search warrant." He asked Massarelli, "What do we need to do now to get assistance from BCI again?"

Massarelli told Boyett, "BCI will need another letter, but send it directly to me in Cleveland and I'll personally oversee any assistance you need."

Boyett thanked Massarelli and told him that this time he was not leaving the case until all the stones were turned.

With that, the call ended and Boyett set about writing a new, updated letter requesting the assistance of Ohio BCI.

He spent the rest of that Friday going through all the reports and photographs in the case file and boxes of notes from 2006. It seemed with every report, a part of his memory was jogged. Although he was trying to keep an open mind, he couldn't get past the phone calls and text on the fateful day where someone utilizing an Ohio number had conversations and the text to meet in the parking lot of July Marcial's hotel. That, of course, was the last time she was seen alive.

***

Upon his arrival at the office the following Monday, Boyett got a call from Jane Bonham.

Jane told him she had some stuff for him to come and see.

When he arrived at the intelligence unit, Jane had Boyett pull up a chair at a table. Methodically, she began bringing out packets of papers.

"First, we don't have a DNA match. This DNA isn't in any of our data banks, which means that the person this DNA belongs to hasn't been arrested for a sex crime. Second—and this is really good, Three B—I ran Russo through a public data base called Info Choice. It's a database of public records plus any random information they can find on a person. It's not always accurate, but it can send help to tell us where we need to look."

Boyett said, "OK, what's it say?"

"Well," Jane said, "this file lists three phone numbers for Russo and one of them is the target phone."

"Wow, that's a big help," agreed Boyett.

"But," Jane interrupted, "for court we'll have to prove that on February 28, 2006, it was subscribed to by Russo, so I'm going to prepare the verbiage for a subpoena for that cell phone. Hopefully, they still have the records we need."

Boyett stood as if getting ready to leave.

Jane Bonham looked up at him. "Where are you going? I'm not done."

Boyett sat back down.

"Are you ready for number three?"

Boyett just said, "Don't tease me."

Jane gave him a knowing smile. "Also according to the Info Choice report, Russo has held a couple different jobs. Delivery driver, auto plant assembly line worker, and... carpet installer."

"Wow," Boyett said again. "Does the report say when and where?"

Jane replied, "Unfortunately not, but that's where good police work is going to come in." Before standing up again, Boyett looked at Jane and asked, "Anything else?"

Bonham replied, "Not right now, but I'm working on it."

When Boyett got back to the office, he immediately began thinking of what information he had that he could base an arrest warrant and or a search warrant on. He began to list the things that pointed to Russo, including the calls between the hotels, the calls between the cell phones, the text message, and the maid who saw July Marcial leave with a white male in his thirties. The fact that Russo had worked as a carpet installer could also explain where the carpet remnant had come from. Boyett knew he was going to have to get some more information in order to write an affidavit for either an arrest warrant or a search warrant.

Boyett decided to reach out to Milton Marcial, just to let him know that he was back on the case. The call went to a message that said the phone had been disconnected. Boyett then called Detective Art Small of the Blowing Rock Police Department.

Upon making contact with the Blowing Rock P.D., Boyett learned that Art Small was now a captain. He was connected to Captain Small, and he reintroduced himself.

Small remembered Boyett and immediately asked, "Was July's murder ever solved?"

Boyett gave Small a short version of his transfer and the lack of serious investigations by his successors. He said he was now back on the case and had some good leads, and he hoped he could get enough probable cause to make an arrest within a month or two. With that, he told Small that he'd tried Milton Marcial's number and got a message indicating the number was no longer in service. He asked Small if there was a way to contact Marcial.

Small told Boyett, "Milton Marcial passed away about two years ago. He'd been having some issues starting about five or six years before that and was diagnosed with dementia and then Alzheimer's. Several times before the diagnoses, I'd run into Marcial in town, and he would ask if I'd heard anything about the case. On one occasion, I even called Mobile and tried to contact you to ascertain the status for Milton Marcial. I was told the case had been closed as unsolved. After Marcial's diagnoses, he hired a housekeeper but as his condition worsened, he would often walk away from the house and get lost, and the department would go out and find him."

He added, "On one occasion, I was on the scene when Marcial was found, and I started talking to him. He didn't recognize me or have a memory of very much at that point. I asked where he was going, and he told me he was looking for his daughter, July, and asked if I'd seen her? It was heartbreaking, to tell you the truth." Small said that about three years ago, Marcial was placed in a facility in Boone, North Carolina, where he eventually died.

Boyett told Small he was sorry that Marcial's life had ended that way. He thanked Small for the information and told him he would let him know about any progress on the case.

Next, Boyett contacted John Hood.

Hood picked up on the second ring.

Boyett attempted to reintroduce introduce himself to Hood, who said, "Detective, I remember you. Do you have some news?"

He told Hood he was back on the case and wanted Hood to know that he was staying on it till he had no other leads to follow up. He told Hood, "I think I'm going to make an arrest in the next few months."

Hood seemed pleased to hear that there may be justice coming after all these years. Boyett ended the call by giving Hood his phone number and telling him that he would keep him notified of any significant developments in the case.

After the calls to Small and Hood, Boyett decided to place another call to Massarelli. He got through to Massarelli and said, "I think we're on to something with Russo."

Massarelli said, "What have we got?"

"Well, did I tell you how the body was wrapped and what the profiler had said?"

Massarelli admitted he did not recall the specifics.

Boyett said, "The body was found partially naked, rolled up in a piece of carpet. The carpet was a remnant that measured about seven feet by eight feet. We have DNA on the body and on the carpet, plus some hair on the carpet that matches the DNA on the body. The DNA isn't in any data bases, but we have phone calls between the victim and an Ohio cell phone. The number of the Ohio cell phone comes out on public records as belonging to Franco Russo. There's also a text message between the phones, where the victim says to meet her in her hotel parking lot. That's the last place she was seen meeting a guy described as a white male in his mid-thirties. But there's one more piece of information I really need to check out."

"What's that?" asked Massarelli.

"The public records indicate that Russo had been employed as a delivery driver, an auto assembly line worker, and a carpet installer. I want to find out when he worked as a carpet installer."

"That shouldn't be too hard, if it's recent. When I get your letter requesting assistance, I can issue a subpoena to the Ohio Department of Treasury and obtain Russo's tax records. On our state records, they ask your occupation and of course the W-2 information for the employer is there as well."

"Wow," exclaimed Boyett, "that almost sounds easy."

Massarelli said, "Hopefully the State Treasury Department still has them. I've never tried to get back more than about five years. But I'll have someone get on it as soon as I get the letter."

Boyett hadn't been able to keep the excitement out of his voice. Massarelli chuckled and said, "Just remember, I get a trip to Alabama for the trial."

Boyett replied, "That won't be a problem if we get enough to charge him."

The conversation ended, and Boyett decided to go over to see Palmer and check the status of the letter.

When he got to Palmer's office, he found Palmer sitting at his desk, going over a budget proposal.

Boyett interrupted him. "J.T., can you check with the chief's office and see whether he has signed the letter to the Ohio BCI?"

Palmer said, "Sure, what's going on?"

Boyett explained the information about Franco Russo and the public records checks, and then his conversation with Massarelli, including the need to get copies of Russo's income taxes. He added, "There's probably going to be a delay of a couple weeks getting those tax returns, so hopefully we don't slow it down on this end."

Palmer motioned for Boyett to sit down and picked up the phone. He talked to the chief's secretary. "Could you

FedEx that if it hasn't gone out yet? OK, thanks." He looked at Boyett. "It's signed and awaiting mailing, as you heard. If it's not already in the mail, they'll FedEx it."

"Thanks, J.T.," replied Boyett.

Boyett went back to his office and began looking at other case files in the file room. He knew he may as well pick another case and begin going through it as the Marcial case would be sporadic. He chose a 2009 case with a female shooting victim named Nancy Gerard. The date of the murder was April 16, 2009. Gerard had lived at 1313 Chester Drive in an upscale neighborhood called Honey Brook. Nancy Gerard had lived in Honey Brook since the neighborhood was developed on the site of an old bee farm.

Honey Brook consisted of about 300 single family homes built in the late 1980s and early 1990s. When Boyett began reading the case, he faintly remembered it as it was unusual. Gerard was a forty-eight-year-old white woman who lived in a good neighborhood in West Mobile and was shot in her driveway as she departed her house one morning.

Boyett began reading the case files, and learned it was another case assigned to Detective Zindell. He read the interviews, which consisted of short synopsis reports, the evidence reports from the crime scene team, and the lab and autopsy reports. He began a spreadsheet of the reports with a synopsis of each report. During the rest of the day, Boyett went through the case file and noticed that some reports appeared to be either missing or never completed. The interview reports only involved a couple neighbors and Gerard's two daughters, Nellie and Jenny, and her ex-husband, Gary Gerard.

In 2009, one daughter, Jenny Mason, was married and living in Pensacola, Florida and the other daughter, Nellie, was a senior at the University of Alabama in Birmingham. Gary Gerard was a business owner who had divorced Nancy Gerard almost ten years before the murder and according to family and friends, they remained friendly. The reports also indicated that Gary Gerard had an alibi, having been out of town on business when the murder occurred. Gary Gerard had made a settlement with Nancy Gerard when they divorced and the only thing he was paying at the time of the murder was child support for his youngest daughter and college tuition that was basically ending since Nellie was due to graduate a month after the murder.

While none of the family were suspects, none of them provided any information about why anyone would want Gerard dead or give any information that expanded the case. Boyett felt something was missing from the case file. There was no computer analysis on Gerard's computer, or even the mention of whether she owned one. No telephone toll analysis on her cell phone. This did not appear to be a drive-by or gang-related shooting,

Working hard to curb his frustration, Boyett wondered how he was going to solve a case where the leads that existed at the time were not even followed up. The good thing about the case was that it was Zindell's last before he retired. Boyett decided that the best thing he could do was start from scratch and begin interviewing family members and trying to expand the leads from there. As he looked through the boxes, he began making a list of where to begin this investigation.

Boyett went to see Jane Bonham again. This time, he requested help locating Nancy Gerard's children as well as ascertaining the names of neighbors who were not interviewed and information on how to contact those people now.

While awaiting the results of Bonham's computer wizardry, Boyett decided to drive over to the former Gerard house and have a look around. It was a twenty-five-minute drive out to that neighborhood, and it was a hot, muggy day, so he drove with his windows closed and air conditioning on. Upon his arrival, Boyett drove the streets looking at the way the houses had been built and the way the streets curved. From just his initial instincts and based on the photographs of the crime scene, it would appear that the shooter would have been parked three or four doors west of Gerard's house, and probably on the other side of the street.

Boyett took down the addresses that were possibly in front of 1308 and 1306 Chester Drive, and went back to the station to see if there were any reports of interviews of these neighbors.

He combed the files again and noticed that none of the neighbors from any of the addresses where it appeared the shots could have come from had been noted or occupants interviewed. Going back and reviewing the autopsy photographs, it was obvious that Gerard had been shot once in the chest after she exited her home and was walking around the rear of her car, which was parked in her driveway, in order to enter it. This would have been the first clear shot a person would have been able to make from the location that Boyett thought the shots were fired from. Prior to Gerard walking around the rear of it, the car would have partially blocked a shooter's view as well as possibly obstructing a bullet.

Boyett also noticed that the single bullet that struck Nancy Gerard was a .308 Marlin express, a bullet used as ammunition for hunting. This bullet could have been fired from a rifle equipped with a scope or just a sight from the distance of a couple hundred feet. Gerard had been an easy target for a decent marksman.

As Boyett continued looking through the files, he could practically feel his blood pressure rise as he grew more and more angry, wondering what the hell Zindell was doing when he should have been following the leads that appeared to be all over the place. As he knew from working with Zindell for only a couple days, Zindell wasn't an investigator, and he recalled Palmer's statement that Zindell couldn't be pimple on a good investigator's ass.

Boyett was scheduled for vacation on August 13. He had plans to take the family down to Gulf Shores, Alabama for a week as they tried to do every summer. The vacation was the one week a year when Boyett and Millie could get away together and not answer the cell phone or emails. This was the week away from the grind that everyone endured fifty weeks out of the year. It was usually enough time to re-charge the batteries and come back to work ready to hit the streets again. The kids were now almost grown and neither lived at home full time. Samantha was a senior at Auburn University and Chris was attending Troy University on a baseball scholarship. Both kids made plans to attend the week at the beach, although last year, Samantha had missed the entire week as she was studying abroad in Ireland.

As was the family tradition, Boyett and Chris fished from the beach almost every day, while Millie and Samantha roamed around the area shopping and took in the sights. Everyone noticed that the entire landscape of the beach was changing. Gulf Shores had gone from single beach houses to small condominium complexes to mega-condominium complexes in the last twenty years. It made Boyett miss the old days.

In the evening, it had become a tradition to build a beach fire, drink beer, and eat lots of seafood. However, it was becoming increasingly hard to find a spot where that was allowed. None of the condo complexes or beach houses located inside of a sub-division allowed open fires. This meant finding one of the individual beach house owners and renting from them. Boyett and Millie had often talked about buying a house and retiring at the beach, but with skyrocketing prices, congestion, and other issues, this didn't seem viable anymore.

***

When Boyett returned to work on August 20, he found a few messages. One was from Massarelli.

He immediately called Massarelli back and asked him what he needed to do to begin getting the tax returns.

Massarelli replied that he'd already made the request for all years available and asked for it to be expedited. He hoped that the returns might be available later in the week. He asked Boyett how he would like to proceed to strengthen up other links to Russo.

Boyett said it would be ideal to get a DNA sample, but he wasn't sure there was enough to get a court order or that if they went that route, whether Russo might flee while they awaited the results of a match.

Massarelli suggested they work on getting a sample of Russo's DNA surreptitiously.

Boyett said he thought that might be a good idea, but it might be a resource intensive endeavor, to which Massarelli replied,

"They're my resources and if using them gets a killer out of my area, they'll be well used."

He told Boyett he was going to dispatch an agent down to Steelton to do some loose surveillance on Russo and see if he could get an idea where he worked and hung out while awaiting the tax returns.

Boyett agreed that was a great idea and asked Massarelli to keep him informed of what was happening.

When he ended the call with Massarelli, Boyett was encouraged. But while waiting on the Ohio BCI, he decided to go back to the Gerard case. He contacted Jane Bonham and found that she had the information about the owners of the properties near the Gerard house as well as contact information for the ones who had moved.

He went over to Bonham's office. He soon learned that the neighbors on each side of Gerard were still living in the same houses. The neighbor directly across the street was still there. The neighbors in all four houses west of Gerard's house had, however, changed hands over the last decade.

He wondered how a rifle could have been fired without someone noticing and whether a person shooting from a vehicle could do so without being heard. He decided it was time to find all the neighbors who had not been interviewed. He took the list of information from Bonham and returned to his office. As he looked over the information, it appeared that one house located approximately where Boyett figured the shot had come from was actually sold before Gerard's house. The other houses had not been placed on the market for a couple years and the last one had been sold just about two years ago.

Boyett decided to go to the neighborhood, start knocking on doors, and just figure out what anyone remembered. He recorded the various addresses and names of people he spoke with. Many people who had moved into the neighborhood were either unaware a murder had ever occurred or had heard something about it, but knew nothing of the details. It seemed that a murder in the neighborhood years ago was not a subject that came up at the neighborhood BBQ.

The one interview that seemed important to Boyett was with Joe Bangle. He was the neighbor at 1311 Chester Drive who had previously been interviewed, though the report indicated he was not home at the time of the shooting and had no relevant information. Bangle was now retired. He recalled that on the morning of the shooting, he'd backed out of his driveway and headed west on Chester Drive. He said he wasn't sure exactly what time he left in relation to Nancy Gerard, but that they almost always left their houses at about the same time and that on some mornings they would say hello across the driveways. Bangle said he didn't hear about the shooting until he got to work, and his wife called him—back in those days, he did not have a cell phone.

Boyett stopped Bangle and asked, "Did you observe anything unusual leaving your house, such as a car or truck parked on the street?"

Bangle shook his head. "No. There weren't any vehicles parked on the street 'cause the Homeowners Association didn't allow that. If there'd been one, I would've noticed as I was always careful backing out of the driveway."

He continued telling Boyett that following the shooting, the neighborhood was distraught and concerned and that for months afterward, everyone in the neighborhood was anxious. That was when several neighbors talked of selling their homes.

Bangle said that the neighbor at 1306 Chester Drive, Timothy Wilson, seemed especially distant from the rest of the neighborhood after the shooting and left for weeks at a time after it. Wilson was the first to sell his home several months later. Bangle said that he figured it was because Wilson and Gerard were close friends, with Wilson often doing yard work for Gerard. He added that Gerard and Wilson were both divorced and that they were the only two "single" people on the street at the time, so they often attended neighborhood events together.

Boyett asked Bangle what else he could tell him about Wilson.

Bangle replied that Wilson had a military background, and he'd apparently done some other type of work for the government before he retired. He said Wilson did not talk about specifics and other than that, Bangle did not know a lot about him.

"Was Wilson a hunter?"

"He sure was. In fact, he had quite a few trophy mounts in his house and during deer season, he'd often supply venison to us neighbors."

Boyett asked, "Do you know where Wilson relocated?"

"I heard he moved to Alaska, but I don't know for sure it's true. Sorry I can't help you more."

Boyett thanked Bangle for his help. As he left the neighborhood, he was thinking that Timothy Wilson needed to be looked at a little more closely.

When he got back to the office, he pulled out the file that Jane Bonham had assembled. According to Bonham's information, Timothy Wilson left Mobile in about the fall of 2009 and relocated to Ketchikan, Alaska. The records indicated that Wilson stayed in Alaska till about 2014 and then seemed to fall off the face of the earth. His Alaskan driver's license expired in 2014 as well as his vehicle registration. He did not transfer his driver's license to another state.

Boyett decided to write his report on the Bangle interview and to try and contact Gary Gerard and the Gerard kids to see if he could set up an interview with each of them. When he reached Gary Gerard, Gerard told Boyett he would be glad to meet with him any time he wished. They set up an appointment for the next morning. Boyett spent the rest of the day writing the report of the Bangle interview.

On Tuesday, August 21, Boyett arrived and prepared to interview Gary Gerard, who arrived a few minutes early. Boyett explained that he'd recently taken over a cold case squad and it was his intent to give every case another look, with fresh eyes.

Gerard expressed gratitude and surprise. He said that after the murder, he'd briefly been interviewed by a detective who was only interested in where Gerard had been. He'd told the detective he'd been in Philadelphia on business. The detective had asked for copies of his plane tickets and hotel receipts. Gerard said that after supplying those items, the detective was almost impossible to reach. Several weeks after the funeral, his youngest daughter, Nellie, came home from school. At the time, they were moving furniture and personal items from Nancy Gerard's house so it could be sold. Nellie said she'd stopped at Tim Wilson's house to see if he had some boxes and while there, Wilson had acted very strangely.

He explained, "Nellie told me Wilson wouldn't look at her. I thought this was odd considering that Wilson and Nancy were close friends. I tried calling the detective on the case several times and never got a call back."

Boyett asked Gerard what he knew of the relationship/friendship between Wilson and Nancy. Gerard said he knew they were close, but he wasn't sure whether it was romantic. He said that as the ex-husband, it wasn't his duty to oversee his ex-wife's friendships.

"Could you supply a phone number for Nellie?" Boyett asked.

"I'll do you one better," Gerard replied. He pulled out his cell and called her.

Boyett heard him tell Nellie that he was at the police station and that they were re-opening the investigation on her mother. He wanted Nellie to talk to the detective and lend whatever information she could. He handed the telephone to Boyett and nodded.

Boyett began by introducing himself and then asked if Nellie could come in for an interview.

Nellie said she would love to, but she was a nurse working at the Cleveland clinic in Cleveland, Ohio. She said she did not know when she would be back in Mobile, but she would be glad to be interviewed either in Cleveland or in Mobile or by phone.

Boyett obtained Nellie's information and told her he would be in touch.

Boyett thanked Gary Gerard for connecting him with Nellie. He asked Gerard if he could supply a telephone number for his other daughter, Jenny.

Gerard said he could, but she was currently living in Spain with her husband, who was a navy pilot stationed there. He told Boyett that it would be easier to make contact with Jenny by email, as there was a seven-hour time difference. He gave Boyett Jenny's email address and said he would email her and tell her to expect communication from Boyett.

Boyett asked Gerard if there was anything else he could add about his ex-wife.

Gerard said that before her death. Nancy seemed happy. She'd recently been promoted at work and had even mentioned that she was dating again. He didn't ask for details as it might seem creepy, and he repeated that it was none of his business.

Boyett thanked Gary Gerard for his help and Gerard left the police station.

As Boyett returned to the files, he decided to go see Jane Bonham to learn what other information could be ascertained on Timothy Wilson.

Bonham said she could delve into more databases, but that these databases mostly compiled public records and about eighty to ninety percent of what one had, they all had. She could, however, make contact with police in Alaska and see if there were any internal data bases that might help them.

Boyett told Bonham that would be a great help and to go forward with it.

After lunch, Boyett emailed Jenny Mason to see if she could expand the investigation. In his communication, he introduced himself and explained that he'd recently been put in charge of taking another look at the investigation. He asked Mason how often she'd visited her mother before her death and what she knew about her mother's personal life, as these things are often interconnected to murders. He asked Mason to simply tell him everything she could and that he would be glad to ask follow-up questions. With that, he hit SEND and decided to head home early.

As Boyett was getting seated with his coffee the next morning, his phone rang.

It was Jim Massarelli in Ohio. He told Boyett that the agent assigned to do a light surveillance on Russo had had a good day. Russo was working at the Chevrolet assembly plant in Lordstown, Ohio, but he didn't know for how long. Chevrolet had already laid off several hundred workers and everyone expected that the plant would be totally closed soon. He could make contact with the security director at the plant, who was a retired BCI agent, and probably get additional information if Boyett wanted it.

Boyett told Massarelli that if he trusted the guy, by all means see what they could get.

Massarelli went on to tell Boyett that after work, Russo left the plant and went to a bar called the Keg and Barrel, about half-way between the Lordstown assembly plant and Steelton. The Keg and Barrel was a blue-collar drinking establishment that had been around for years and catered to the union guys because it was only about a quarter mile from several union halls that served the industries in the area. It was also located near the former union hall of the UAW, which had moved recently.

Massarelli went on to say that the Keg and Barrel might be a place to try to get a sample of Russo's DNA as the police had several "in's" at the establishment, including the fact that it had been owned by a retired police chief who died a few years ago and was being operated by the former chief's son, who was always cop friendly. He said it might take a few days and some creative thinking on how to get the DNA sample, but he would be thinking about it.

Boyett asked Massarelli how long it might take and Massarelli said he would discuss some potential ideas with his agents and try to come up with a concept to get the DNA. Meanwhile, he would be in touch as soon as he had the tax records.

Boyett turned on his computer and went through his voice mails and messages. One message was from Jane Bonham, who said she'd made contact with the Alaska

Bureau of Investigation. She'd placed a call and was awaiting a call back.

He then went to his emails and found a response from Jenny Mason.

Mason had written a long message that seemed to detail every aspect of her mother's life. She said she and her mom had been very close and talked almost every day. Her mom and Tim Wilson were close friends and to Mason's understanding, her mom had recently signed up to an online dating service. She said her mom shared some of the dating prospects with her, but she never met any of them and her mother had only actually gone to dinner with one of them. She said her mom had confided in her that Wilson had been upset that Nancy Gerard had signed up for online dating. Her mom and Wilson had been intimate, but it was just a "friends with benefits" relationship as far as Nancy Gerard was concerned, though Wilson apparently was upset with her about the online dating. Mason said the two stopped seeing each other several weeks before Gerard was murdered. She further said she'd tried to tell the detective who interviewed her about the relationship between Gerard and Wilson and that he told her he only wanted to know what she personally saw, not hearsay.

Boyett responded to Mason, thanking her for her email and telling her he would get back to her if he had any further questions or if he had some news. With that, he called Jane Bonham and asked for the Alaska Bureau of Criminal Investigation's phone number.

Bonham gave Boyett the number of the agency's office in Ketchikan. She reminded him that Alaska was three hours behind Mobile, so he shouldn't expect anyone till about noon Mobile time.

It was just past 9:30 a.m., so Boyett decided to go visit J.T. Palmer.

Palmer was sitting in his office when Boyett approached. He asked how things were going with the cases and Boyett just looked at Palmer. "Do you remember we said something about Zindell not being a real detective?"

Palmer nodded.

"Every time I read another report or interview another witness, I think, could this guy be this bad?"

"What did you find now?" asked J.T.

"Well, when the Gerard shooting happened, several of the family members thought the police should look at a neighbor she'd been having an affair with. They told Zindell, who wasn't interested," said Boyett. "The shot appears to have come from the area of this neighbor's house, and it turns out the neighbor had some sort of military or government background and was an avid hunter. Then immediately after the shooting, the neighbor makes himself scarce and within a couple months, he sells his house and moves to Alaska."

"That sounds suspicious," said J.T. "So where are we now?"

"I'm going to call the Alaska Bureau of Investigation when they open in a couple hours and see if they can assist in locating the guy."

"Think there's enough for an arrest?" asked Palmer

"Not yet, but I think we might have enough for a search warrant to look for his gun and maybe some other evidence," said Boyett. "Zindell sure didn't make these cases easy." With that remark, he told Palmer he would keep him updated on what he learned.

It was now a little after 10:00 a.m. and Boyett decided to walk to the district attorney's office to see Gloria Wood, who was now the first assistant district attorney and in charge of the criminal division. Boyett and Wood had seen each other numerous times over the last decade, and she was always as helpful as ever. Upon entering the D.A.'s office and going to Wood's office, her assistant told Boyett she was in a meeting with the district attorney and should be back momentarily.

After about ten minutes, Wood came down the hall and greeted Boyett. She asked what was up and Boyett asked if he could give her a briefing on two cases he was working.

She said sure, they entered her office, and she shut the door.

Boyett told Wood he was now running the cold case squad.

Wood nodded in approval. "The department needs that. Too many cases are dropped without proper investigations."

Boyett agreed and told Wood he'd already pulled two cases and may need some help. He asked her if she remembered the dead girl on Mardi Gras day back in 2006.

Wood said she did. She remembered going over to the hotel and then issuing a bunch of subpoenas for records, but she didn't recall anything coming of it.

Boyett told Wood, "After I got transferred, Zindell caught the case. A lot of good information came in from the subpoenas and Zindell did nothing. He just closed the case."

Wood said, " I understand. I had a couple cases with him. One was so poorly investigated that Michael O'Brien went to Major Coachman and complained about Zindell's lack of ability and professionalism."

Boyett brought Wood up to speed on where the case was now and said that with any luck, they would be able to get a DNA sample from Franco Russo and hopefully that could lead to an indictment.

"Good. That case is long overdue to be solved."

Boyett then explained the case involving Nancy Gerard.

Wood ran Gerard's name through her computer system and said that nothing about the case had ever been referred to the district attorney's office.

Boyett explained that while it was still in the basic investigative stages, a former neighbor looked like a fair suspect, and he was in the process of locating him now. If they did, there might be some legal work such as search warrants or subpoenas to do on the case.

Wood said she would be glad to open a case on it, or they could wait until there was a real request for something.

With that, Boyett asked Wood whether she would be handling the Marcial case or whether it would be re-assigned since she'd been promoted.

Wood looked at Boyett and said, "Our case file still has it assigned to me and I see no reason to re-assign it."

Satisfied, Boyett thanked her and excused himself.

By now, it was 11:15 a.m. Boyett decided to kill time by going to eat lunch in the cafeteria. When he returned to his office with a coffee to go, it was just past noon. He took a chance and sat down to dial the Alaska Bureau of Investigation number.

The phone was answered by a man who identified himself as Investigator Edwards.

Boyett introduced himself and explained about the murder and the fact that a neighbor who was a tentative suspect had moved to Alaska and then seemed to disappear several years ago.

Agent Edwards asked for all the information Boyett had. When Boyett supplied the information, Edwards said that the address Boyett had was actually not in Ketchikan, but way out in the country. He said some of the addresses were so far out that residents had to have a post office box to get mail because the post office couldn't even get there to deliver mail. Most of these areas were not accessible by car and some only by boat or sometimes even by private plane. Edwards said he would get with the postmaster and determine where Wilson actually lived and try to ascertain whether he was still there.

Boyett thanked Edwards and gave him his call back number. Now it was just wait and see what the Alaska Bureau of Investigation could find.

He sat in the office going through the many boxes and files and reviewing them again. He decided that it was time to begin affidavits on each case, as a complex case like these may involve affidavits totaling thirty to fifty pages. He knew from his DEA days that while simple cases were often worked locally in Mobile, the lengthy affidavits might total five or even ten pages, that as cases were more complex and involved many facts, the affidavits could grow dramatically. He decided to start with the Gerard case, outlining the facts that made him believe Timothy Wilson was a suspect and then listing various items he would hope to find and seize, including any rifle that could fire a .308 Marlin express round. He also would seek any documents or papers, including electronic data, that were exchanged between Nancy Gerard and Wilson as well as any that mentioned Nancy Gerard or a shooting.

Boyett spent the rest of the day typing up the affidavit, which was about fifteen pages when he decided to call it a day and go home.

The next day, Boyett arrived at the office to find a message to call Jim Massarelli. He placed the call immediately.

Massarelli said he'd heard two things from his agent on the ground in Mahoning County. The first was that the auto workers union was having a general membership meeting concerning the Lordstown plant the next week, on Labor Day, September 3, at 5:00 p.m., and it should be presumed that most of the membership would attend, including Russo.

The second thing was that Massarelli had contacted Bob Bigham, the owner of the Keg and Barrel, the place where the union members hung out. He said Bigham had no problem cooperating with the BCI in any way, shape, or form, except he wanted to be assured that none of his personnel would be required to go to court. Massarelli said his idea was to have some BCI agents undercover in the bar, offering samples of products, and to single out Russo to see if they could get his DNA. He thought it would be good if Boyett came up to Ohio so he could take possession of the sample DNA and send it to the Alabama lab so that if there was a match, the same lab would be using the same chemist to testify. Massarelli said that if Boyett could arrive Labor Day afternoon, there would be plenty of time to get to the Keg and Barrel.

"I'll talk to the captain about flying up to Ohio," Boyett agreed.

"Perfect," said Massarelli. "I'll help you get a hotel and have an agent assigned to help you while you're in Ohio."

Boyett thanked Massarelli and told him he would get back to him as soon as he had an answer.

Upon hanging up with Massarelli, Boyett went to see J.T. Palmer.

Palmer was sitting at his desk talking on the phone. He motioned Boyett in and to a chair. After hanging up, he asked Boyett what was going on.

Boyett related his conversation with Massarelli.

J.T. told Boyett to write up a memo outlining the reason for the trip and to emphasize that Russo was the prime suspect in the case and that the DNA sample, if positive, would seal the prosecution. Then he looked hard at Boyett and said, "Three B, you know there are going to be people questioning the travel, thinking that you're just scamming a trip at the city's expense. But I've been to the Cleveland area several times, and I know from personal experience there isn't a whole lot there. Well, except for the Rock and Roll Hall of Fame."

Boyett laughed.

"Get it to me ASAP, so I can walk it through," said Palmer.

Boyett went back to his office and began the memo requesting travel to northeast Ohio. He spent several hours researching the best airline routes and airfares from Mobile to Cleveland. It seemed it was a route that made it "hard to get there from here." Some routes went through Atlanta or Dallas and neither had very good connections. He made a couple more calls to Massarelli to ascertain prices for hotels and ensuring that Boyett would need a rental car.

Boyett eventually finished the memo, which had him departing Mobile on September 3 at 7:00 a.m., routing through Dallas, and arriving in Cleveland at 2:00 p.m., which should give them time to drive to the Keg and Barrel before the union meeting. He finished his request and took it over to J.T. Palmer's office.

Palmer wasn't in, so Boyett left the papers his desk. He headed home, only to be contacted by Agent Edwards on his cell during the drive.

Edwards told Boyett that Timothy Wilson lived out in the Alaskan wilderness, where he had several hundred acres over toward the Canadian border. Edwards had some direction coordinates and had checked the borough's land records, and he believed he could find Wilson's place. He also said that the property taxes had been paid several years in advance, which was unusual, but that the tax bill from the prior year had gone unpaid. He said Wilson had not been to the post office in some years, and he confirmed that both the Jeep registration and Wilson's driver's license had expired. This was highly unusual, but he was working on finding a partner to accompany him to try to find Wilson's property.

Edwards said it might take several days to reach Wilson's place. He explained that many of the areas were inaccessible by vehicle because of everything from dense forest to mountains, creeks, and bodies of water. If Wilson made it into town, there was obviously a way to get to his place, although as he was going to map it out and try and determine the best way to do so. He asked Boyett to send him any information or synopsis of the case that he had, so he could review them and make his supervisors aware of the reasons for his trip.

On Friday, Boyett went into the office and found an email from J.T. Palmer saying that the travel request to Ohio had been approved. Boyett then emailed Edwards the affidavit he'd started. This affidavit gave an overview of the investigation and particularly the points that made Wilson appear to be a suspect. After sending Edwards that email, he decided to begin the affidavit that would be needed for the arrest and / or search of Franco Russo.

The week of August 27, 2018, was uneventful but a bit busy. Boyett had been subpoenaed to court on two different cases he'd had worked in patrol. One was a federal civil case involving an accident between a tractor trailer and a Mini Cooper. The tractor trailer had literally driven over the Mini Cooper, crushing it to a height of about three feet, as if it had been put into a car crusher at a junk yard.

The driver of the tractor trailer had committed several vehicle violations and had been charged and convicted in state court with criminally negligent homicide (by vehicle). Because the truck was owned and registered to an out-of-state trucking company, the personal injury attorneys representing the victim's family had filed their actions in federal court. Boyett's participation had been minor, but he'd been the first officer on the scene, therefore the plaintiff's attorneys wanted him there to describe the scene when he arrived.

The federal case took two days, and the other case was in state court. This case was a possession of controlled substances. The defendant had been a passenger in a vehicle that was reported stolen and had fled when officers had attempted to pull it over almost three years before. The chase had gone about seven miles through the center of Mobile and out to West Mobile, where the vehicle had wrecked, and the occupants fled. Boyett had given chase on foot after the passenger of the vehicle, while other officers had given chase on foot after the driver. Boyett had caught the passenger, who was found to possess a small quantity of methamphetamine. The driver got away. The passenger claimed he'd been picked up hitch hiking just before the chase and when the accident occurred, he panicked and fled because the driver fled. The district attorney's office had said the passenger couldn't be charged with stealing the car unless there was more evidence. He couldn't be charged with the chase, since he obviously was not operating the vehicle. They did agree that the possession of meth was illegal. Boyett had checked in and was placed on "stand-by" and would be called at least thirty minutes before he was needed, so he spent two days at the federal courthouse.

On Wednesday, when Boyett got back into his office, he had messages from Agent Edwards in Alaska as well as Massarelli. He called Massarelli first.

Massarelli told Boyett that he had lots of news on Russo. First of all, a subpoena to Sprint cellular had determined that the number Russo had used in 2006 was still subscribed to him. The number was active. Secondly, the information on Russo's taxes had come back from the state, and they only went back five years. They showed that Russo had been employed by General Motors all five years, but they also did show that Russo employed an accountant to prepare them. Massarelli said that in his experience, the accountants held records longer and that they could subpoena the accountant and see if he had any additional years of records on Russo's taxes. Thirdly, Massarelli said he'd also gotten copies of Russo's original employment application from the security director at the Lordstown GM plant. When Russo had applied to GM in 2011, he'd indicated that he'd previously worked as a carpet installer at Boardman Carpet and Tile Works in Boardman, Ohio from 1998 till 2009, and then as a delivery driver for Steelton Pizza on a part-time basis from 2009 until 2011. Massarelli said he'd checked and learned that Boardman Carpet and Tile Works went out of business during the recession in 2009. He was attempting to locate the former owner of the business,, but it appeared he'd left the state.

Massarelli said he'd come up with a couple scenarios involving several of his agents working undercover at the Keg and Barrel that he was sure would work, as long as Russo showed up at the bar. He said one undercover female undercover agent would be walking around offering free shots of a supposed new liquor. The liquor was non-alcoholic, but the people drinking it wouldn't know that. It was going to be billed as a promotion and every guest would be given the drink in shot glasses. That undercover agent wouldn't hit the floor until Russo entered the bar. When he entered, the undercover agent would work her way over to Russo and whoever he was with and offer him or them a free shot. The shot glass Russo used would be segregated to save his DNA. Another female undercover agent would be offering customers a new "rum" flavored gum and like the other female, would hit after Russo entered the bar. The gum was horrible tasting and most people chewed it for about five seconds before spitting it out, and the undercover agent would recover the gum from Russo in a napkin. The third undercover agent was a male who was going to be working the bar and move to whatever part of the bar that Russo ended up in so he could grab any glasses or bottles that Russo used. Massarelli told Boyett that he and Boyett would be in the bar watching Russo and when they saw him leave DNA with an undercover agent, they would retrieve it and place it in evidence bags for analysis.

Boyett was extremely impressed by Massarelli's creativeness and plan. He told Massarelli he looked forward to working this operation. Before hanging up, Massarelli asked Boyett to email him whatever updated affidavit Boyett had, so that he could add any relevant information to it, including the information from General Motors as well as the tax returns. Boyett said he would do so as soon as they hung up. He found his affidavit on the computer and updated as much information as he could before sending it to Massarelli.

Next, Boyett called Agent Edwards at the Alaska Bureau of Investigation.

Edwards informed Boyett that he and another agent had gone out to Wilson's house. It had taken them about sixteen hours roundtrip, utilizing a four-wheel drive. The agent said the cabin where Edwards lived appeared to be unoccupied because the brush and growth had not been cleared in probably a year or more. He said Wilson's Jeep was parked in the driveway, the cabin was locked up, and they couldn't see anything through the limited view they had through the windows. The house was furnished, but it did not appear anyone had been there in a while. Edwards would be glad to use Boyett's information to try to obtain a search warrant to enter the house and see if there was a .308 Marlin and if so, seize it for ballistics testing. Other than that, Edwards said that Wilson may have moved on and he had no idea how he might be tracked.

Boyett thanked Edwards and said that if he could obtain a search warrant based on what probable cause they had it would be great, and if they found the rifle it would be great evidence. If they did not find the rifle, Boyett may have to go back to square one in the case. Edwards agreed to begin the affidavit but cautioned that it might take up to a week for him to write it and obtain the warrant and get back to execute it. Boyett told Edwards he appreciated anything that Edwards could do. They ended the call with Edwards telling Boyett he might be calling to get some additional information and he would certainly call when he had something to report.

Boyett spent the rest of that day and the next day updating his reports and making copies that might be needed and available while he was travelling. He cut out of work early on Friday, since he was going to have to travel on the holiday Monday.

CHAPTER 6 - THE STING
(GETTING HIS DNA)

Monday, September 3 started early with Boyett saying an early goodbye to Millie and leaving his house at 5:00 a.m. to get to the airport. He was lucky as there was designated parking for police in the employees' lot at the Mobile Municipal Airport. The time he saved parking was used up once inside the terminal, however, where Boyett had to file an array of forms in order to carry his firearms on board the aircraft. Luckily, Mobile Airport was small in comparison to others. It only took about twenty minutes of bureaucracy to get everything done.

Once on the plane, Boyett was offered an upgrade to first class by the pilot, whom he was introduced to as per protocol. He knew this meant there were no TSA Air Marshals on the flight and the pilot wanted the armed cop as close to the cockpit as possible. Boyett took the upgrade although being armed, he was forbidden from indulging in the free alcohol that goes with first class. But at least the seat was wider and more comfortable.

The plane departed Mobile and landed in Dallas, where Boyett had a four-hour layover. Since he had not really eaten breakfast that morning, he decided to eat a snack as he wouldn't be landing in Cleveland until 2:00 p.m.. He placed a call to Massarelli's cell phone and made sure Massarelli had his flight information and knew what he was wearing.

Boyett's flight to Cleveland was not a nice as the Mobile to Dallas segment. There was no upgrade to first class and his seat was the middle seat in an exit row where the seats did not recline.

Oh well, he thought as he tried to make himself comfortable. *You win some and you lose some.* He hoped the losing part wouldn't apply to today's plan at the Keg and Barrel.

Upon landing at the Cleveland Airport and deplaning, Boyett was approached by a rather dark Hispanic man in his late thirties who introduced himself as Special Agent Carlos Gomez with the Ohio BCI. In the slightest of accents, Gomez said he'd been directed by Massarelli to pick up Boyett, make sure his needs were met, and that he was checked into his hotel before heading to the meeting set for 4:30 p.m. at the BCI Office in Youngstown. Gomez told Boyett that they'd reserved a hotel room for him at the Holiday Inn in Boardman, a few miles from the BCI Office in Youngstown as well as a few miles from Russo's house and the Keg and Barrel Bar. The hotel was surrounded by places to eat and plenty of things to do just in case the trip got boring.

On the way to the hotel, Gomez told Boyett some stories about the Youngstown area, which he knew well as he'd lived there since coming to Ohio from Puerto Rico with his parents when he was fourteen. He mentioned that the Holiday Inn where Boyett was staying had been owned by Eddie DeBartolo, the former owner of the San Francisco 49ers football team. DeBartolo made millions in the construction business, building malls, then bought the team. Gomez said DeBartolo eventually was convicted in federal court on charges relating to bribing Louisiana governor Edwin Edwards in a case involving building a casino when Louisiana legalized casinos.

By the time Gomez and Boyett arrived at the Holiday Inn, it was 3:30 p.m. and they decided they should grab a bite to eat before heading to the meeting. They entered and Boyett registered. He put his bags in his room and he and Gomez left to get a quick bite before the meeting at the BCI Office. Although it was Labor Day, there were plenty of places to eat.

Gomez asked Boyett what kind of food he might want.

Boyett said that Mobile's food consisted of lots of seafood, home cooking, and Cajun food. He would like to try something more exotic.

Gomez suggested Aladdin's Eatery, which was almost across the street from the Holiday Inn and specialized in Middle Eastern food.

Boyett agreed that would be a good change, and off to Aladdin's they went.

After leaving Aladdin's with their bellies full, Gomez and Boyett drove to the BCI office. The office was situated in downtown Youngstown, in an area that appeared to be in the midst of revitalization. Upon entering the BCI building, Gomez took Boyett to meet Massarelli, who was in the squad bay.

The agent was five or six years older than Boyett, with black, wavy hair and neatly trimmed beard that screamed Italian heritage. He wore a perfectly-fitting grey blazer and an easy smile, which he immediately aimed Boyett's way.

Boyett and Massarelli shook hands and talked about the case. Massarelli told Boyett that from the very beginning, he'd had a feeling that this case was much bigger than a single murder in Mobile. As the BCI agents filtered in, Massarelli began the briefing.

Massarelli started with a background on the July Marcial murder back in 2006 and a description of the evidence pointing to Franco Russo. He went over Russo's brief criminal background and the individual assignments for each of the BCI agents. He had three agents assigned to the Auto Workers Union Hall, where they would locate either Russo's vehicle or Russo himself, if necessary, inside the union hall. At the Keg and Barrel, Agent Gomez was assigned to work behind the bar. Two female agents, Jill Baker and Sandra Loundes, were assigned to the undercover positions of offering free shots and free rum-flavored chewing gum.

Massarelli brought out some props for the female agents. One included a leather holster type apparatus that held two bottles, one on each side of her waist where a gun would go on a cowboy. Above the holster were straps that crossed the chest and held shot glasses. Baker was already dressed for success, wearing a short, black skirt and a white blouse. When she put the holster on, she was stunning, looking like a Mexican gun fighter, but armed with two bottles of liquor and plenty of shot glasses. Massarelli said each shot glass had been sanitized at the lab and if Russo drank a shot, the empty glass was to be put into a vacant place in the top of the belt.

Loundes, meanwhile, was given a tray of gum, each contained in a small plastic cup. She was told to offer the gum to patrons, but the target was Russo. Massarelli said if Russo took the gum, that as he was putting it in his mouth to mention that she, Loundes, had tried it and didn't like it. If Russo attempted to spit the gum out, Loundes could hand him one of the small cups and tell him she would dispose of it for him.

Gomez was instructed that when the surveillance agents informed the team at the Keg and Barrel that Russo was in the parking lot, he should get a view of the door and try to work the bar directly in front of Russo. Gomez was to secure any glasses or bottles that Russo used below the bar until Massarelli and Boyett retrieved them. Massarelli and Boyett were to keep an eyeball on Russo until DNA was secured and placed into evidence. Unless something went wrong, Russo was not to be stopped or questioned. Any change in this plan would require Massarelli's approval. With that, the meeting ended, and agents shuffled out of the

BCI office to their various cars and matched up with various partners they were assigned to work with.

Boyett accompanied Massarelli out of the building and got into Massarelli's 2017 Mercedes GLE SUV. He grinned at Massarelli and asked, "Seizure?"

Massarelli grinned back. "Of course. The State of Ohio isn't buying anything that costs more than $25,000."

"We used to get some decent ones when I was on the DEA Task Force too. But my department made me drive a city car, which was often a Ford."

Massarelli said, "Around here, we grab the best, least police-looking cars we can get, especially if they're free."

As Massarelli and Boyett drove the seven or eight miles to the Keg and Barrel, they could hear the various teams on the radio discussing their locations. As they pulled up to the bar, the team at the union hall radioed that they had a "eye" on Russo's vehicle, which was parked on the side of the union hall. Several other units near the union hall were taking up positions to pick up surveillance when Russo left the union hall.

Massarelli decided to park in an adjoining parking lot. He said that being that he was driving the Mercedes, he did not want the car to attract any attention. After parking, he suggested that he and Boyett go into the Keg and Barrel so he could let Boyett get an idea of the layout and where things were.

After entering, Massarelli went back to the manager's office, where he met Bob Bigham, the owner of the place. He introduced Boyett to Bigham. During their small talk, Bigham told Massarelli and Boyett that no one on his staff knew anything about the investigation. He'd told them that the liquor supply company was sending some girls out to promote some new products and that's all the staff knew. As for Gomez working as a bartender, Bigham had said they were hiring a new bartender and that when he failed to come back a second day, Bigham was just going to say that it did not work out. He did say he thought it best that his cooperation be kept low key as some patrons may object to the bar cooperating with the police, even if it were for a murder investigation.

Massarelli promised not to let out about the cooperation, especially if it resulted in something that would result in media attention. With that, he and Boyett went back to his vehicle to listen to the radio traffic.

About 7:10 p.m., the surveillance teams at the union hall reported that members were beginning to filter out. As the members began to leave, it became easier to see Russo's vehicle. At 7:25, Russo exited with several other union members and talked for a couple minutes outside the union hall. A couple minutes later, surveillance reported Russo had entered his vehicle and was backing up. As the surveillance agents stayed with Russo's vehicle, the agents assigned to the Keg and Barrel began getting ready for their participation.

Massarelli and Boyett waited while Gomez, Loundes, and Baker got ready for their parts. Gomez, dressed in black slacks and shirt, entered the bar when the surveillance team said they were about two miles away. Meanwhile, Massarelli and Boyett also exited their vehicle and headed toward the bar. As they walked from the adjoining business and across the Keg and Barrel parking lot, they observed Russo's vehicle pull in followed by one of the surveillance vehicles. Massarelli and Boyett entered the bar, which now had over 100 people in it, mostly from the Auto Workers Union. Massarelli and Boyett took up a position at the bar from which they could see the front door.

Within a minute, Russo walked through the door. Boyett thought he looked fairly unassuming and maybe even innocent. An inch or two shorter than Boyett's own six feet, he was slightly overweight, with light-brown hair just past his ears and fair skin, almost like a baby face. As Russo stepped toward the bar, he looked around and walked within ten feet of Massarelli and Boyett before beginning to talk to several other patrons who were obviously union members. Russo ordered a beer, and Gomez was there to serve him. Although the bar was loud, Boyett could distinctly hear parts of their conversations about how GM was going to "fuck us." The conversation apparently was about how GM had notified the union that there would be more cuts at the plant and that a determination had not yet been made whether they would close the plant, but that it was a real possibility.

Russo seemed especially despondent about the possibility. Boyett heard him say it had taken him a decade to finally get hired and that because he did not have seniority, the positions in other GM plants wouldn't be offered to him. As he was listening to Russo and the others discuss the plant, he noticed Agent Baker walking toward them. She stopped at Massarelli and Boyett and offered shots, which they took. She then moved over to Russo and his friends and offered free shots to them.

Boyett noticed Russo's level of interest rise as Baker talked to them. Russo was telling Baker how pretty she was and asked whether she would want to "run away with him?"

She asked, "What are you running away from?"

He replied, "This stinking valley." He told Baker that they'd just come from the union hall meeting, and it looked like they would all be laid off soon. As Russo was saying that, Baker poured shots for each of them. They all raised the glasses to their mouths and swallowed the juice. Russo asked for a second and set his glass on Baker's tray.

Baker said, "No problem. Maybe it'll help chase the blues away."

Russo asked Baker for her phone number and Baker told him she couldn't give it to him because she had a boyfriend, then added, "But I'm not sure how long that'll last. How about you give me yours and if I decide I want to run off,

I'll call you?" With that, Baker handed Russo a napkin and a pen and Russo scribbled a phone number.

Baker collected the shot glasses, placing Russo's separate from the others, and departed the group. She stopped and gave one other patron a sample before heading toward the back of the bar, where Massarelli and Boyett met her. They bagged the shot glass that Russo had used and also took possession of the napkin sporting the telephone number.

Meanwhile, after taking the evidence to Massarelli's vehicle, they re-entered the bar and were met by Agent Loundes. She gave them a plastic cup with a partially chewed piece of gum in it.

"He didn't like it," she said, laughing. Then she looked at Massarelli and asked, "Where did you get this shit?"

"In a gag gift store online," said Massarelli. "The ad says it's the worst tasting gum in history. But did it work?"

Loundes said, "It worked, all right," and laughed again.

Massarelli and Boyett packed the partially chewed gum into another evidence bag and secured it in Massarelli's vehicle.

Upon re-entering the bar, they observed that Russo was still with the group he'd met up with earlier.

Gomez motioned them to the end of the bar. There, he said he had two beer mugs and one shot glass from Russo. It was only 8:20 p.m. Not even an hour had passed, and they had numerous DNA samples from their suspect.

Massarelli told Gomez to collect the mugs and shot glass and meet them in the parking lot next door. With that, he led Boyett to the manager's office again, where they met Bob Bigham again. They thanked Bigham and told him everything had been successful, and they were clearing out.

Bigham said, "Good luck with whatever you got. Just keep me out of it."

Massarelli and Boyett left the bar.

In the parking lot, Gomez, Massarelli, and Boyett placed each mug and shot glass into different envelopes and carefully labeled them. Massarelli told Gomez to take Boyett back to the BCI office to secure the evidence and then take him back to the Boardman Holiday Inn.

Massarelli got on his radio to thank all the investigators. He told them they could head home, and they could complete their reports the next day. He told Gomez not to forget to pick up Boyett the next day and to bring him to the office to get his evidence then to the Cleveland office. He asked Boyett, "Is there anything else you want to do while in Cleveland?"

Boyett thought a minute. "Well, there's an interview in an unrelated case I might try to get in, and then there's the Rock and Roll Hall of Fame."

"If you can arrange the interview, we can handle that," Massarelli replied with a nod, "but the Rock and Roll Hall of Fame isn't a problem."

Boyett went with Gomez back to the BCI office to secure the evidence and then returned to the Holiday Inn. They agreed that Gomez would pick up Boyett at 8:30 the next morning.

Back in his room, Boyett was amazed at the creativeness and efficiency of the Ohio BCI and thought about how lucky he was to have made contact with them. He finished his evening by sending an email to Nellie Gerard, telling her he was in the Cleveland area on another case and asking if an interview would be possible. After sending that email, he called Millie to see how things were at home. By this time, it was after 10:00 p.m. and he hit the sack, exhausted from his flight and the long, busy day.

The next morning, Boyett was up early again, and he immediately checked his emails and voice mails. He had a message from Nellie Gerard that said she was working at the Cleveland Clinic if Boyett wanted to stop during her lunch hour or meet after work for the interview. Gerard left her cell and work number for him to call if he decided that either of those times worked.

He packed his bag and went down to the lobby to check out as he was not sure whether he was going to catch a late flight that day or wait till the next day. He grabbed a complimentary coffee and muffin in the lobby while waiting for Gomez.

Gomez arrived about 8:40 a.m. and apologized for his lateness. He told Boyett he'd been delayed in traffic on the interstate.

"No need to apologize," Boyett said easily.

They drove to the BCI Youngstown office, where they retrieved the evidence and placed those evidence envelopes into a box, sealing that box with evidence tape, so Boyett could carry it onto the airplane. On the drive to Cleveland, he asked Gomez where the Cleveland Clinic was located in comparison to the BCI office.

Gomez said that the Cleveland Clinic had several different locations in the area and asked Boyett if he knew which one.

Boyett said he did not, but he would find out. He called Nellie Gerard and asked her which location she worked at. She told him it was the main campus on Euclid Avenue.

Gomez said it was maybe fifteen or twenty minutes away, and that it wouldn't be a problem to head that way.

Boyett asked Gerard what time would be good for her to take lunch.

Gerard told Boyett to be at her office at noon and she would make sure she was available. She gave him her office wing and suite number and said she would see him then.

Gomez asked Boyett what the interview was about.

Boyett filled him in on the Gerard case and how it was just a coincidence that the daughter was in Cleveland, and he was there on another case. He hoped it would save him a second trip later.

Gomez and Boyett arrived at the Cleveland BCI office and took the sealed box of evidence inside to check it into temporary storage pending Boyett flying out. Boyett sat down at an empty desk and began making calls as well as using his phone to determine what flights would be available later in the day or the next day. After about thirty minutes, it became obvious that the best flight was the next morning at 10:30 a.m. He would arrive back in Mobile about 2:15 p.m., which would give him time to drive to the Alabama Forensic Sciences and check in the evidence.

After making the reservation, Boyett approached Gomez about going over to the Cleveland Clinic. Gomez said it wouldn't be a problem, but that they had a little over an hour to kill before heading there. He suggested they could either eat an early lunch or make a hotel reservation for Boyett in Cleveland for that evening. As he and Boyett were discussing the options, Massarelli walked into the squad bay.

He offered to take care of booking Boyett's hotel room as he had hooks at the Cleveland Hilton, which was located downtown. He said it was about a ten-minute walk to the Rock and Roll Hall of Fame, if Boyett wanted to spend the afternoon there. As Boyett was going through his briefcase, Massarelli reappeared and told him and Gomez that the hotel reservations were made. He asked what they intended to do for lunch.

Boyett explained that they were going to the Cleveland Clinic for an interview with a potential witness in another case. Massarelli said that if they decided to get lunch immediately after the interview to let him know. If not, no problem, Massarelli would see Boyett the next morning before his flight. With that, he excused himself to go to his office and field some phone calls.

Gomez and Boyett left BCI and went to the Cleveland Clinic, arriving about 11:50 a.m. Gomez utilized his blue light and placard to park in a spot near the main building that was reserved for police. Upon entering the building, they found Nellie Gerard's office and went in. There they met Nellie, who was waiting for them. She suggested they could do the interview there or even go to the cafeteria and find an out of the way table and conduct the interview there. They opted for the cafeteria and followed Nellie through the halls and corridors to the ground floor and the cafeteria.

After getting some food, they sat down at a table at least twenty feet from any other tables. There, Boyett began asking Nellie about her mother and what she remembered concerning the murder. Nellie told Boyett that she was a student at the University of Alabama at Birmingham School of Nursing when her mother was murdered. She explained that her first two years at school she'd lived in the dorm, but her second two years she had an apartment with roommates. She said once she got an apartment she did not need to vacate during holidays and the summer, she visited Mobile less often. In her senior year, the year her mom was murdered, she also was doing practical assignments in the UAB hospital and was even less available to take the four-hour drive to Mobile.

Nellie said she and her mother were close and were in contact almost every day. It was common knowledge that her mother had a relationship with Tim Wilson, but it was pretty much not talked about. She told Boyett that just before the murder, her mother did mention that Wilson was mad at her because her mother had decided to sign up for an online dating service. She said she never saw any animosity or bad feelings between her mother and Wilson and that Wilson was often over at the house doing chores or helping her mom out. Nellie did say that whenever she showed up, Wilson would usually excuse himself and either go and do something that needed doing or go back to his house.

Boyett asked Nellie, "Do you know anything about Wilson's hunting activities?"

"Not really," she replied. "I was only at his house about a half dozen times, but I remember he had numerous hunting trophies such as deer heads, and there was a large, wild boar's head above his fireplace. I never thought much of his hunting since in southern Alabama, it's a fairly common activity."

Boyett then asked her about the story when she and her dad were cleaning out the house, after her mother's death. Nellie said that between the end of classes and graduation, she'd had about a week off school. Her dad and sister had decided it would be best to sell the house and put the money in the bank to be divided up later. Her dad had talked to some auction companies about selling off the contents in order to empty the house and get it ready for sale.

"My dad suggested that the two of us girls go to the house and determine what each of us wanted. We were free to take anything as the rest would be sold at auction. I hadn't been living there in several years, and I didn't realize how many things in the house had special memories. I went in with five or six empty boxes, but I soon found that Mom had saved childhood toys, souvenirs from vacations, and even our report cards from grade school. It didn't take long to fill all the boxes I'd brought. Wilson had already placed his house up for sale by then, which I thought was strange, but I went over to his house to see if he had any extra boxes."

Nellie went on to say that when Wilson answered the door, he seemed startled to see her. He seemed obviously uneasy with her there and did not want to look at her. At the time, she took it that he was upset about the murder. She said that as she later thought about it, it seemed weird, and she mentioned it to the detective. She said that after that incident, she did not see Wilson again or have any contact with him.

"Are you making any progress in the case?" she asked Boyett.

He told her he was unravelling some things, but it was too soon to know whether there was a prosecutable case. He would be in touch with her if anything positive developed. He thanked Nellie for her time and he and Gomez departed the Cleveland Clinic.

On the way back, Gomez told Boyett he would take him to the hotel to get registered and be glad to wait if Boyett wanted a ride to the Rock and Roll Hall of Fame. He said he then needed to get back to the BCI office and complete his reports on the undercover operation at the bar so that Boyett could take it with him when he departed the next day.

Boyett told Gomez that he would be fine to check in and walk to the Rock and Roll Hall of Fame, since it was less than ten minutes away.

Gomez said he was not sure who would be picking up Boyett the next day, but he would make sure someone would be there and asked what time Boyett wanted to be picked up.

"Is 8:00 too early or late to be picked up, get to the BCI office, and then to the airport?" Boyett asked.

"Nope, 8:00 should be fine and if things get tight, the BCI cars all have lights and sirens so they can hustle you through airport security fairly quickly."

With that, Gomez was pulling up to the Cleveland Hilton.

Boyett got out and entered to check in. Once checked in, he went to his room and found that he'd been given an upgrade to a suite. He decided he should drop his bags and get to the Rock and Roll Hall of Fame before the day was over. On the walk over, he decided to call J.T. Palmer and tell him what had transpired.

The call went to J.T.'s voice mail. Boyett left a short message saying that everything was well in Ohio and that he would be back in Mobile Wednesday afternoon. He would fill J.T. in when he got there.

That afternoon, Boyett relived some of his childhood memories, seeing the displays and rock and roll memorabilia from the many bands he'd listened to growing up. The afternoon was one of his favorites of the trips he'd taken as a cop. The mission had been accomplished gathering the DNA, he'd interviewed Nellie Gerard, and now he was enjoying a free afternoon before returning to Mobile and the stress that awaited him there.

On Wednesday morning, Boyett walked out of the Cleveland Hilton at 7:55 a.m. and heard a horn beep. He looked over to see Massarelli's Mercedes SUV. He walked over and threw his bag in the back seat and saw the sealed evidence box already there.

As Boyett slid into the front seat, Massarelli said, "Good morning. As you can see, I already retrieved the evidence box. Here are copies of the reports from all my undercover agents. I'm now in the chain of custody, so you have to subpoena me to Alabama."

Boyett just laughed.

On the drive to the airport, Massarelli said that if the DNA was a positive match, he and his team wanted to do a thorough search of Russo's house.

Boyett said he agreed, and that he would make the search warrant request as inclusive as he could to gather as much evidence as possible.

As Massarelli pulled in at the Cleveland Airport, he maneuvered the Mercedes around to a spot marked "police" and threw a BCI placard on the top of the dashboard. He escorted Boyett through the maze of the Cleveland Airport to a back hallway leading to the TSA director's office. Walking inside, Massarelli greeted a white man in his late fifties. He introduced Boyett to Bill Rankin.

Rankin was the TSA security director for the airport, overseeing the TSA screeners as well as TSA air marshals assigned to Cleveland.

Massarelli told Rankin that Boyett was carrying evidence and a weapon, and he wanted to ensure that Boyett wouldn't have any issues with the evidence.

Rankin assured Massarelli that he would personally walk Boyett through the security checkpoints with the evidence. With that, Massarelli bid Boyett goodbye and told him to call as soon as the lab had an analysis on the DNA.

After Massarelli departed, Rankin asked Boyett what time his flight departed.

Boyett said 10:30.

Rankin said, "Come on, let's get you through security and checked in at the gate. Maybe we'll have time for a cup of coffee." He walked Boyett through a series of hallways that exited near the screeners checkpoint. He took Boyett around the checkpoint to a small office, where he had him sign a book listing his name, weapon make and model, and department's name and badge number. With that, they were through the checkpoint and walking down the concourse toward the gate. Once at the gate, Boyett checked in and went with Rankin back down the concourse to a Starbucks coffee shop.

While waiting on a boarding call, Rankin and Boyett talked about police work. Rankin asked what brought Boyett to Cleveland and Boyett gave him an overview of the case and how great Massarelli had been assisting in it.

Boyett learned that Rankin had begun his career right out of college in Eastlake, Ohio, a suburb of Cleveland. After a few years there, he'd begun as a special agent with Ohio BCI. After a five-year stint with BCI, he'd applied to the FBI and was hired as a special agent. He loved working for the FBI, but when he was fifty-six, a year from mandatory retirement, the position had come open at the TSA and he said that under a special program he could retire from the FBI and still work for the TSA. He said the job was much less stressful than the FBI, but more bureaucratic. He'd been with TSA almost three years and was hoping to get a few more in before being tossed out.

As Boyett finished his coffee, he heard the boarding call for his flight. He said goodbye to Rankin and told him he might be seeing him again, depending on how the evidence turned out.

Rankin gave Boyett his business card and told him if there was anything he needed at the Cleveland Airport to just call.

Boyett boarded his flight and found his seat, placing the evidence in the bin above his seat, and hoped for an uneventful flight. With little issue, he landed at the Mobile Airport about five minutes ahead of schedule. After departing the plane and exiting the airport, Boyett was on the way to the Alabama Department of Forensic Sciences with the box of evidence.

Upon arrival at the lab, Boyett met with the intake technician and asked to see the lab director, Ron Weiss.

The director came out to meet Boyett, who explained the case and said he would send the original reports over, but he had numerous possible samples of a person's DNA that needed to be analyzed and compared to samples found in 2006.

Weiss, the technician, and Boyett went to an intake room and opened the sealed box containing the evidence. Boyett explained that they had numerous samples of Russo's DNA.

Weiss said it would only take longer to analyze all the exhibits, and that the best exhibit should be the partially chewed gum. He suggested the gum be submitted and Boyett retain the other exhibits. He said the test, which would be a Y-STR test, would also be fairly quick, with a rush, and could possibly be done in a week to ten days. If there was no DNA on the gum or if it did not match, other exhibits could be submitted. He said this route would be the quickest since they were only analyzing one exhibit versus multiple.

Boyett agree to the plan put forth by Weiss and placed the unused samples back into the box to go to the Mobile Police Department evidence room.

He arrived back at the police department about 4:30 p.m. He stopped into J.T. Palmer's office but found he'd left for the day. He re-sealed the box containing the unused DNA samples and placed it under his desk until it could be turned into the evidence room the next day. He did not even check his messages before going home to enjoy the evening with his family.

The next day, Boyett arrived at the office at his usual time, just before 8:00 a.m. He grabbed a cup of coffee and went to see if J.T. Palmer was in yet. This time, he found Palmer at his desk.

Boyett sat down and spent the next thirty minutes telling Palmer how the Ohio BCI had treated him like royalty and how they had so many samples of DNA, the lab decided he should bring all but one back. That they would only use one, and keep the others in case they were needed.

Palmer asked Boyett if he'd heard anything back from the Alaska Bureau of Investigation on the Gerard case.

Boyett told Palmer he had not, but that he had that on his list of things to do that day.

Palmer said it was good that Boyett was making cases, as if a couple cold cases could be solved, Palmer would have an easier time justifying additional resources for the squad.

Boyett said that with some luck, they might have both cases solved within weeks. He returned to his office to type up an evidence sheet before taking the sealed box containing the DNA samples down to the evidence room. After checking the box in, he returned to his desk and began going through messages and writing reports concerning his participation in the DNA samples in Ohio.

Just after lunch, Boyett's phone rang.

It was Agent Edwards from the Alaska Bureau of Investigation. Edwards started the conversation with, "I think we've solved your murder."

Surprised, Boyett asked, "You think so? How?"

Edwards explained that the prior day, they'd executed a search warrant at Timothy Wilson's cabin. After they'd gotten into the one-and-a-half-story cabin, he said, "We found Wilson's almost mummified body in the second-floor bedroom. He appeared to have died from a self-inflicted gunshot wound to the head about two years ago. At the desk where he died, there were numerous newspaper articles from Mobile papers about the murder and some notebooks where Wilson had scribbled various notes and writings including that he was sorry and that he wished he could turn back the clock.

"It's fairly obvious that Wilson killed himself with a handgun and that he was in some state of depression about the murder. He also possessed an array of weapons, including a .308 Marlin."

He told Boyett that the investigation was just a death investigation at this point, but added that it appeared the writings would make a reasonable man believe Wilson had been remorseful over Gerard's death and in a moment of depression, probably during the long winter months, had committed suicide.

Boyett asked Edwards what the procedure would be from there.

Edwards said he was sending the .308 Marlin to his forensics lab for a ballistics test and that those results, along with a fired bullet, would be sent to Boyett. Other than that, there would be an investigation into Wilson's death and when completed, if Boyett needed more evidence, Edwards would be glad to send him Wilson's composition books and writings for review. He told Boyett there was little doubt that there was probable cause to believe Wilson committed the murder and the ballistics would corroborate that, but that the best Boyett was going to get was a "cleared by exceptional means" statistic out of the case.

Boyett thanked Edwards for his help and returned to Palmer's office to brief him.

After Boyett briefed Palmer on the information from Edwards, Palmer said, "I have no doubt that Wilson committed the murder. After they confirm the ballistics tests, it would be a good idea to issue a press release that shows that the cold case squad is having some success in clearing unsolved murders."

By the time Boyett got back from Palmer's office, it was time to head home.

The following day, Boyett worked to clear up more paperwork on both the Gerard case and the Marcial case. He decided to not pull another cold case because he was due to attend a week-long advanced homicide investigators school in New Orleans. Although he'd worked homicides for several years, Palmer thought it would be a good idea to send Boyett to the school because so many things had changed while they'd been assigned to patrol. Technologies like DNA, blood splatter, and even GPS and cell phone technology had evolved greatly since Boyett had last worked homicides.

***

During the next week, Boyett attended the homicide school and learned a few new things, but he realized that no matter what information was given, it was usually available from experts in the field. He figured what he'd learned was worth about eight hours, not the thirty-six hours he spent in the class.

The one advantage of attending these regional training schools was that it was a chance to meet investigators from different cities and states and trade business cards. Boyett was careful to make notes on the backs of the cards to jog his memory later in case he needed to call the person. Spending lunches with these other investigators and listening to "war stories" was just as important as sitting in the class. He came away with about twenty different cards, each with notes on the back, some with a description of the detective who gave it to him and others with a sentence or two about a war story that detective had told.

When Boyett returned to work on Monday, he had a FedEx package waiting for him from the Alaska Bureau of Investigation containing a fired projectile. The accompanying evidence report indicated that the projectile had been test fired from a Marlin .308 rifle, serial number 04598711. The report further reported the Marlin .308 had been recovered during a search of Timothy Wilson's home. Also inside the package was an envelope addressed to Agent Edwards at the Alaska Bureau of Criminal Investigation.

Boyett signed and dated the receipt and placed it in the envelope in order to return it to Agent Edwards. He then went down to the evidence room to retrieve the original projectile that had killed Nancy Gerard, in order to take both to the lab for comparison. After retrieving the evidence and writing up a new evidence sheet and request for the laboratory, Boyett took the evidence to the lab for submission. After checking in these pieces of evidence, he checked on the status of the DNA evidence in the Marcial investigation. He learned that the DNA Y-STR tests had been completed the previous day and that the report had been dictated for typing. He asked if he could get the results, pending the report being typed, which could take a couple days.

Boyett learned that the DNA taken from Russo matched the DNA found on the carpet and July Marcial's body. The certainty of the match was no less than one in one hundred million. Boyett felt a strange sigh of relief. He asked the lab personnel to call him when the report was typed, that he needed it right away, and he headed back to the office. On the way back, he called J.T. Palmer.

Palmer answered his phone with the usual, "Palmer."

Boyett burst out with, "J.T., we got a match."

Palmer knew exactly what Boyett was excited about. "When are you going back to arrest that scum?"

"I'm not sure, J.T. I need to see Gloria and discuss whether we want to indict first or whether we should just pick him up."

"Let me know," responded Palmer.

Back at the office, Boyett placed a call to Gloria Wood, who wasn't in. He asked Wood to call back as soon as possible as he had an urgent matter. He then called Massarelli.

"Jim, the DNA matched," he said when Massarelli answered the phone.

"Did you ever really doubt it would match?" responded Massarelli, but Boyett could hear the excitement in his voice.

"I always knew he was the best suspect, but it's good to have confirmation," said Boyett.

"So, when you coming back to put the cuffs on the guy?"

"I'm working on that now. I just got the lab confirmation orally and I want to see whether they want to indict or just obtain a warrant. Either way, it won't be long. I'm going to start the affidavit for the search warrant today. I'll email it to you in sections so you can review it. Are you and I going to be co-affiants?" asked Boyett.

"I wouldn't have it any other way, partner," said Massarelli.

"I'll be in touch later today, hopefully," said Boyett

After hanging up with Massarelli, Boyett broke out the case file and began the affidavit for the search warrant. All affidavits begin with an introduction of the person writing it, which is called the affiant. Boyett gave a brief synopsis of his career. He went into his promotions and assignments and his being the affiant on over fifty search warrants, and that he'd testified in over 100 trials in various courts including the state of Alabama as well as federal courts.

The next twenty to twenty-five pages would be an overview of the crime, including how the Marcial case developed, the victim's background, and what evidence was found at the crime scene, including DNA on the body and on the carpet, the abrasion on Marcial's toe, and the fact that she was found without any ID or cell phone. The affidavit would include a brief synopsis of the investigation as it centered around the hotels within the downtown area during Mardi Gras 2006. The affidavit concentrated on the pieces of evidence that pointed to Franco Russo as a suspect, including the fact that he was driving a van and that the FBI profiler thought the perpetrator would have utilized a truck or SUV to carry the body, the fact that the body had been wrapped in a carpet remnant, and the subsequent investigation determining that Russo had worked as a carpet installer at the time of the crime. The toll and text information between Marcial and Russo's phones were also detailed. The interview with John Hood where Hood described July Marcial's toe ring and the initials engraved in it was also included.

Lastly, Boyett detailed how the investigation in Ohio had allowed them to retrieve Russo's DNA, how the sample had been submitted to the Alabama Department of Forensic Sciences lab and compared with the DNA taken from Marcial's body and the carpet, and how it had matched within one and one hundred million.

Boyett spent most of the day with the evidence box and reports, making sure he had his dates and his quotes from those reports correct. As he was beginning to list the items to be searched for and seized, he received a call from Gloria Wood.

Wood told Boyett she was in her office if he needed to see her.

He told her he would be right there. He arrived in Wood's office within fifteen minutes and sat down. "We have our killer in the Mardi Grad murder case," he announced.

Wood's eyes popped open, and her jaw dropped. "Tell me what you got."

Boyett went over the same items he'd just listed in the probable cause for the search warrant.

Wood listened intently. As Boyett finished, she asked, "So, how do you want to proceed here?"

Boyett said he intended to finish the affidavit and work with Ohio BCI to obtain the search warrant and search for any souvenirs Russo might have saved. He asked Wood whether they should indict Russo or get a warrant from a circuit judge and make the arrest based on that.

Wood said she would prefer the indictment for an interstate extradition, as it might be a better legal document. She could probably get Boyett into the grand jury before the end of the week and have the indictment before the next weekend. She suggested that any evidence relating to the murder be brought back to Mobile with Boyett if possible as in the past, she'd seen other departments lose evidence.

Boyett told Wood the Ohio BCI had been very cooperative, and he was sure that wouldn't be an issue. As he departed her office, Wood said she would check with the district attorney and try to add Boyett to the grand jury.

After speaking with Wood, Boyett returned to his office and continued on the affidavit. As the day was ending, he sent a copy to Massarelli via email, asking Massarelli to add in his biography, to review the information about the crime, and to add any facts Boyett might have omitted. After sending the email, Boyett headed home, looking forward to a relaxing evening.

Over the next few days, Boyett and Massarelli sent emails back and forth several times a day. Each of these clarified particular points of what, when, and how certain things had been determined. By Thursday, they agreed that the affidavit should easily suffice for a search warrant and that it should stand up to any motions to suppress by a defense attorney.

CHAPTER 7 – THE INDICTMENT

Thursday afternoon, Gloria Wood called Boyett and told him she'd arranged a meeting with District Attorney Barry Mueller for 9:00 a.m. Friday morning to go over the case and determine which direction they should take concerning the arrest of Franco Russo.

The next morning, Boyett was at the D.A.'s office about 8:30 a.m. with the case files. These were mostly lab reports and investigative reports dating back from 2006. He also had the latest draft of the affidavit that Massarelli had sent for the search warrant. He sat outside Wood's office while she was in a meeting with department heads and Barry Mueller that was running late.

At about 9:20 a.m., Wood appeared at her office and apologized for the delay. She said Mueller was going to see them in about ten minutes and the meeting would probably be short. She asked Boyett if he could synopsize the evidence against Russo in ten minutes or less.

Boyett handed her the affidavit. It was now twenty-seven pages long and growing. He directed her to start on page four, which was where the probable cause section began.

Wood read the document without saying a word. When she finished, she said, "It looks like we have a great circumstantial case. It'd be great to find some direct evidence linking Russo as the last person July was with, but I'm sure we can go with this."

So, off to Mueller's office they went.

Barry Mueller had been elected district attorney in 2010, after Michael O'Brien had decided not to run again. O'Brien, a Democrat, had held the position for over a decade. Mueller was a lawyer who had earned his fame as a plaintiff attorney in personal injury cases. Before being elected as the district attorney, Mueller had commercials on TV about once an hour in Mobile for several years. He was a household name. When O'Brien decided to retire, the Democratic Party floundered finding a competent candidate and the Republicans united around Mueller. By this time, Mueller was a multi-millionaire, and his personal injury firm was raking in millions per year. When Mueller won the election, he turned the firm over to his brother and his son, a recent graduate from the University of Alabama Law School.

Mueller was not as well-liked by the cops as O'Brien had been, as O'Brien had often responded to the scene of police shootings and knew most of the senior cops, such as J.T. Palmer, by name. Mueller rarely responded to shootings or got involved in cases, unless there was the opportunity for "face time" with a TV camera. Then Mueller would have a speech prepared, and he would deliver that speech like a TV commercial, informative and very polished. He rarely took questions from the press, opting to ask them to email them to the district attorney's public information officer, who was an ex-television reporter and infomercial spokesman. That way, responses could be accurate and polished. One thing Mueller hated was being caught off guard.

Upon his entering Mueller's office, Mueller greeted Boyett and offered him a chair. Boyett and Wood sat on sofa along the wall next to Mueller's desk. Mueller asked for a quick briefing and Wood handed him the affidavit and told him to start with page four.

Mueller popped on his glasses and seemed to speed read the document. He was done in about three minutes. Then he began asking questions. "Gloria, what do you think the defense will be?"

Wood responded, "Their best defense is going to be either that the strangulation was part of some kinky sex act and the strangulation was purely accidental, or that he had sex with her but didn't kill her, thus accounting for the DNA."

"How will he explain the carpet?" asked Mueller.

"If he claims he had sex with her and he left and someone else killed her, he doesn't have to explain it. If he claims the strangulation was accidental, then he can say he got scared and didn't know what to do and panicked," said Wood.

"Do you think we can win it? What are the percentages?"

"Well, if we charge him with several different counts such as manslaughter, it can give the jury an out, allow them to convict him of a lesser crime, but not capital murder. But if we charge just capital murder, then it's an all or nothing proposition. I think we still have a ninety percent chance of convicting on capital murder. If Three B finds some more evidence, that percentage will go up," said Wood.

"Let's roll the dice. Prepare an indictment charging just capital murder. If things turn to shit, we can always plea it down," said Mueller. He peered at Boyett over the top of his glasses. "Good job. Let's get this guy indicted and in handcuffs."

With that, Wood and Boyett went back to Wood's office, where she got on the office computer to look at the grand jury schedule. There was an opening for Tuesday morning. Wood asked Boyett whether that worked.

"It should be fine," he said. "When do you think the warrant will be available?"

"Probably Wednesday or Thursday," Wood said.

Boyett said he would work with Thursday so they could plan on the execution of the warrant as soon after that as possible. He went back to his office and called Massarelli.

"We're going to indict on capital murder next week," he said as soon as Massarelli answered his cell.

"Great," said Massarelli. "Do you think you can get here next week?"

"I'm not sure yet. I guess it depends when I have the warrant in hand."

Massarelli said, "A favorite arrest day of mine is Friday. If we arrest him Friday afternoon, there's no chance he'll see a judge until Monday, which gives us all weekend to get ready for court and also to try and get a confession."

"Let's plan for that and see if we can make it happen," Boyett agreed.

"That'll be easy. I just have to run it by a deputy A.G. in my office, then go before a judge. I'll need you with me for that, but it shouldn't take more than thirty minutes," said Massarelli.

"OK. We might be able to get that done and be ready on Friday. I'll let you know as we proceed here."

"I'm going to send you the latest update of the affidavit in a few minutes. We updated that Russo is still living at the house," Massarelli told Boyett.

Boyett spent the remainder of that day and the next Monday going back and forth with the affidavit and making copies of reports to corroborate what information was contained in the affidavit. Most judges would accept facts as stated, but there were the few who wanted copies of reports attached as part of the affidavit. Boyett did not know what the judges in Ohio might want.

He was at the courthouse Tuesday morning at 9:00 a.m. and met up with Gloria Wood outside the grand jury room.

Wood asked Boyett if he was ready.

He smiled and said, "Absolutely." They sat for about fifteen minutes, until another assistant D.A. exited the room and told Wood she was next.

Wood told Boyett to wait there and she would be ready for him in about ten minutes.

Upon entering the room, which held a grand jury of about twenty-five people, Gloria Wood introduced herself. She then started explaining a little about the case.

"On Mardi Gras night in 2006, Detective William Boyett was working the evening shift at the Mobile Police Department. He received a call about a body that had been discovered and responded to the scene. There he found the body of a white female, rolled up in a piece of carpet. This female was subsequently identified as July Marcial, a visitor to the city who had been attending Mardi Gras. The crime scene team found semen on both the carpet and Marcial's body.

"Detective Boyett worked this case through the spring of 2006, subpoenaing telephone phone records, interviewing potential witness as well as friends, and attempting to figure out who had killed Marcial. Boyett was promoted and re-assigned to patrol and the case was assigned to another detective. Over the next few months, the case went cold.

"Recently, Boyett was re-assigned back to major crimes, where he's working cold cases. One of the cases he pulled was the Marcial case. Boyett is going to tell you that when he was re-assigned to patrol in 2006, they were in the process of narrowing down the number of suspects. Upon being re-assigned the case, Boyett began reviewing the old material as well as additional material that had come in over the years. That evidence pointed to one suspect named Franco Russo, who lives in Ohio.

"You will hear Boyett explain how working with Ohio authorities, he got a DNA sample from Russo and that this DNA sample matched the DNA left by the killer on the carpet and Marcial's body. We will be asking for a capital murder indictment in this case. Are there any questions for me before I bring Detective Boyett in?"

No member of the grand jury responded, so Wood went to the door to call Boyett.

***

Boyett was sworn in by the court reporter. Wood asked Boyett his name and rank and how long he'd been with the Mobile Police Department. After Boyett responded, Wood asked him if he was the lead investigator into the murder of July Marcial, to which he answered yes. She then asked Boyett to tell the grand jury just what facts and circumstances made Boyett believe that Franco Russo had killed Marcial.

Boyett began the story with the initial call and crime scene, explaining how he'd begun working the case before being transferred back to patrol and how recently, after being reassigned to cold cases, he'd found July Marcial's name on a box in the file room and decided to start with that investigation. He explained that the box now contained many records that he'd subpoenaed, but which had not been received by the police department prior to his transfer back to patrol. He explained that these records almost totally convinced him that Russo was the culprit. He told the grand jury about his trip to Ohio over Labor Day and how he'd obtained Russo's DNA sample. He said the Alabama Department of Forensic Sciences had matched Russo's DNA sample with the DNA on the carpet and the body.

After Boyett's testimony, Wood asked the grand jury if anyone had any questions.

One young man raised his hand. "Can you tell us what the odds are of this being the DNA of another person?" he asked.

Boyett responded, "The lab has told me that it's one in a hundred million."

"Why do you believe the person who left DNA is the one who killed her? Couldn't she have been killed by another party after she had sex with this person?"

Boyett responded again. "The DNA wasn't just on and in her body. It was also smeared on the carpet. That indicates whoever had sex with her, did it on that carpet and then rolled her body in it and dumped it in the parking lot."

At this point, it seemed like the grand juror was getting ready to ask another question when Wood stepped in. "This is the evidence we have. We will be asking for an indictment on capital murder charges. Detective, you're excused."

Boyett exited the grand jury room and waited outside for Wood. A few minutes later, she came out and another A.D.A. entered.

Boyett asked Wood, "What was with that guy?"

Wood shrugged and said with a bit of a smirk, "It happens more and more often these days. Grand jurors watch *CSI* and *NCIS* and think we can just pull up anything and everything on camera. They aren't living in the real world, they think this is a script and we're in Hollywood. After you left, I told them that if they don't think there's probable cause, to vote against the indictment. I doubt even he will."

"When can I expect a warrant?" asked Boyett.

"Probably tomorrow. The grand jury should report about noon, and I'll get the clerk's office to put a rush on Russo's warrant. Check with me tomorrow afternoon. When are you planning on going to Ohio?"

"As soon as possible. We're hoping to execute the search warrant sometime Friday."

"OK. Good luck and call me tomorrow afternoon," said Wood.

With that, Boyett left Wood and the courthouse. Back at the police station, he began looking at airline ticket prices as well as rental car information for Cleveland as he did not want to have to be driven around by the BCI guys. He placed a call to Massarelli to tell him he was planning on flying to Cleveland on Thursday.

Massarelli said he would book Boyett into a hotel for Thursday night and that they could go to Mahoning County on Friday morning. He also said he was thinking about having Agent Jill Baker call Russo to see if he wanted to meet her for coffee on Friday. This call could help determine whether Russo was working or at home and help them put the cuffs on him.

Boyett agreed with that idea, since they were not going to be kicking his door at o'dark-thirty. He would let Massarelli know what time he would arrive and Massarelli would arrange for a Cleveland hotel as well as the Boardman Holiday Inn for Friday night through Monday morning.

Boyett spent the rest of Tuesday and Wednesday exchanging emails with Massarelli, refining the search warrant as well as making copies of many of the reports in the case file, just in case they were needed. By Wednesday afternoon, he was just about ready. The search warrant had been finalized. The list of items to be searched for and seized included July Marcial's cell phone, her North Carolina driver's license, and her green toe ring, as well as any papers, documents, or writings that would indicate that Russo had been in Mobile, Alabama in February 2006 or that he had contact with July Marcial in February 2006.

Just after lunch, Boyett called Gloria Wood and asked about the issuance of the arrest warrant.

Wood told Boyett she would meet him at the clerk's office, and they would get the warrant even if they had to wait on it.

Boyett left the office and met with Wood. The criminal clerk had not yet processed the grand jury's indictments as they had come in just before lunch. She found the Franco Russo indictment and precipe requesting the warrant. She began typing the warrant and mentioned to Wood, "Well this one is easy, it's only one charge." As the clerk finished the warrant, Wood asked if she could also make a certified copy of the indictment.

She said to Boyett, "This will make any court hearings in Ohio easier."

As they left the clerk's office, Wood told Boyett to keep her informed about everything that occurred in Ohio.

Boyett promised he would do so.

When he returned to the office, he called Massarelli. "I've got the warrant and copies of the indictment in my briefcase."

Massarelli said the final draft of the search warrant affidavit was being reviewed for a final time and there was no reason to believe it was not going to be a go by the time Boyett arrived.

Boyett told Massarelli he would be arriving at about 1:30 p.m. in Cleveland and was going to get a rental car.

Massarelli said he would text the BCI address and a gate code for the BCI parking lot.

Before leaving the office, Boyett stopped to see J.T. Palmer and let him know that everything was a go.

Palmer asked Boyett to keep him informed if he needed anything or if anything unexpected happened.

Boyett told Palmer he knew he would, and told him to keep his cell phone on him Friday afternoon as that was the time they planned on executing the search warrant.

CHAPTER 8 – THE ARREST
AND CONFESSION

Boyett was back at the Mobile Airport on Thursday for an 8:30 a.m. flight to Cleveland. This time, the connections were a bit better, with the plane change at Dallas/Ft Worth. Everything went well and he landed on time, grabbed his luggage and rental car, and punched the BCI address into his phone's GPS system. By 2:20 p.m., Boyett was pulling into the BCI parking lot. Upon entering the BCI Office, he was met by Jim Massarelli.

"Been waiting on you," Massarelli said with an easy smile. "We're set up to have Jill call Russo and see if she can arrange a meet with him tomorrow afternoon. We're hoping he'll tell her a time and we can either nab him at his house or when he goes to meet her."

"Sounds like you've been planning," said Boyett.

"A little," said Massarelli, leading Boyett into a room where Jill Baker was waiting with a phone hooked up to a computer driven recording device. "Ready?" he asked, looking at Baker.

"Sure… I'm all prepped," Baker replied.

Massarelli hollered into the hallway, "U/C call being made from interview room," then he closed the door. He sat down at the table and motioned for Boyett to take a seat, handing him a set of headphones.

Baker punched in the number she'd written down and turned on the computer recorder.

Boyett listened as it rang… One, two, three times.

Then, "Hello, Franco?" asked Baker in a sweet voice.

"Yeah," said Russo. "Who's this?"

"This is Jill. I met you at the Keg and Barrel a couple weeks ago. I was your waitress. You asked me to run away with you."

"Hi, I remember you. Although I don't recall giving you my number, but I got pretty drunk that night," replied Russo with a chuckle. "So, what's going on?"

"Well, you told me to call you. I've been thinking about you, but I had to leave town for a few days. I just got back," Baker explained.

"Hope you were having fun wherever you were," Russo said. "So, when do you want to get a drink?"

"Well, that's why I was calling you, Franco," Baker said. "I was wondering what you were doing tomorrow and thinking we might be able to meet someplace."

"Tomorrow I work from seven to three. I usually get home about 3:30, and then I'll need to shower and dress and meet you, or you could just come over and we could shower together," Russo said, laughing.

"That might be interesting, Franco, but I'm not sure I know you that well… yet." Baker rolled her eyes. "How about if I call you about 3:15 tomorrow afternoon and we'll set up when and where to meet?"

"I'll be listening for your call," said Russo. "We should have some fun tomorrow."

"I agree," said Baker. "Listen for your phone. Chat then."

As Baker hung up the phone, Massarelli said, "Good job, Jill. It looks like we'll brief at the Youngstown office at 1:30 p.m. tomorrow and then wait on the asshole to get back from work and cuff him either when he arrives or goes inside. Then we'll execute the search warrant and see what we find." He turned to Boyett. "Are we ready with the affidavit?"

Boyett replied, "My final copy is what I sent to you yesterday."

"We're good, then. So, tomorrow you and I will go down to Youngstown about 9:00 a.m. and we'll have an appointment with a judge for between 10:30 and 11:00 a.m. I'll set that up."

"OK, sounds good."

"I'll also get you a reservation down at the Holiday Inn in Boardman, since we'll definitely be working later than usual. We may even end up working the weekend, if he decides to talk," said Massarelli.

"Sounds good," Boyett said again. "So, what time do you want me here tomorrow morning?"

"Why don't I call you in the morning? I'll run by your hotel, and you can follow me down to Youngstown?"

"Sounds good to me. Anything else for today?" asked Boyett, thinking to himself that everything about this case seemed to be coming together just fine. He hoped the good luck would continue.

"Nada," said Massarelli.

"I'll head to my hotel and await your call in the morning," said Boyett

"See you then."

Boyett departed the BCI office, drove back to his hotel, and checked in. He did not bother to unpack, just threw his bags down and set out his clothes for the next day. While he was preparing his clothes and items in his briefcase, his phone rang.

It was the Alabama Forensic Sciences with the results from the Wilson ballistics tests. The bullet fired from the gun recovered from Wilson's house was a perfect match for the bullet that killed Gerard.

Boyett thanked the lab clerk for the phone call and asked her to forward the report to him at the police department. He then called J.T. Palmer to inform him of the ballistics results.

Palmer said it was good that the match occurred, and although they couldn't make an arrest, it was going to count as a clearance and one less unsolved murder on the books. He asked Boyett how things were progressing in Ohio.

Boyett told him how things had gone and that they intended to make the arrest and execute the search warrant the next day.

Palmer told Boyett that when he got back, depending on how things went, they might hold a press conference to announce that the cold case squad was making progress. He said that "good press" might get the city council to free up some more money for the investigation's unit as well as the police department overall.

Boyett replied, "J.T., use these cases any way you want. Just don't expect me to go in front of a TV camera."

Palmer responded, "Don't worry Three B. I'll handle the cameras. But we do need to push the good news when we can. The media sure pushes the bad when we fuck up. Call me tomorrow after the asshole's in custody."

Boyett confirmed that he would do so and ended the call. He continued getting ready for the next morning, then he went out for a drive around Cleveland and to get something to eat. A call to Millie followed, ending with her usual caution to be careful tomorrow.

Friday morning began early for Boyett, who had not slept well, waking up throughout the night and looking at the hotel alarm clock to see what time it was. Ever since his days with the DEA, he'd had trouble sleeping before a big operation.

About 5:00 a.m., he decided to quit fighting the short naps and long awake periods and just get up and make some coffee, before going down to the hotel restaurant for breakfast. It also gave him time to shower and make sure everything he needed was in his bags.

He was the second person in the restaurant. It was a made to order restaurant as opposed to the popular buffet styles in many hotels.

Boyett ordered bacon and eggs and while waiting, he scanned a copy of the *Cleveland Plain Dealer* to see what was happening in Cleveland. Like every city, there were reports of political malfeasance. Murders, shootings, and mayhem. The newspaper was much larger than the *Mobile Press Register*, which had been downsized several times over the last couple decades. When he finished his breakfast, he went back to his room and watched NBC's *Today Show* while waiting on Massarelli to call.

The call from Massarelli came in about 8:40 a.m. He told Boyett he was enroute and about fifteen minutes away.

Boyett said he would check out and meet Massarelli in the parking lot. He proceeded to the front desk, checked out, and went to his rental car. A few minutes later, Massarelli pulled in and waved to Boyett, and off they went in tandem toward Youngstown.

By 9:30, they were parking at the BCI building. Massarelli told Boyett it was best to leave his car in the BCI parking lot for the day, while they obtained the search warrant as well as took the enforcement action. Inside the building, Massarelli called Bob Dunlap, the assistant attorney general who worked in the Youngstown office.

Dunlap told Massarelli they had a 10:30 appointment with Judge Vicki Newman at the county courthouse. He told Massarelli he'd reviewed the search warrant affidavit, and everything looked good. That gave Boyett and Massarelli time to get more coffee and discuss how the day might go.

Massarelli said that depending on how much and what evidence they found, Boyett might just carry it back to Mobile. If there was something too big to carry, Massarelli would take it into custody and arrange for delivery or transfer as it would be needed in court. Boyett agreed with both those points and they chatted about their families and baseball until it was time to leave.

As 10:15 came, Massarelli and Boyett walked the two blocks to the courthouse. Upon entering, they had to go through security. Massarelli badged the deputy, who waved him through. The same deputy stopped Boyett and demanded to see ID. Massarelli told the deputy that Boyett was an out-of-state officer working a case with BCI and that it was OK.

The deputy still refused to let Boyett enter with his weapon. Boyett, not wanting to cause a scene, agreed to check his weapon into a lock box located at the security checkpoint.

After clearing the checkpoint, Massarelli and Boyett went to the attorney general's office. There, Bob Dunlap was waiting for them. Dunlap and Massarelli shook hands and Massarelli introduced Boyett. Dunlap said he was very impressed by the cooperation, and he did not anticipate any issues with the obtaining the search warrant.

The trio proceeded to walk the halls of the courthouse until arriving at the chambers of Judge Vicki Newman. Upon entering the judge's chamber, the judge's secretary asked them to have a seat and called the judge on the intercom. After hanging up, she told Dunlap they could go in and see the judge.

Judge Vicki Newman was in her forties. She'd been elected a few years before and was from the east side of Mahoning County. She'd been in private criminal practice for a couple decades before running for office. It was rumored she'd been handpicked by local Democratic leaders when a judge from the east side of the county had decided to retire. In Mahoning County, there were few independent politicians. Most were party people who were hand selected for the job by the political machine.

Dunlap told Newman they were there to present an affidavit for a search warrant for a subject's house and that the subject was also going to be arrested for murder on charges out of Alabama.

The judge asked for the search warrant application and affidavit. Dunlap handed them to her, and everyone sat quietly as she began reading it. Fifteen minutes later, she peered at Dunlap and asked, "Are the Steelton Police aware of this investigation?"

Massarelli piped in. "Your Honor, Steelton police were notified of the investigation. Because it involves an out of state agency and the potential for someone needing to travel to Alabama to testify, BCI has taken the lead."

Judge Newman said, "All right. I just like to make sure we don't overstep our local officers. You know I was born and raised in Steelton, and I still have relations there."

Massarelli said, "I wasn't aware of that, but I assure you we'll keep them in the loop."

"Do you really think you will find any evidence after this long period of time?" asked Judge Newman. The frown on her face and the tone of her voice suggested she was doubtful.

"Your Honor, I've found evidence in defendants' houses years after the fact. In this case, the perpetrators often keep souvenirs. There's no reason to believe that the defendant would dispose of a souvenir such as the toe ring after going to the trouble of pulling it off her toe," said Massarelli.

Judge Newman responded, "You are the experts. I'll take your word for it. But if this guy still has evidence, he may be able to claim insanity as a defense, because he surely is crazy."

"Your Honor, we'll see when we make our warrant return," said Massarelli.

Judge Newman proceeded to sign the various documents and seal them with the seal of the court. She handed the approved warrant to Massarelli. "Happy hunting, agents."

"Thank you, Your Honor," said Massarelli, and the three departed the judge's chambers.

As they were walking down the hall, Boyett looked at Massarelli and asked, "Steelton... aware of the investigation? Really?"

"Didn't you call them when this case first started? Didn't you let them know you were investigating a murder and a suspect lived in their town?" asked Massarelli.

"Yeah," answered Boyett, "I did."

"Then they were informed. Don't worry. After we get him in cuffs, we'll call them and invite them over."

"OK," said Boyett with a grin.

As Massarelli and Boyett departed from Bob Dunlap and headed back to the BCI office, Massarelli pointed out some of the older buildings located in downtown Youngstown. One was Powers Auditorium, which he explained had been the Warner Theater before being renovated back in the 1960s. The theater had been built by the Warner Brothers of movie fame, who were originally from Youngtown, but who had departed as the movie industry grew. He explained to Boyett that Youngstown was once a thriving steel industry city, but as the ore dried up and the steel mills closed, the town fell into disrepair and most of the more prosperous residents fled to the suburbs. At one point, the city had a population of 170,000 but had shrunk to about 65,000. He said that Youngstown had begun to revive in the last few years, although it still had a long way to go.

When Massarelli and Boyett got back to the BCI office it was only 11:30, and Massarelli suggested they take a ride and get lunch.

Boyett readily agreed and they headed to Massarelli's car. As they pulled out, he asked, "Where're we going?"

"I'm taking you somewhere special," replied Massarelli. "It's called Cassese's MVR and it's real Italian food."

"Is there a difference between Olive Garden and real Italian?" asked Boyett, feigning innocence.

"You'll see," said Massarelli.

The drive to the MVR from the BCI office was less than a mile. The MVR wasn't anything fancy, just a store front. They entered, took seats near the front door, and began looking at the menu.

"Calamari?" asked Boyett.

"Yeah. That's squid," answered Massarelli with a wink.

"I know. Down my way, we call it bait," said Boyett, grinning.

"Try it, it's great."

As they looked over the menu, Boyett decided to play it safe and ordered a meatball sub with fries.

Massarelli decided to go more Italian and ordered the MVR Italian melt, which consisted of several Italian meats and cheese. He also ordered calamari as an appetizer in order to get Boyett to try them.

As they ate, Boyett had to admit that the food was much better than at any of the franchise places where he'd eaten. He told Massarelli that when Massarelli came down to Mobile, he would take him out for some southern cooking and fresh seafood. After they finished their lunch, they headed back to the BCI office, where agents were assembling for the operation.

Massarelli had already given out assignments, including to the team that would take custody of Russo and process him. Another team was assigned to take custody of all the evidence. Agent Gomez was assigned as documenter and photographer.

The briefing began at exactly 1:30 p.m., with everyone in the room bringing their needed tools and supplies. The agents were wearing tactical gear with "BCI" and "State Agent" clearly written across the bullet proof vests. Boyett felt naked. Only Jill Baker was wearing street clothes—a pretty blouse and skirt—just in case she had to meet Russo somewhere. During the briefing, she said she was going to call him and catch him on the way home, and tell him she'd just come to his house to meet him. The presumption was that this would induce him to go directly from work to home. Agents Gomez and Kelly were going to the GM plant to try and find Russo's vehicle in order to follow him.

As everyone acknowledged their assignments, agents filtered out of the room toward their vehicles. Massarelli said he and Boyett would surveil Russo's street from a block or two away, in case he arrived unannounced. He and Boyett departed the BCI office and drove to Steelton.

Steelton was an old town. Most of the houses were single frame, two-story structures on small lots in narrow streets, built in the 1920s and 1930s. Some of the houses in Russo's neighborhood appeared vacant, and several were boarded up. It was obviously a working-class neighborhood that had seen better days. Many of the houses had sidewalks that were cracked or just missing completely. Cement steps leading to the front doors were cracked or had pieces broken off. Front yards had become makeshift driveways, probably because the streets were not wide enough to accommodate the number of vehicles in the neighborhood.

Russo's house was one of the houses in better shape on the street. It was clean and well kept, although the peeling white paint and faded shingles indicated that it had not had any major renovations in years, if ever.

Massarelli and Boyett found a surveillance location in the front yard of a vacant house about one block down from Russo's, from which they had a clear view of the front of the suspect's house. As they were parking, agents reported that they'd located Russo's vehicle at the GM plant and were sitting on it. Other agents assigned to the team set up in various locations around the area, spread out so as not to alert anyone in the neighborhood.

At 3:05 p.m., agents at the GM plant radioed that Russo was in his vehicle and rolling. Over the next ten minutes, they radioed Russo's position and the fact that he was heading toward Steelton. As Russo passed through the town of Austintown, Jill Baker dialed his phone.

"Hello," Russo said as he answered the phone.

"Franco, it's Jill," said Baker in a sweet voice. "I was calling to see if we can still get together today."

"I'm on the way home from work now. I'll need to shower. Where do you want to meet?" "Well, I'm just hanging out down in Boardman, so if you'd like I can come meet you at your house. Where do you live?" asked Baker.

"I live in Steelton. I'll text you my address, and sure, come on over. I may be in the shower, though, so if I don't answer, come on in. I'll leave the front door unlocked," said Russo.

Baker responded, "OK... I'll be there about 4:00."

"See you then," said Russo before hanging up.

About 3:25 p.m., the agents following Russo radioed that he'd exited Interstate 680 and was heading into Steelton. Agents previously parked throughout the area around his house began moving into position to ensure that if Russo tried to flee, they had all the streets blocked. When Russo's vehicle passed Massarelli, that was his cue to pull out and block any exit in Russo's rear.

When Russo pulled into his yard, two BCI cars pulled up directly behind him with agents exiting, guns drawn and shouting orders to exit his vehicle. Massarelli pulled in behind the first two vehicles and allowed his agents to handle the arrest.

Russo followed directions, exiting his vehicle with his hands up. As agents had him place his hands behind his back and were cuffing him, he tried to tell them that there must be a mistake.

The agents asked him if he was Franco Russo and he replied, "Yeah. That's me."

The agents then told him they did not have the wrong guy.

By this time, Massarelli and Boyett had exited Massarelli's vehicle and walked to where Russo was standing handcuffed. Russo continued to proclaim his innocence and demanded to speak to whoever was in charge.

At that point, Massarelli stepped up with Boyett by his side.

"Mr. Russo, you're here because a warrant has been issued for your arrest out of Mobile, Alabama," said Massarelli.

"Mobile? I haven't been to Mobile in over ten years," replied Russo.

"Well, did you do something in Mobile when you were there that could be behind this?"

Russo glowered at Massarelli and fell silent.

Massarelli said, "And by the way, let me introduce you to the guy you're going to get to know real well over the next year or so. This is Detective Boyett from the Mobile Police Department." He pointed to Boyett.

Boyett then addressed Russo. "Mr. Russo, you've been indicted in Mobile for first-degree murder relating to the death of July Marcial on Mardi Gras day in 2006. Before you say anything else, I want to read your Miranda rights to you." He recited the Miranda warnings by reading them from a card, even though he knew them by heart.

When Boyett finished, Massarelli told Russo they had a search warrant for his house. He asked Russo if he could have the key to the front door so they wouldn't have to force it open. Russo told Massarelli the key was on his key ring. Massarelli then asked if there was anyone or any animals in the house. Russo replied that there was not.

Massarelli took Russo's keys and gave them to Agent Gomez.

Gomez and other agents went up to Russo's door and opened it. They went into the house and did a sweep of the rooms to make sure they were empty. As Massarelli and Boyett were ready to lead Russo into the house, Jill Baker walked up.

Russo immediately recognized her and not realizing she was part of the team, said, "Hey, sorry… I'm going to have to take a rain check on our date."

Neither Massarelli nor Boyett said a word.

Jill Baker feigned surprise with wide eyes and hesitation in her voice. "Oh! Well, maybe next time, then."

As Massarelli and Boyett escorted Russo toward the house, Massarelli asked Russo, "Who was that?"

Russo groaned. "She was going to be my future girlfriend. But I guess that'll have to wait, huh?"

"Yeah, maybe until your next lifetime," said Massarelli.

As they were about to enter the house with Russo, a Steelton Police car pulled up. Two officers got out and approached Massarelli. The younger one couldn't have been more than twenty-five. The older one was about fifty-five, with a salt-and-pepper crew cut and an expression of superiority on his face. Hands on his hips, the older officer asked Massarelli what was going on.

Massarelli identified himself and explained that BCI was executing a search warrant on Russo's home and arresting him for a murder in Alabama. The older officer identified himself to Massarelli as Captain Jonas Pappas. He asked Massarelli why his department had not been informed there was a murder investigation involving a resident of Steelton and why the department had not been notified before any action was taken.

Massarelli motioned to a BCI agent to take possession of Russo and for Boyett to join the conversation with the Steelton officers. When Boyett walked over to the Massarelli and the Steelton officers, Massarelli introduced him.

"Detective Boyett, did you ever have contact with anyone in the Steelton Police Department about this murder case?" asked Massarelli in his best official-sounding voice.

"I did," replied Boyett.

"Do you remember when and who you spoke to?"

"A detective named Pappas, in early March 2006," replied Boyett.

"And what did he tell you?"

"He said he was too busy to assist... Then he hung up on me. I never heard from him again."

At that point, Massarelli confronted Pappas, whose air of superiority had promptly evaporated at mention of Boyett's name. "Because you refused to help, BCI got involved. If it ever gets out how incompetent you were, Captain, you might become the laughingstock of cops all over the Mahoning Valley. If I were you, I'd just leave and hope the word doesn't get out." He then focused on the younger Steelton officer and added, "Make this a learning experience: don't blow off simple requests or information. It can come back and bite you in the ass."

CHAPTER 9 – THE SEARCH

As the Steelton officers left with their tails between their legs, Massarelli and Boyett returned to Russo and entered the house. They sat Russo down on his sofa in the living room. "We want you here while we search, in case we have any questions about things we find and also so you can see what we're taking. Don't worry. We'll give you a detailed receipt for any items we take."

As the other agents entered the house, Massarelli went outside to see Jill Baker. "Jill, why don't you hang outside? He doesn't realize you're one of us and maybe in the future, we can use that to get more information."

"Sure, boss. I can't believe he hasn't caught on yet," said Baker.

When Massarelli returned to the house, he sat down with Russo and Boyett. "Do you understand what's going on?" he asked Russo.

"Yeah. I'm in handcuffs and you're searching my house," replied Russo.

"You've been read your Miranda rights. Are you willing to talk to us?"

"I guess so. I'm not totally sure what you're looking for. I don't think you're going to find any bodies or anything in my house," he said with a faint attempt at humor.

"I'm not sure what we'll find. We'll have to wait and see, won't we?"

As this conversation was taking place, BCI agents began a methodical search of the house—two stories and a full basement. The second floor consisted of three bedrooms and one bath. The ground floor consisted of a living room, dining room, and kitchen, with an addition on the rear containing a half bath and a covered porch. The basement had been partially finished, in what would be best described as a "man cave" and a laundry room, with the remainder unfinished. The basement had an outside entrance from the back yard. This outside entrance led down some steps to a door that opened into the unfinished area of the basement. This further led to the laundry room and into the man cave.

As agents searched each room, they went through items and made notes of their finds. Gomez was kept busy running from room to room photographing items and having them recorded on the receipt. About twenty minutes into the search, Massarelli heard his name, along with Gomez's name, bellowed from the basement. He left Boyett and Russo and went downstairs. There, Agent Sandra Loundes pointed to a small wooden crate under a desk located beneath the steps leading from the floor above. The wooden crate, which measured about twelve inches by eighteen inches, was found upon opening to contain about a dozen manila envelopes standing on end.

Loundes said, "Boss, these are all his souvenirs. It appears there were a lot more victims than the girl in Mobile."

Agent John Gomez, arriving on Massarelli's heels, began photographing the crate and each envelope as it was removed. Most of the envelopes had some sort of writing on the front. Some contained names and others appeared to be places, like "Slidell" and "Pensacola." Each envelope contained several items. In one envelope marked "July in Mobil," the contents included a cell phone, a North Carolina driver's license , and a small, green ring.

Massarelli immediately knew what he had. "Sandra, great job! This is the mother lode. Go relieve Boyett and have him come down here."

"OK, boss," replied Loundes. She went up the stairs and moments later, Boyett came down.

"It looks like July was one of many," Massarelli told Boyett. He shook his head in disgust. "This should make your case sign, sealed, and delivered."

Boyett stared at the items from the envelope marked "July in Mobil." "Wow, that's pretty damning. How many others?"

"Looks like about a dozen, but now to try and identify them all," answered Massarelli. "I think this is going to be big news. You might want to call your captain or chief and give them a heads up."

***

Boyett went outside and placed a call to Palmer. "J.T., you're not going to believe this." "What?" asked Palmer.

"We're doing the search warrant on Russo's house. We found a box containing a bunch of manila envelopes. Each contains personal items from women, including July Marcial. We have her phone, driver's license, and toe ring. This guy is a serial killer. Massarelli wanted me to tell you what's happening because it'll probably hit the news," said Boyett.

"Good god," was all Palmer said. After a few seconds of silence, he added, "Call me whenever you get done the search. I'll call the major and the chief, let them know what's happening, and begin to prepare for questions if the press calls."

"It may be tomorrow, J.T. We're not even close to being done on the search yet."

"Three B, just keep me up to date as best you can. Good job. Now, let me get with the major and the chief."

Before going back in, Boyett called John Hood.

After three rings, Hood answered. "Hello, Detective," he said, apparently recognizing Boyett's telephone number.

"John, I wanted you to be the first to know. We've arrested the man we suspect is July's killer," said Boyett.

"You gotta be kidding!" said Hood, his voice rising half an octave with excitement. "When? Where?"

"We arrested a guy named Franco Russo in Ohio about an hour ago. I also recovered July's toe ring. When this is over, I'll try to get it back to you."

"Thank you, Detective," said Hood, his voice thick with emotion. Boyett suspected he was weeping.

"John, I'll call you early next week and give you more details."

The phone call ended with Boyett wondering how Hood was going to make it through the next few days.

Poor guy, he thought, *finally getting news after all this time.*

Back inside, Boyett made his way back to the man cave in the basement. By now, the BCI team had gone through most of the envelopes, photographing each envelope as well as their contents. The search through the rest of the house had ceased and most of the BCI personnel were in the man cave. Massarelli was on the phone. When he got off, he told Boyett he'd called in two analysts to work in the Youngstown office for the weekend in order to try and determine who the missing souvenirs belonged to. "I think this may be as big as Gacy or Bundy," he said. He looked and sounded disgusted.

"I actually hope not," admitted Boyett.

As Boyett was talking to Massarelli, he noticed the carpet on the man cave floor looked a lot like the carpet remnant that July Marcial's body had been wrapped in. He mentioned that to Massarelli.

Massarelli said, "Let's roll it up and take it."

"Wouldn't a sample tell us whether it's the same?" asked Boyett.

"Yes, but if he cut it off this piece, the remnant may actually match the cut edges. Let's take the whole thing." He barked orders to his agents, who began ripping the carpet up from the tack strips along the walls. As they completed separating the carpet from the tack strips and rolling it up, the padding fell apart under the carpet. The cement floor, which was painted burgundy throughout the basement, was observed to have about a three by four foot patch in the center that was not painted.

Massarelli immediately became suspicious. "I wonder why he would patch the center of the floor? Let's go have a chat with Russo," he said to Boyett.

They returned to the living room, where Sandra Loundes was still babysitting Russo.

Massarelli spoke. "Franco, we saw you've done some cement repair work on the floor of your basement. Can you tell me when and why?"

Russo looked at Massarelli in a sort of despair and said, "I'm not sure. I think there were some plumbing problems some years ago. I really can't recall for sure."

"How long have you lived in this house?" asked Massarelli.

"My whole life. I grew up here and inherited it from my mom when she died," replied Russo.

"When did she die?"

"She died in September 2001, right after 9/11," said Russo.

Massarelli walked back toward the stairs to the basement. Boyett followed. In the basement, Massarelli walked into the laundry room and then to the unfinished area.

Boyett asked, "What are you thinking?

"I'm thinking he's lying."

"About when his mother passed?"

"No. About the floor being ripped up by a plumber. Look here. This is the drainpipe coming down from the kitchen and second floor bathroom." Massarelli pointed to an iron pipe running down from the ceiling of the basement. "It runs along this outside wall into the laundry room, where it has a connection for the washer. Then it goes down into the floor and presumably runs along the wall under the floor and exits the house and goes to the sewer. Why would a plumber dig up the center of the floor if there shouldn't be a pipe there?"

"Honestly... I'm not a plumber. How do you know about plumbing? asked Boyett.

"When I was in college, I worked some construction work and then I did a complete renovation on my first house. These are the things you learn," replied Massarelli.

"Okay, then." Boyett shrugged. "I'll trust you on this one."

Massarelli said, "Well, I've got to call Bob Dunlap to discuss whether I need another warrant to jackhammer the floor." He excused himself and went outside while his agents continued to gather, log, and photograph evidence.

Boyett went back upstairs to the living room. "Well, Franco, it looks like things are not going well for you. Do you want to talk about any of this?"

Russo squinted up at Boyett. "I guess you're going to find out everything. Can I ask a question?"

"Sure," replied Boyett.

"What took you so long to find me?"

Boyett sighed. "That, Franco, is a long story," he replied.

CHAPTER 10 – THE CONFESSION

"So, you want to talk?" asked Boyett after a moment of silence.

"I guess," said Russo.

"OK then, Franco, let me lay down the ground rules. I won't lie to you, but there may be some questions I can't answer. In return, I expect you not to lie to me. If you don't know for sure or can't remember something, just tell me. If there's something you don't want to answer, just say you don't want to answer. We agree?" asked Boyett.

Russo nodded.

"I'm going to record this, so we don't have any misunderstandings… OK?" he asked again. "You understand?"

"I understand," replied Russo in a low, defeated voice.

Boyett took a digital recorder out of his pocket and began a preamble. "This is Detective Sergeant William Robert Boyett of the Mobile Police Department. I'm with Franco Russo, who is going to be interviewed, and Sandra Loundes of the Ohio Bureau of Criminal Investigation, who is also present. We are at Russo's home in Steelton, Ohio. Mr. Russo has been arrested for the February 2006 murder of July Marcial. Mr. Russo has previously been advised of his Miranda rights… Is that correct, Mr. Russo?"

"Yes," replied Russo.

"Now, Franco, before we get into the questions involving July Marcial, Special Agent Massarelli is in the process of obtaining another search warrant, if needed, to tear up your basement floor. Are you at all concerned about what he might find?"

"Well, what he finds won't help me," replied Russo.

"So, he will find something?" pressed Boyett.

"Yeah. He might."

Boyett told Loundes to go get Massarelli, who was outside.

Within a minute, Massarelli was back in the living room.

Boyett asked Russo, "What is he going to find under the basement floor?"

Russo suddenly looked scared. "Probably some bones."

"Bones? Really? Tell us how they got there," said Boyett.

"Well, back during the recession, maybe 2009 or 2010, I couldn't afford to go to Mardi Gras anywhere, so I met a couple girls at a bar here in Steelton. They were flirting with me, trying to get me to buy them drinks. I told them all about Mardi Gras, how girls lifted up their tops to attract guys on the floats to get beads thrown their way. I told them I had beads at home and they should come back here with me, and we could have a Mardi Gras Party. They came back with me, and we started drinking. They ended up topless with lots of beads. One of them passed out and the other started stripping and we had sex. I realized she was just a little slut. That's when the demon came out of me, and I strangled her." Russo related this in a disturbingly matter-of-fact way.

"The demon?" asked Boyett. "What do you mean?"

"Yeah, it seems during Mardi Gras season I get the urge to participate in the celebration. And when I do, especially if I'm drinking and with a slut, a demon inside me appears and tells me to rid the earth of her. That she's an unworthy sinner. I think it may relate back to my mother, who was very protective of me when it came to women. She was always worried I'd get some slut pregnant, and the slut would ruin my life. My mom was very Catholic," said Russo, as if this explained things.

"So, you killed the girl who had sex with you. What about the other one?"

"The demon told me I had to kill her, too, because she would tell people, so I strangled her while she was sleeping," replied Russo.

Boyett was getting a bad taste in his mouth. "So, now you've got the bodies of two young women in your basement. What did you do?"

"Well, at first I thought about putting them in my van and driving them somewhere to drop the bodies. But they weren't light. And I couldn't get my van into the back yard. I didn't want to carry a body around to the front of the house, so I decided to break the cement up in the floor and bury them there."

"How did you do that? asked Boyett.

"Well, first I took the carpet up. I tried breaking up the cement with a sledgehammer, but that was really hard work. So, I went down to the Home Depot in Boardman, and I rented a jackhammer from their tool rental department. It took me about seven or eight hours to get through the cement with a hole that was big enough. Then I had to dig with a shovel about three or four feet down. It was hard work and took me a couple days. By the time the hole was deep and wide enough, the bodies were starting to smell and had gotten stiff. It was a lot of work," Russo repeated, sighing wearily at the memory.

"So, you were finally able to get the bodies in the hole?"

"Yeah, but it wasn't easy and the one on top was only about two inches below the floor. When I cemented the floor, her arm was literally getting cement poured on it."

"After getting the bodies in the hole, what did you do?" asked Boyett.

"I used dirt to fill most of the hole. I ended up with a bunch of dirt left on the floor and had to carry it out to the back yard in buckets. If you look back by my fence you'll see a small mound of dirt, that's where I dumped it. So, after filling the hole with dirt, I went back to Home Depot and bought bags of concrete. I tried mixing the cement in buckets and it wouldn't mix well, so I called a friend who knows a little about cementing. He didn't know why I was doing this, I just told him I needed to patch a large hole from fixing a pipe. He told me to put water in the hole and to dump the concrete mix in and it would eventually harden. He told me to leave about an inch on top to mix and put on a finish coat. So that's what I did."

Do you remember the girls' names?" asked Boyett.

"I remember the little slut. She said her name was Tina. I remember calling her 'Tina with Tits' as she liked showing them off. Neither one of them had any ID, but I did keep Tina's necklace and the other one's bracelet," replied Russo.

"What bar did you meet them at?"

"Oh, uh... It was Patty's Sports Bar, here in Steelton."

"Did anyone ever interview you about them? Do you know if they were reported missing?"

"Apparently they were reported missing. I was in the bar a few weeks later and the bartender told me that right after the girls had been in the bar and I was talking to them, that they'd run away from home."

"But no one ever came and interviewed you?" asked Boyett.

"No. Never did."

Boyett paused to let this all sink in. "So, after you mixed the cement and water in the hole, what did you do?"

"I waited till the next day and made a small batch of cement in the bucket and mixed it real well and made a topcoat that was level with the floor. After it dried a couple days, I reinstalled the carpet," said Russo.

"Speaking of the carpet, is that the same carpet you used to wrap July Marcial's body in?"

"I'm not sure. Back when I was doing carpet installing, I'd often end up with remnants. Sometimes they were big enough to carpet a whole room. I'd give some to friends, throw some away. It wasn't unusual to have carpet remnants in my van," said Russo.

"OK. Let's turn to July Marcial. How did that take place? What exactly happened?" Boyett pressed.

Russo took a minute to think about it before starting the story. "Well, I went to Mobile for Mardi Gras, because New Orleans was closed. I'd spent a night in Pensacola a couple years before and that's when I learned that Pensacola and Mobile had Mardi Gras. I'd planned my trip to New Orleans but the hurricane hit, and everything got cancelled. Since I hadn't been to Mobile, and I knew they had a fairly large Mardi Gras celebration, I decided to go there. I drove my van there and spent about five days there. The night before Mardi Gras Tuesday, I met that girl, July, at a bar across the street from the big hotel. There was a band playing at the bar and she apparently knew them. When they took a break, she went up on stage, used their piano, and began singing. She was better than the band. She got a standing ovation when she was done. Afterwards, she was sitting at the bar, and I went over and started talking to her. She seemed real cool, but she was too involved with the music that night. I asked her if she'd be interested in lunch or dinner the next day. She said yeah. We exchanged numbers and I called her the next day. I thought she was going to blow me off, but she'd apparently been out late, and she said she'd be glad to meet me about 2:00 in the afternoon.

"I don't recall whether we texted or talked, but I walked over to her hotel, and we went off to catch a couple parades. We watched the parades and then went to get something to eat. There weren't many restaurants open, just street vendor food. She wanted some real food, so we went to my hotel and got my van and drove out toward Mobile Bay. We ended up at a seafood restaurant near the water. We'd already had a few drinks and she started drinking a few more. By the time we finished dinner, it was dark and she was pretty drunk, I asked her if she had a boyfriend. She said, 'Kind of.' She told me he was more like her daddy, always looking after her. She said sex with him had fallen off probably because of his age. I asked if she liked sex and she said she loved it. At this point, we were driving on the road down near the water. There was a restaurant by that battleship. I turned into it and parked in the parking lot. I told her to get into the back and I'd give her the best sex she's ever had. She wanted it and jumped right back there. Before I could even get back there, she was almost naked on the carpet. I think I made her happy, as she was moaning all the while we did it. Then the demon in me came out.

"The demon told me to kill the slut. As I was still fucking her, I put my hands around her throat and started choking her. She actually liked it, I think. At least at first."

"So, you strangled her during the sexual act?" asked Boyett.

"Yes," replied Russo.

"So, she's now almost naked and dead in your van. What do you do next?"

"Well, I saw she had a toe ring and thought it was cute. So, I took it off her toe. It was on there pretty tight, but I finally got it off," replied Russo. "Then I dressed and drove back into Mobile. It was dark, but there were still some people milling around downtown, so I parked at my hotel and went in and showered. About an hour later, I went back out and drove around downtown looking for a place to drop her body. I found a vacant parking lot that was filled with some trash and things. I pulled up along a building next to the lot and drug the carpet out with her body on it. Then I rolled the carpet up and left it. I went back to my hotel and slept and the next morning I drove back to Ohio. On the drive back, I kept hearing something in the back of the van. When I was probably in Tennessee, I was gassing up,

I heard the noise again and I realized her clothes were still there. I went through them and found her driver's license and cell phone and some cash she had. The noises were her cell phone alerts for texts. I turned the phone off. I dumped the clothes in a trash can at the gas station. As you probably already know, the toe ring, driver's license, and cell phone are downstairs."

At this point, Massarelli, who had not said a word so far, interjected. "Franco, are you hungry?"

"Getting there," replied Russo.

"OK, then. Why don't I order some pizza and drinks and then we can go back to the story?" suggested Massarelli.

"That'd be great," said Russo. He licked his lips at the thought.

Massarelli gave Boyett a meaningful look. "Come outside so we can get this pizza order right." With that, they both exited the house, leaving Russo with Sandra Loundes.

Outside, Massarelli told Boyett he wanted to continue the interview as long as they could go, but that it was obvious they weren't going to finish before the day was done. He also told Boyett he was going to have his agents obtain another search warrant to break up the floor in search of skeletal remains. Meanwhile, he was going to call the Mahoning County jail to make sure that Russo was isolated for the night, and that they could retrieve him the next morning to continue the interview at the BCI office.

"I'm going to have Gomez take all the photos of the envelopes and souvenirs and give them to the analysts to try to identify as many victims as possible before we interview him tomorrow," said Massarelli.

"Sounds great," said Boyett, following up with, "When you order that pizza, can I get anchovies on mine?"

"Anchovies? I took you more for a ham or pineapple type guy," replied Massarelli with a chuckle.

As Massarelli got on his phone, Boyett went back into the house for round two of Russo's confession. "So, Franco,

216 | Doug Lamplugh

is there anything else about July Marcial that we didn't cover?"

"I don't think so. But she really was nice with great musical talent," said Russo. "I just don't understand why she had to be such a slut."

"I remember seeing an envelope that mentioned Pensacola. Can you tell me about that?" asked Boyett.

"Yeah, that was back a year or two after my mom died. It was one of my first trips. When she was alive, I often had to hang around and take care of her. She was pretty sick her last couple of years. About a year after she died, I'd gotten some insurance money. I bought a motorcycle and had heard how Daytona's Bike Week was so much fun. I decided to go down. I remember it was the end of February and still snowing here. Daytona wasn't what I'd hoped for. It was a bunch of hard-core bikers, they weren't friendly, and everything was crowded. I left a few days early. I was going to drive up I-75, but there were some snowstorms coming in through the Tennessee and Carolina mountains, so I decided to go across the Florida panhandle and up I-65 since I had a few extra days. I stopped in Pensacola the first night. That was when I found out they had Mardi Gras.

"I went to the parade downtown and that's where I met that girl. She said her name was Mary, but she didn't have any ID. We went out in my van and drank a few beers I had in an ice chest and drove out into the bay on an old bridge that people use for fishing. We parked and got in the back of the van. She was a monster in bed, or back of the van in this case. She was so demanding. After I came in her twice, she demanded more and got upset when I couldn't perform again. That's when the demon told me to kill her. I started choking her, and she really liked it," said Russo. "She had that look of terror in her eyes as she lost consciousness. When I went through her clothes, she didn't have any ID, but I took her necklace with a cross on it. Why would a slut like that have a cross?" He seemed genuinely puzzled.

"What did you do with her body?" asked Boyett.

"The bridge or pier or whatever it is was basically empty. So, I drove to the end of it and turned around and backed up to the end barrier. I pulled her body out and dumped it in the bay."

"What did you do after that?"

"I went back to my hotel, re-hooked up my motorcycle trailer, and left in the morning. It was on the way back through Mobile, after going through the tunnel, that I saw Mardi Gras floats lined up on the streets. When I stopped in Mobile to get gas, I talked to some people at the gas pumps about Mardi Gras in Mobile and they told me Mardi Gras parades were a nightly event," said Russo.

"Now, can you tell me about the girl in Slidell, Louisiana?" Boyett pressed on, looking for more. However, just as he said those words the pizza arrived, and they took a break from the interview.

As they were eating pizza, Russo asked, "Can I get a beer from my refrigerator?"

"No. No alcohol, sorry," replied Boyett, although he could have gone for one or three, himself.

"So, what's going to happen to me?" asked Russo as he ate pizza and drank a Coke that Massarelli had ordered with the food.

Boyett hesitated. "Well, that isn't up to me. That's going to be a decision made by prosecutors and then eventually a judge. The best I can do is make your cooperation known to the prosecutors and the court, if they ask."

"Do they listen to you?" asked Russo.

"The prosecutors always listen. They don't always do what I want, though. Sometimes they cut plea deals with defendants who don't cooperate that I'm against, but they always listen. In this case, I'll make them fully aware of your cooperation," replied Boyett.

By now it was after 7:00 p.m. Massarelli came in and said he was going to leave Sandra Loundes at the house to maintain possession overnight. He said Boyett needed to finish up and they would get Russo out in the morning to continue the interview. He then asked Russo what he wanted for lunch the next day.

Russo's eyebrows shot up in surprise. "I get a choice?"

Massarelli said, "When we sign you out of jail, we have to feed you, so I figured I'd see if you had some favorite food that I'd make arrangements to get."

"Can we get Popeyes' fried chicken?"

"Sure, that's an easy one. Is there a Popeyes in Youngstown?" asked Massarelli.

"Yeah, it's on Midlothian, just off Market Street. I think that's Boardman. But right where Boardman and Youngstown meet," said Russo.

"Okay, we'll find it," said Massarelli.

Boyett decided to stop with the Pensacola incident in order to try and get more details on the other incidents in the morning. By this time, Massarelli had several more agents arriving to transport Russo to the Mahoning County jail. He specifically instructed them to ensure that Russo was isolated for the night with no contact with anyone.

As the agents departed with Russo, Massarelli told Boyett, "I'm going to leave you to do the interviews tomorrow. You and he apparently have a good rapport. Sandra is staying here tonight. Tomorrow I'll meet you at my office about 8:00 a.m. and hopefully we can get briefed by my analysts, who will have uncovered some information about the various victims. Tomorrow I'm going to be between the office, where you'll interview him and here, where we'll be digging up the floor and conducting a full crime scene. I've already reserved an electric jackhammer and a couple sledgehammers from Home Depot. I'll leave Gomez with you at our office and the rest of my crew will probably be here."

Massarelli called an all hands meeting in the living room. He told his agents they would be meeting back at Russo's at 9:00 a.m. He instructed Gomez to be at BCI Youngstown at 8:00 a.m. to assist Boyett and also to get Russo from the Mahoning County jail. He told the other agents to wear crime scene clothes and to bring body bags and evidence envelopes as well as video cameras and indoor artificial lighting for the next day.

It was just after 8:00 p.m. when the evening broke up, and Boyett knew he was going to be in for a long day on Saturday. On his way back to the hotel, he called Palmer. "J.T., it's been an interesting day."

"Yeah, what's happening up there?" asked Palmer.

"Well, first off, Russo and I have a good rapport and an understanding. So far, he's admitted to Marcial's murder, the murder of two local girls up here, whom he buried under his basement, and another girl in Pensacola."

"Wow," replied Palmer. "That's... good. Good work, I mean."

"We just took him over to the jail and we're getting him out tomorrow morning to continue the interview," said Boyett.

"Why not continue it tonight?" asked Palmer.

"Well, we have these souvenirs from more victims. Massarelli has a couple analysts who are going to work all night trying to get identities and reports by morning so we can talk intelligently to him. BCI is making arrangements to dig up the floor tomorrow while I continue the interview."

"Sounds like it's going to be a big case and an important one," said Palmer.

"Yeah, it's turning into a lot more than I ever thought it would," Boyett agreed.

"Call me tomorrow and update me?"

"Will do, J.T.," Boyett replied and hung up the phone.

He arrived at the Holiday Inn in Boardman and checked in. After getting settled, he called Millie and they discussed his day. He told Millie he'd expected to be back either late

Monday or Tuesday, but considering what was happening with Russo, he did not know whether that would happen.

Millie told him to take whatever time was needed to make the case. She passed the phone to Chris, and Boyett chatted with his son for a few minutes before ending the call. Then he hit the shower and went to bed. It had been a long day physically and mentally, and he expected tomorrow would be just as exhausting.

CHAPTER 11 – THE CONFESSION, DAY TWO

Saturday morning started after a night of restless sleep that had Boyett rolling over

throughout the night, looking frequently at the bedside clock to see what time it was. He kept edging in and out of sleep with thoughts and dreams involving July Marcial and Franco Russo. About 5:30 a.m., he decided to give up on the sleep and get up. After dressing and going downstairs, he found the restaurant in the hotel just beginning to open. After a breakfast of pancakes and two cups of coffee, Boyett decided to drive to the BCI office early in case anyone had arrived early. He arrived about 6:45 a.m., finding Massarelli's Mercedes already there.

He went to the door and rang the buzzer.

Massarelli buzzed him in. He told Boyett the analysts had made quite a bit of progress with the information found in Russo's home and that there had been a total of twelve girls apparently involved in Russo's murders. The analysts had positively ID'd eight as deceased, not including the two missing girls believed to be buried in the basement floor of Russo's house. Three other victims had been reported as missing, but were not listed as deceased.

He took Boyett back to the room where the analysts were working and introduced them. He handed Boyett eleven envelopes, seven of which contained the details of the bodies found. These seven packages contained information of every murder or body found and included dates, autopsy reports if available, and details about how and where the bodies were found. Three files containing the reports on the missing persons that the analysts believed were victims of Russo. The remaining file was the one marked "July in Mobil", which the analysts had not researched knowing that Boyett had the complete file. The deaths / murders covered included:

1) File marked "Pensacola" – file contained a necklace. The analysts believed the deceased was Mary Murphy of Cantonment, Florida. Murphy was a white female 24 years old. Details of investigation were a female body was found washed up on a beach in Pensacola Bay on March 26, 2003, on the west side of the city of Gulf Breeze, Florida. The body was in a state of decomposition. Autopsy determined that the subject died before entering the water. The body was bloated, and cause of death couldn't be determined. There were no stab wounds or gunshot wounds. Cause of death was ruled as suspicious. On April 11, 2003, the body was identified as Murphy, who had had been reported missing on March 2, 2003. She had last been seen leaving her house on February 28 about 5:45 p.m. to attend the Mardi Gras parade in Pensacola. Murphy worked as a clerk at a heating and air conditioning company.

2) File marked "Metairie" – File contained a bracelet, a cell phone, and a Louisiana driver's license in the name of Carol Hamilton, which described her as a white female, born 10/23/1980, 5'5", with red hair. Also some strands of hair were in the envelope. According to what could be found, Carol Hamilton was reported missing to

the Metairie Police Department on February 27, 2004. She was last seen leaving her apartment the morning of February 24, 2004. She told her roommates she was going to get a bite to eat and intended on walking down to the Metairie Mardi Gras parade. Her body was never located.

3) File marked – "N.O." – File contained a necklace, a bandana, and a University of New Orleans student ID in the name of Belinda Sharp. On February 10, 2005, Sharp, a white female, age 22, 5'07", 125 pounds, with blond hair, was found murdered on the shore of Lake Pontchartrain. Autopsy determined that she was strangled, and the time of death was approximately February 8, 2005.

4) File Marked "Mobile" – Analysis not done.

5) File Marked "Marie" – File contained an alligator ring and a Louisiana driver's license in the name of Marie Lartigue. Lartique was determined to be a 25-year-old graduate student who lived alone in Lafayette near the University of Louisiana at Lafayette. She was found dead of strangulation in her apartment on February 22, 2007. Crime scene investigators recovered several partial fingerprints, but none which were classifiable. Police initially suspected an ex-boyfriend, but enough evidence couldn't be gathered to result in his arrest.

6) File Marked "B.R. 2008" – File contained two rings, dried skin that appeared to have been the cut nipple portion of a breast. Analysis of these objects appear to lead to the body of Roberta Masters. Masters was a 31-year-old stripper who worked in various strip joints in the Baton Rouge

area. Her body was found along a road that runs parallel to the Mississippi River in Baton Rouge on February 7, 2008. When the body was found, part of Masters' left breast had been cut off.

7) File marked "Tina the slut" – File contained a bracelet and a necklace. This file appears to be related to the two bodies believed to be buried under Franco Russo's floor. It appears the two victims were Tina Watson (age 20) and Janet Crowe (age 21). Both subjects were last seen in Steelton on February 24, 2009. Both girls were reported missing to the Steelton Police Department on February 25, 2009, by their parents. Steelton police did a missing person's investigation. According to the Steelton police, they interviewed several of the girls' associates and without reporting the names of those associates, learned that the girls wanted to run off to Florida. Steelton police reported that at least one associate told them the girls had said they were going to go to a truck stop in Austintown, Ohio and try and catch a ride south toward Florida. The Steelton police told the families that because both girls were over eighteen and there was no evidence of foul play, the missing persons case was closed.

8) File marked "Amanda" – File contained a Missouri driver's license in the name of Amanda Plank (a white female, date of birth 03/21/80, 5'04", 115 pounds), and a pink tank top shirt. Analysis of the investigation determined that Plank was reported missing on February 19, 2010. Her parents who lived in Kansas City reported her missing when they had not received any calls or texts from her in several days. Plank was a legal

secretary for a local law firm. She was still listed as an active missing person.

9) File marked "Autumn" – File contained a key marked Island Shores 117 and a scarf. This file is believed to contain the scarf and a key to a rental condo rented by Autumn Bradley. Bradley was a white female dob: 07/23/1989. Her body was found in Shelby Lake in Gulf State Park, Alabama, on March 13, 2011. Bradley had originally been reported missing by her parents on March 5, 2011. Her parents had contacted the Gulf Shores Police after failing to hear from their daughter since the evening of March 3. Bradley had been staying at a condo the family co-owned in the Island Shores Condo Complex and had gone to the beach because she was off from college for the Mardi Gras weekend. A subsequent search of the condo revealed that Bradley's clothing, computer, and personal effects were there, although she was not. Her vehicle was located on March 6, parked on East Second Avenue. On March 13, 2011, Bradley's body was found by a fisherman. At the time the body was found, it had been mutilated and partially eaten by alligators. An autopsy was performed but a cause of death could not be determined because of the extreme mutilation.

10) File marked "Galveston" – File contained a necklace bearing a cross and a turquoise bracelet. The analysis determined that the items most likely belonged to Isabella Herrera. Herrera's body was found in a dumpster on March 5, 2014. According to the Galveston Police report, Herrera's body was found by workers at the Mexican restaurant when they were taking trash out at the end of shift

on March 5, 2014. Herrera was identified by her driver's license also found in the dumpster. An autopsy determined Herrera had been strangled. The investigation is open but considered cold.

11) File marked "Biloxi" – File contained a $1 chip from Harrah's casino, a blindfold, and a pair of restraints. These items may be connected to the murder of Jacklyn Harper, who was found dead on February 18, 2015 in Ocean Springs, Mississippi. According to police reports, Harper's body was found along Front Beach Drive, just south of Highway 90 in Ocean Springs. At the time the body was found, it was naked. The autopsy determined the cause of death was strangulation. The autopsy also revealed marks on both wrists. indicating there may have been some sort of restraints involved. Semen was found during the autopsy, although no matches had been made.

"Goddamn. Well, these points will sure be a conversation starter," said Boyett. "It gives me a whole lot more to talk to Russo about than I had before. Thanks."

Massarelli asked him, "Are you ready for today?"

"As ready as I can be. Why?"

"Because I've had our interview room furniture changed out for this interview, so Russo is a little more comfortable. We're going to have video running through the entire interview. Let's get him to go for every one of these murders," replied Massarelli.

"Hopefully, he'll still be willing to cooperate," said Boyett.

When you go in, turn your digital recorder on. Give the preamble like you did yesterday. I want him to think he's only being recorded on your recorder. He was comfortable that way."

"OK," said Boyett, "show me the interview room."

"Right this way."

They walked down a series of halls toward the front of the office. Inside the room were a sofa and several nice armchairs.

"Where'd these come from?" asked Boyett.

"The sofa's from the agent in charge's office. The chairs are from the lobby," replied Massarelli. "Gomez will be running the audio and video equipment. He may stop in the room now and then, but I think leaving you alone with Russo will be best. Gomez will be in the next room viewing and listening. The door won't open from the inside, so if you need out you need to call Gomez. That way, Russo won't know we're listening and recording."

"Got it," said Boyett with a quick nod.

With that, Massarelli told Boyett he was going to head down to Russo's house to continue the search. He said Gomez was at the jail, awaiting them to transfer Russo to his custody.

Boyett sat in the BCI office reviewing the analyst files. At about 8:15 a.m., Gomez arrived with Franco Russo shackled and handcuffed. He was escorted to the interview room, where his restraints were removed. Gomez told Boyett that if he needed anything, just to call, and he left the room.

Boyett started the conversation off by asking Russo, "How was your first night in jail?"

"It could've been better, " Russo said matter-of-factly. "I didn't have a cell mate, so it was quiet, except when there was some echo of a door slamming somewhere."

"Have you ever spent any time in jail?"

"Not really. I spent a night in Steelton's jail one time and another night in Warren, but nothing more than small town jails for a night," replied Russo.

"Did you get breakfast this morning?"

"Yeah, they brought a tray to my cell. Wasn't very good, but I'm looking forward to Popeyes for lunch."

"Well, give me an hour or so notice before you want to eat. It may take some time to get here," said Boyett.

"Yeah, sure," responded Russo.

"Let's continue our conversation from last night. OK?" asked Boyett.

"Sure, that's why we're here... Right?"

"That's the reason," confirmed Boyett.

With that, Boyett removed his digital recorder and began his preamble. "This is Detective Sergeant William Robert Boyett of the Mobile, Alabama Police Department. Today is September 29, 2018, and I am at the Ohio Bureau of Investigation office in Youngstown, Ohio to interview Franco Russo. This is a subsequent interview of Mr. Russo, which began last evening when Mr. Russo was arrested. Is this correct, Mr. Russo?"

"Yes," replied Russo.

"Mr. Russo was given his Miranda rights yesterday, but I'm going to include them again on this tape," Boyett said, and he began reading Russo his rights. Upon completion of the preamble, he got down to the interview. "Franco, last night at your house we found eleven envelopes containing various items in your basement. Are you familiar with what I'm talking about?"

"Yes," Russo replied again.

"Can you explain what they are?" asked Boyett.

"They're items I took from the women I killed."

"Can I ask why you took items from those women?"

"It makes it easier to remember them," replied Russo, as if this should have been obvious to anyone.

"So, last night we spoke about the women in Mobile, Pensacola, and the two girls in Steelton. Today I'd like to go in a chronological order of the events. We've done some research, and we believe we've found more information on each of the women. Is that OK?" asked Boyett.

"I'm not sure what you mean by chronological, but we can talk about them in any order you want," replied Russo.

"OK. Now, the first folder was marked Pensacola. That's the case where you said you met her at the Pensacola Mardi Gras parade and later killed her and dumped her off the fishing bridge. Is that right?"

"Yeah, that's her."

"Do you remember any more about the incident? Maybe what day of the week it was when you met her? Where you met her? pressed Boyett.

"I met her on the street watching the parade, and then I suggested I buy her a drink. We went to some bar... Or actually, it was a building with a series of bars a few blocks from the parade route. We had a couple drinks and I mentioned I had beer in my van, and we should get to know each other better. She was all in, she followed me right to my van," replied Russo.

"Then you drove her to that fishing pier or bridge?"

"Well, not directly. We rode around a bit. Maybe twenty or thirty minutes and then as we were along the bay, she directed me on how to go to that fishing pier."

"And as you told me last night, you had sex with her in your van. Then you strangled her and dumped her body in the bay?" asked Boyett. He knew he was repeating things, but he wanted to be absolutely certain of everything.

"Yes."

"Was this the first time you killed someone?" asked Boyett.

"Yes," replied Russo.

"What led you to do it?"

"I'm not sure how to explain it. I heard a voice in my head, telling me she was a slut, not worthy of living, that she could ruin my life," said Russo. "It told me these girls would never stop being the sluts they were. These were the kind of women that ruined my father. He left my mom for a young slut when I was a baby. They use sex to ruin men's lives."

Reflecting that Russo was in serious need of psychological help, Boyett said, "OK. Let's go to the next envelope. By what I can tell, your next event was in the Metairie, Louisiana area. Can you tell me about it?"

Russo began, "I don't remember the year, but I think it was the year after I was in Pensacola. I went to New Orleans for Mardi Gras. I couldn't get a hotel for a reasonable price anywhere in New Orleans, so I ended up out by Metairie, not far from the New Orleans Airport. I drove into New Orleans for a couple of parades, but the traffic was terrible, and parking was worse. So, after I went downtown a couple days, I found out that there were going to be parades in Metairie on Fat Tuesday. Instead of fighting the traffic into New Orleans, I decided to attend the parade in Metairie. I met a girl—I think her name was Carol—at the parade. She was beautiful. She was about half drunk when I met her.

"After the parades, me and her went to a bar and drank some more. She had beautiful red hair. Well, after the bar, she went back to my room with me and we had sex several times, and that lasted into the night. She was pretty kinky. So, she stayed the night. While we were sleeping, the demon came to me in my dreams and told me that she was a whore and a slut. I woke up, saw her sleeping beside me and strangled her. I remember her waking up as I was strangling her. There was terror in her eyes as she passed out and died. After she was dead, I moved her body to my van. There was an open parking spot just outside my door and it was the middle of the night. I backed my van up to the room and drug her body out to the van. After I got her body in the van, I saw a guy in the parking lot. I didn't know if he'd seen me or not, so I decided to leave. I grabbed my bag, which was almost packed, cleaned out the room in, like, five minutes, and left the key in the room and drove off. When I got into Alabama, almost to that place where the University of Alabama is..."

"Tuscaloosa?" interjected Boyett.

"I think so. I remember seeing signs for the University of Alabama. So, right before that city. It was just getting daylight. The interstate crossed a river. I got off the interstate at the next exit and tried to find my way back to that river. I got lost. I was on some rural road and could see the interstate. I just pulled over and dumped her body on the side of the road. I did take off her bracelet and cut some of her hair, it was so beautiful. I also found her cell phone in her clothes later. I kept the cell phone and dumped the clothes in a trash can at a truck stop on the way home. I think I made it home about eight or nine that night," said Russo.

"OK," said Boyett. "So, the next envelope says 'New Orleans.' Tell me about that one."

"Well," started Russo, "after having the hotel and traffic issues and staying out by the New Orleans airport, the next year, I did my reservations in advance and also planned better. I was able to get a motel out near the New Orleans Zoo. I didn't have to fight traffic or parking. I did take the streetcar a few times to get over to the French Quarter and walked quite a bit to the different parade routes. I met her on the trolley one day when I was there. She was very pretty and was wearing a bandana around her neck. We took the trolley over toward the French Quarter and got off and walked to the parade route together. During the parade, she lifted her top and showed her tits to get the attention of the guys on the floats. She had some nice boobs, and they threw a lot at her. We were drinking during the parade and I was getting pretty loose, and I think she was too. As the parade ended, I mentioned that she had nice boobs and she said thanks. Then she said it was a shame that they didn't get enough attention from anyone. I told her that I'd love to give them some attention and invited her back to my hotel.

"On the way back to my hotel, on the trolley, we flirted about sex and things. She told me she was a student and lived in a dorm and couldn't get any privacy from her roommates. She also mentioned liking older guys because they were more discreet. When we got back to my room, we had mind-blowing sex. She stayed in my room well past midnight. It was real early morning, maybe about five. I woke up and she was giving me a blow job. She looked at me and said something about finding a fun way to wake me up. She asked me if I could give her a ride back to her school, as she had an 8:00 class. We left the hotel about six and drove toward her school. During the ride, she asked me how long I was going to be in town and whether we could meet up after she was done classes. She talked a mile a minute. By the time we got back to her campus, the demon was whispering in my ear about how she was a slut and didn't deserve to be on this earth. When we pulled onto her campus, we parked, and she leaned over to kiss me. I put my hands around her neck and choked her. After she was dead, I moved her body to the rear of the van and drove out the back of the campus to the lake or bay that's there. I drove along the water and found a place that was a bit remote and backed up to the water and dumped her body in. I kept the bandana, a necklace, and her school ID."

"OK," said Boyett. "So, the next envelope was Mobile. We talked about July Marcial last night. Is there anything you might want to add to that?"

Russo looked hard at Boyett. "Yeah, I remember you were asking about the carpet in my basement. When I was in jail last night, I got to thinking about that question. Back about that time, the carpet company I was working for got a contract to carpet houses in a new subdivision in Canfield. I was working there about three or four days a week for several months. That carpet was what we used in almost all of those houses. I'm not sure the carpet in my basement came off the same roll as what I used to roll her body in, but

I'm pretty sure that was the carpet from that subdivision. I remember we had so many remnants, I could've carpeted a couple houses if I wanted to piece it together."

"You think it'll match?"

"It might. It could depend on whether it came from the same roll as what was in my basement. We probably went through over twenty rolls of carpet in all. I'm not sure how they do the manufacturing, but sometimes two rolls of the same carpet have a slight difference in color," replied Russo.

"OK, let's move on to the next file. It had the name 'Marie' on it. Can you tell me about her?" asked Boyett.

"Yeah, I remember her well. It was in Lafayette, Louisiana after Hurricane Katrina. New Orleans was still recovering and it had been over a year, so I heard Lafayette had a good Mardi Gras, so I went there. I met Marie in a bar not far from the university there. She was a local, Cajun girl. I parked in one of those lots where you pay to park. When I was on the way back to the parking lot after the parade, I stopped in a bar a couple blocks from the parking lot. That's where I met Marie. She was in the bar, getting drunk, and was very talkative. She said she was in college for some master's degree, I don't recall what. She told me she'd broken up with her overbearing boyfriend who she'd been with for a few years. She said she was exploring her sexuality and the next thing you know she was inviting me back to her apartment. I left my van in the parking lot and we walked the eight or ten blocks to her place. She lived in a house that had been converted into several apartments near the university We spent the night together and she seemed fine. She wasn't as kinky as I expected her to be. Nothing more than missionary-type sex.

"The next morning, she seemed to have changed her mood. Next thing you know, she said it was time for me to leave. I'd hoped to spend a couple days with her. When I didn't jump up and leave right away, she started getting mad. In about two minutes, she started telling me to get out.

She was getting loud. It was just before noon. She began shouting for me to leave. At that point, I grabbed her by the neck and choked her. After she was dead, I realized my fingerprints may be in the house, so I wiped down all the surfaces I might've touched—her bedroom, the bathroom, even the doorknobs. I took a ring I saw on her bureau in her bedroom and her driver's license. After I left, I walked back to the parking lot only to find that my van had been towed. Apparently, the parking lot owners towed it to get the lot cleared for the next parade. I had to go to a towing company and pay like a hundred bucks to get my van back."

"Did you leave Lafayette that day?"

"No, I stayed until the day after Mardi Gras day," replied Russo. "I even walked by Marie's apartment house once and expected to see police, but there wasn't anything."

As they were finishing the discussion, it was now approaching noon. Russo asked Boyett if they could order the Popeyes chicken.

Boyett called Gomez, who was listening live in the adjoining room, and asked if they could order the Popeyes. Gomez said to ask Russo what he wanted in his order and Russo replied that he wanted some of everything. Lots of chicken, fries, and red beans and rice. Gomez said he would call Massarelli and see about getting it delivered. While Boyett prepared for questions from the next envelope, Gomez placed the call to Massarelli.

Massarelli said he would pick up the chicken on the way to the office as the crime scene team had begun excavating the bodies from the basement floor.

***

As Massarelli left Russo's house, which was now surrounded with mostly unmarked police vehicles as well as the BCI crime scene van, the first of what would be many news crews arrived and began setting up cameras. Before he could get out, one news reporter who knew him from previous cases walked up with a microphone and asked what was going on at the house.

"I can't comment at this time. I'm sure when we finish up the investigation, we will be providing information," said Massarelli.

"Is it drug-related?" asked the reporter.

"No comment beyond what I've just told you," repeated Massarelli. "I'll be sure to contact you when we have something to release."

With that, he got into his vehicle and departed Russo's house. On the way, he called Gomez, confirmed the Popeyes order, and asked how cooperative Russo was being.

Gomez told him that Russo was answering every question in great detail and pretty much hanging himself.

Massarelli told Gomez he should be there in about forty-five minutes.

At Popeyes, Massarelli decided to order some extras to keep Russo happy and cooperating. He ordered the sixteen-piece family meal with sides of french fries, red beans, and coleslaw. He added five hot apple pie desserts and five soft drinks. The bill came in at just over $50.00. What a small price to pay to clear a dozen or so homicides.

***

Back at the BCI office, Boyett was continuing with the questions. "Franco, there's an envelope marked 'B.R.' Tell me about her."

Russo began, "Well, I don't recall her name. It was in Baton Rouge, probably the year after Lafayette. I went down for their Mardi Gras. It wasn't nearly as good of a Mardi Gras celebration as the other places I'd been to. The people weren't nearly as friendly. I ended up attending the last parade, then driving to a strip joint. The place wasn't very busy that night. So, I'm sitting there nursing my beer and this dancer comes over and starts flirting with me. She's not really that great-looking, but she did have great tits. She keeps trying to get me to go to a private room for a lap dance. I remember asking her how much a lap dance was, and she said it was $100. I told her the only way she would get $100 from me was if she gave me a blow job. She said they weren't allowed to do that. Then she said she'd already done her last set on stage and if I wanted to meet her after she left, she'd be glad to make $100. I told her I'd be in my van, and she told me she'd be checking out in about fifteen minutes. So, I finished my beer and left. She came out to my van about twenty minutes later. She told me she wanted to be paid first. I gave her the $100 and we climbed in the back of the van. She kept telling me how she had the most beautiful tits of any of the dancers and how they were all natural. After she give me the blow job, she spit it out on the carpet of my van.

"After about fifteen minutes, I started getting hard again and told her she needed to go to work again. She said that would cost another $100. I tried to get her to do it for free, arguing she was already making more than $100 per hour. She refused to negotiate and wanted the money up front. I told her I didn't have the cash and would have to go to an ATM. We went to an ATM, and I got more money, and right there in the parking lot of the bank she sucked me off again. This time, she pulled away before I came and my jizz shot across the van. I told her for a hundred bucks she needed to be swallowing that cum. She got nasty about that comment and told me to take her back to her car, which was at the club. At that point, I had enough of her shit and grabbed her by the neck and strangled her. Because she was so proud of her tits, I decided to take my carpet knife and cut her nipple off as a keepsake. I remembered I'd gone across the Mississippi River bridge, so I worked my way back toward the bridge and dropped her body on a road down by the river."

As Russo finished with the story about Baton Rouge, Massarelli arrived with the Popeyes chicken, and they took a lunch break.

Massarelli motioned Boyett outside the room and Gomez came in while Russo dug into the food. Outside the room, Massarelli asked Boyett if he had any additional information on the bodies in the basement.

"They're next on the list."

Massarelli said he would like to sit in, since they were Ohio murders and because someone from Ohio may need firsthand information about the confession at a later date.

Boyett agreed that would be a good thing. He suggested they return to the room and eat with Russo, in order for Massarelli to try to build a relationship with the suspect before the interview.

They re-entered the interview room and sat down to eat with Russo. As they were eating the chicken and dishing sides onto some paper plates that Massarelli had gotten from the office lunchroom, Massarelli casually asked Russo, "Do you like apple pie?"

Russo stopped chewing to look across the table at him. "Sure, why?"

"Because you look like an apple pie kind of guy. So, I got some apple pie for dessert," replied Massarelli.

"Nice, I'll have to save some room," Russo replied easily, as if he had not just been talking about all the women he'd killed.

As they continued eating, Boyett mentioned that Massarelli was going to sit in for part of the next interviews.

"Huh," said Russo without interest, and he dug into his apple pie.

As lunch was finished, Gomez went back to the room where they were filming and Boyett and Massarelli got back down to discussing the envelopes and souvenirs. Boyett set his digital recorder down and began his new preamble, adding, "With me during this part of the interview this afternoon is James Massarelli, agent in charge of Ohio BCI. Franco Russo has previously been informed of his Miranda rights. Is that correct, Franco?"

"Yes," replied Russo.

"You're willing to talk to us again?" asked Boyett.

"Sure, why not?" responded Russo with a shrug.

With the preamble complete, Boyett started the conversation. "So, before lunch we discussed the murder you committed in Baton Rouge, Louisiana. Do we need to add anything to your prior statement?"

"I don't think so."

"OK. Let's go to Tina the Slut. Last night you said back in 2009 or 2010, you couldn't afford to go to Mardi Gras anywhere, and you met a couple young women at a bar in Steelton. You invited them back to your house started drinking with them and had sex with the one named Tina. You killed Tina and then strangled her friend, who was sleeping. You didn't know how to get rid of the bodies, so you eventually dug a hole in your basement and buried them there. Is that right?"

"Basically, that's it," said Russo.

"Do you have anything to add?" asked Boyett.

"There were more details in what I told you last night, but you've got the basic facts right."

At this point, Massarelli interjected with some questions of his own. "Franco, did you ever see these girls before you met them that day?"

"I can't say for sure. I see a lot of people around Steelton that I don't know by name."

"But you weren't friends or never dated them or had any type of relationship or friendship with either one before that day?" asked Massarelli.

"No."

"Did you ever tell anyone about this incident?"

"No," Russo said again. He was beginning to sound bored.

"Did you ever see any of the posters that were posted around Steelton by the girls' families reporting them missing?"

"I don't think so. I've seen posters people put on telephone poles and things, but I never stop to read them. If someone put them up about Tina and that other girl, I don't know."

"Franco, we're digging in your basement right now. We've found the bodies. Is there anything you want to tell me now, before we find out for ourselves?" asked Massarelli.

"I don't think so. You'll find two bodies. I've told you how it went down and who they were to the best of my knowledge," answered Russo.

"OK," replied Massarelli. "When we're done at your house, we'll lock it up. Is there someone we can give the key to, who can look after your property? You may not get back to Steelton for a while. You'll need someone to take care of everything, from utilities to taxes. Or we can just secure it and bring you the key and it'll be put in your personal belongings."

Russo frowned. "I have some relatives, most of whom I don't trust, so let me think about that."

"Well, let me know what you want to do. If I don't hear anything by Monday, I'll bring you the key," said Massarelli.

At that point, Boyett said, "Let's move onto the next envelope. It's marked 'Amanda.' What do you remember about her?"

Russo started, "That was St. Louis. Did you know they celebrate Mardi Gras in St. Louis? It was after I got laid off when the carpet store went bankrupt. I was on unemployment. Bored, nothing to do and not much money. I heard they had Mardi Gras there and since it was only a day's drive, I decided to go. I drove out there and stayed a couple nights at a motel. I got there late the night I arrived and found a bar near my hotel. I went in and had a drink, but the place was dead. The next day I went to a parade

It wasn't bad, but it wasn't anything like New Orleans or down south. After the parade I went back to the hotel, and I went back into the same bar wearing my Mardi Gras beads. That's where I met Amanda. She was a cute one. She was also wild. She wanted my beads. I told her she'd have to earn them. She said that would be fun. So, before you know it, she's kissing on me, sucking my fingers, right at the bar. It's now dark outside and I tell her we should go back to my hotel. She says OK. As we're walking through the parking lot, she grabs me and goes down on her knees and unzips my pants. We're out kind of behind a dumpster. I remember it was cold and I'm wondering why here and not back in the room. She starts giving me a blow job right there in the parking lot. That's hot. Then, for no reason at all, she chomps down on my cock. I mean really biting it hard. I grabbed her hair trying to pull her off it. It didn't do any good, like she was getting revenge for something. I couldn't get her to let go, so I used her hair to bang her head into the dumpster. She eventually let go and fell to the ground with her head bleeding.

"I jumped on that bitch and strangled the shit out of her. After I was sure she was dead, I picked up her body and threw it in the dumpster. I found her purse on the ground and carried it back to my hotel. In it I found the pink tank top and her driver's license. I threw everything else in a trash can in the hotel walkway. When I get in the shower, my cock had teeth marks that drew blood. It was like being bit by a goddamn dog, or maybe a vampire. I showered and packed up and left that night. I stopped at a rest area in Indiana and slept a bit in the back of the van."

Boyett and Massarelli looked at each other. "The next envelope said 'Autumn' and contained a key from some place called Island Shores. Can you tell me about that?" asked Boyett.

"Yeah, that was probably in 2011. It was during the recession. I remember I was delivering pizzas and not making shit. I still had a little money left from when my mom died. I decided to get away from the cold and headed down south. I ended up staying a small hotel just outside of Gulf Shores, Alabama. It wasn't much, but it was cheap. I drove up to Mobile one day and to a small town about twenty-five miles away for a parade. But Gulf Shores also had a small Mardi Gras parade, so I went there. Mardi Gras in Gulf Shores is different than everywhere else. It was full of old people they call snowbirds. They go to the beaches in Florida and Alabama for the winter from everywhere up north.

"I'm in Gulf Shores and the average age of people is probably seventy to eighty. I saw this cute girl in her early twenties, alone, so I went over and started talking to her. She said she was visiting for the Mardi Gras weekend. This was the weekend before Mardi Gras Day, if I remember right. We're, like, the youngest people there, so we went off to get some drinks. I don't remember the exact names of the places, but one was a place right on the beach in Gulf Shores. We went up some outside stairs and it was fairly crowded, so we sat on a balcony overlooking the beach. The place was so crowded, we couldn't even get a second drink, so she said she wanted to go to another place. She had me drive about five or six miles along the beach, to a bar located on the Florida/Alabama state line. At the time, it was still being rebuilt from a hurricane. It was a real dive, but at least we could get a beer. We actually got pretty drunk.

"We ended up in my van, in the parking lot of this bar. She wanted me. We screwed for an hour, and she kept calling me "Daddy." We actually fell asleep in the back of the van in the parking lot of the bar. I woke up and it was dark. She was laying there naked. That's when the demon told me to kill the little bitch. I strangled her right there. She woke up and I had my hands around her neck. I could tell she liked it at first, thought it was a game. Then she realized she was losing consciousness. I remember getting dressed and pulling out of the bar, and driving maybe eight or ten miles and nothing looked familiar, then I realized I'd turned the wrong way coming out of the parking lot and was going farther into Florida. I turned around and headed back into Alabama. On the way back, I took a shortcut through a state park. I found a place to pull over next to a lake or bay. I pulled her body out and dumped it right on the shore. When I got back to my hotel, I cleaned out the van and found her jeans with the key in them and kept her scarf. I dumped the rest of her clothes in a trash can at a gas station near my motel." Russo finally paused.

"Do you remember the name of the hotel or where it was located?" asked Boyett.

"Kind of," said Russo. "It was off the main road that leads into the beach area. About ten or fifteen miles north of the beach. It was small, not a brand name. It was near a bunch of stores, like an outside mall. I think there was a Home Depot and a bunch of fast-food places near it."

"OK," said Boyett. "The next file was marked 'Galveston.' Can you tell me about that envelope and woman?"

"I remember Galveston, although I don't remember her name. I met her in this Mexican restaurant when I went down there. It wasn't the year after Gulf Shores, it was a couple years after that. I'd started working at GM. When I first went to work there, I couldn't get the days off I wanted, so it took a couple years to get the days off. So I went to Galveston, just because it was there. I heard they had Mardi Gras, which they do, but it's not a big event like Louisiana or even Alabama. I remember getting a hotel down by the water, by the seawall. I went to the parade. I'd seen a sign for $1.00 margaritas at this restaurant. So, after the parade, I ended up at the restaurant eating and drinking. There were some girls sitting in the restaurant and since margaritas were cheap, I sent them a round. As they were leaving, one of them came over to me and thanked me for the drinks.

She was obviously Mexican and spoke with an accent. I was feeling pretty good and I'm pretty sure she was too. I offered to buy her another and that led to several more. We got to talking and she told me she was from Mexico and loved the United States and was hoping she could get to stay here. I got the vibe from her that she was lonely and sexually frustrated."

"Why's that?" asked Massarelli.

"Well, while we sitting in the booth drinking the margaritas, she took her shoe off under the table and started rubbing my leg with her foot. Then she moved it up to my crotch and was rubbing it there, while looking into my eyes and smiling," said Russo.

"That explains that," said Massarelli.

Russo continued, "So, I told her to come back to my hotel and she agreed. When we got to my van, she said something about not needing to go to the hotel, we had the back of the van. So, we climbed back there, and she used me to end her sexual frustrations. After probably an hour of sex, she said she'd love to come with me and live. She basically wanted me to bring her home and I think marry her so she could become legal."

"And you didn't like that idea?"

"Hell, no!" Russo exclaimed. "I'm not marrying an illegal Mexican!"

"Of course not," said Massarelli in a sarcastic tone.

Russo did not seem to notice, and he went on, "So, when I told her I couldn't bring her back with me she started crying and kind of throwing a tantrum. I told her to get dressed and I'd take her home. She continued to cry, but got dressed. As she finished, I got behind her and put my arms around her and after she calmed down, I moved them up and began choking her. I was afraid she might scream rape or something, since she didn't get her way. After she was dead, I backed up to the dumpster, opened the back doors of the van, and got her body into it. Right after I got her body in the dumpster, I could hear voices in the parking lot near the rear of the restaurant. I got in the van and drove off. I left Galveston the next day. After I got home and was cleaning my van, I found her necklace on the floor where she was when I killed her. She must've either dropped it or not gotten it back on when she was dressing."

"Do you remember the name of the hotel you stayed in? How far it was from the Mexican restaurant?" asked Boyett.

"I think it was a Knight's Inn or Red Carpet. Not a high-end hotel," said Russo, "and it was a couple blocks from the restaurant."

Nodding as he took this all in, Boyett said, "The last file I have says 'Biloxi.' " Tell us about that one."

"Well, that was the next year, if I remember right. I managed to get off work for a few days plus the weekend. I couldn't find a reasonable price on any hotels in New Orleans or even Mobile, so I ended up finding a real good deal in Biloxi instead. You know they have a bunch of casinos in Biloxi, and they're always offering deals on rooms. I got a room at one of the casinos for, like, $60 a night, I guess because it wasn't the beach season yet."

"Do you remember which casino you stayed at?"

"I don't recall the name, but it wasn't a brand name like MGM or Harrah's or any of those. It wasn't right on the beach. It was back on a bay behind the main beach area," explained Russo.

"What happened in Biloxi?" asked Boyett.

"Well, I checked into my hotel, and it was a bunch of old people apparently there for the buffet. So, I ended up driving over to the beach area and parking at the Harrah's casino. I went into Harrah's and sat down at the blackjack table and started playing. I played about an hour and wasn't doing very well, so I got up and went to the roulette table. I'd never really played roulette, although I understood the concept. There was this girl there and she had a pile of chips, but was only playing sporadically. A chip or two here and there, like she was waiting on certain numbers. I sat down and we started talking. She explained that she played the outside bets like odd/even and red/black, but only after they'd been three in a row of something, then she played the opposite figuring it would come up. If she lost, she'd double down and if she lost again, she'd quadruple down. I followed her lead and we won, not a lot, but probably fifty to a hundred dollars an hour, while they were feeding us free drinks. During the game, she asked if I was visiting, and I told her I was.

"We played a couple hours, and I was up by about maybe $175, and she asked me if I was hungry. I was, so we cashed out and went to eat. At the buffet she told me she was a local and she began asking about my life, whether I was married, etc. When she heard I wasn't married, she remarked that there were three things a man needed. She said they were food, sex, and sleep. She said she knew I was getting plenty of food, but was I getting enough of the other two? I laughed and said I bet she could help me with at least one of them. She just smiled and said we should go to her place. She lived across the bridge from the Harrah's casino. I followed her to her house, where she led me to the bedroom, and I saw that she was somewhat of a sex freak. She had restraints on her bed posts, a mirror on her ceiling, and some kind of stock in the corner to restrain people. She went into the bathroom for a minute and came out completely naked. She actually wanted me to use restraints on her, which I did. I tried not to make them too tight, but she insisted they needed to be tighter, like tight enough to cut off circulation to her hands. She wanted to be made to feel pain. I was having sex with her, and she was telling me to choke her. I did, and she really got into it. I'm not sure what happened, I really didn't mean to kill her. I liked her, but I was doing what she said and next thing you know, she wasn't breathing."

"So, this one was accidental?" asked Massarelli, his voice rising slightly in surprise.

"I guess you could call it that. It's the one time the demon didn't tell me to kill," said Russo. It was the first time he'd sounded at all remorseful.

"Why didn't you just call the police or 911?" asked Massarelli.

"Do you think the police would have accepted that? Here she is restrained, choked by a guy from Ohio who doesn't even know her name?" countered Russo.

"Yeah, probably not," said Massarelli.

"So, what did you do?" asked Boyett.

Well, I didn't want to leave her there, because if the cops found the body, they might find my fingerprints. So, I undid the restraints from the bed, grabbed the blindfold, and carried her body out to my van. It was dark and I was pulled up on the side of her house. I put her body in the back of the van and drove away. When I was safely away, I got in the back of the van and took the restraints off her hands. I was driving back toward the casino and right before the bridge, I veered off the road that went back along a road that ran along the bay. It was close to midnight, so I pulled over and pulled her body out, and drug it into some weeds. I drove back to my hotel and left the next morning. The items in the envelope are the restraints and blindfold and the chip is one that was in my pocket that I must've forgot to cash in. I left early the next morning and drove all day, arriving about midnight so I could be at work on Thursday."

"So, that appears to explain everything in the envelopes we found at your house. Is there anything else you haven't told us? Did we cover everything you've done?" asked Boyett.

"How deep do you want to go?" asked Russo.

"What does that mean?" asked Massarelli.

"Well, if you're looking for every crime I ever committed, we could be here for weeks."

"Everything? Like what?" asked Massarelli.

"Well, if we start when I was in high school, me and some friends broke into the school and stole some stuff," said Russo. "Then there was the time I was driving drunk and hit another car and left the scene."

"No, not bullshit stuff like that. Let's stick to things like maybe robberies, rapes, and murders."

"Well, there was one more. But I was only involved in the sex part. I didn't kill the girl or anything," said Russo, actually pleading innocent after everything he'd admitted to.

"So, tell us about it," said Massarelli.

"Well, back in the late 1990s, I don't recall the exact year, my cousin in Pennsylvania was getting married. It was my mother's brother's daughter. So, being the big Italian family, my mother insisted we go. We drove, like, six hours to Philadelphia. Actually, it's an area just south of Philly. So, we went to the wedding, which was in a small town where my mother's family was from, a place called Marcus Hook. The wedding was in a Catholic church that was right next to an oil refinery. It was kind of strange, with this church sitting on a corner and an oil refinery with big, tall smokestacks less than a hundred yards away. After the wedding, the reception was at a fire hall a few miles away. I'm there, my mother's with her relatives, most of whom I don't even know. I end up with some distant cousins and other people my age. We start drinking. There were all these girls, mostly Italian girls. One of my cousins started getting one of the bridesmaids drunk. Next thing I know, one of the guys said we were going to this guy named Bruno's house and do a train on this girl. I didn't know Bruno. I got into the car with some of the cousins and we drove maybe a mile to Bruno's place.

"When I got to the house, there a couple guys there taking turns screwing this girl. She was almost out cold from drinking, but they were having their way with her. I joined in. So, we're there about an hour still drinking and she's laying on the bed, with her clothes half torn off. She starts coming to, she realizes what's happened and she's still pretty drunk, but she starts shouting about what we did to her, she was going to tell her father. The guys I'm with told Bruno this was his problem, that he needed to solve it. We left. As we were getting in the car, I heard a bang. It could've been a gunshot, I dunno. We went back to the reception. Later, one my cousins, Billy, told me Bruno had taken care of the problem. I presumed that meant he'd killed her. I didn't ask any more questions about it and never heard anything," said Russo.

"What was your cousin's name, the one who got married?" asked Massarelli.

"Lucy Genovese, that's my mother's maiden name," said Russo. "I haven't even spoken to any of those people since my mom died, except for her brother and a few cousins who came to her funeral."

"Where did you stay when you went to the wedding?"

"I don't recall the name of the hotel, but it was down the interstate in Delaware, just across the state line. It was pretty big, maybe eight or nine stories high. My mom made the arrangements."

And you don't really know what happened to the girl or even what her name was?" asked Massarelli.

"No, sir, I told you what I know, but I'm pretty sure she was a bridesmaid," said Russo.

It was now getting close to 4:00 p.m. Massarelli told Russo to eat whatever leftover chicken was still in the box, as it was sure to be better than the meal they had at the jail that evening. He asked Boyett to step outside.

"So, do you think we got everything we need?" he asked when they were out of the room.

"Jim, easily enough to convict him in Alabama. Now the question is, who's going to run down all these other leads?" Boyett asked his own question.

"Well, when I left his house, the news crews were already showing up. When we get back there, I'm fairly certain there will be more news reporters begging for some sort of statement," said Massarelli. "I'm going to call Bob Dunlap and let him know what we have. I'm thinking the best way we can handle this is to take Russo to a hearing on Monday. If he'll waive and agree to go back to Alabama, you get him first. That will give us time to do our forensics on the bodies and put together our case. We can then file and get him back for trial here when you're done with him. Meanwhile, we'll make his confession available along with the evidence and send it out to the other jurisdictions, and they can get in line to take a shot at him."

"What if he won't waive back to Alabama?"

"Oh, I think he'll waive; you and he are buds," Massarelli said, laughing. "If he doesn't waive, it'll probably take a month to get Russo through the system and I doubt we'll have all our forensics together before then. I think you're going to get him first. Now, you go back in and explain to him that we're going to take him back to the jail and we probably won't see him until Monday at the courthouse. I'm going to make the call to Dunlap."

With that, Massarelli went to his office to call Dunlap while Boyett returned to the interview room, where Russo was scarfing down the last pieces of chicken and apple pie.

"So, what happens now?" he asked Boyett around his mouthful of pie.

"Well, when you're done eating, we'll take you back to the jail. Tomorrow, you'll spend the day in jail and Massarelli and I will be busy going over your statement and also meeting with the attorney general's office people, getting our paperwork ready for a hearing with you on Monday," said Boyett.

Russo swallowed and asked, "What's the hearing about?"

"Well, I'm not from Ohio, but if this is like anywhere else, the government will appear before a judge, and you will be there too. The government will present the judge a copy of the indictment for you in Alabama and ask the judge to send you back to Alabama," said Boyett.

"Well, I already admitted I did it," said Russo.

"Well, this judge isn't determining if you did it, just that the paperwork is correct," explained Boyett. "At the hearing, you'll probably have an appointed attorney. You should consult with him or her and if you want to go back to Alabama, you can waive the hearing and the judge will order you returned to Alabama."

"Will you be taking me back?"

"I'm not sure. If they order you back, and if it's possible, I'll personally take you back," said Boyett.

At that point, Gomez entered the room and told Russo it was time to get moving. He handcuffed and shackled Russo and Boyett accompanied them through the BCI office to Gomez's car, where he was loaded into the back seat for transport back to the Mahoning County Jail. After Gomez departed, Boyett walked to his car, threw his briefcase into the trunk, and took a deep breath. Even with all his experience in homicide, Russo's confession weighed on him.

On the way back to Russo's house, Boyett called J.T. Palmer.

"J.T., I just got done with an all-day interview. The scumbag went for twelve murders. Most were down our way: Gulf Shores, Pensacola, Biloxi, and Louisiana. He may have been involved in a rape and a thirteenth murder in Pennsylvania."

"Thirteen? That's impressive. So, when do you think you'll be back with him?" asked Palmer.

"We'll have a hearing on Monday. If he waives extradition, Massarelli thinks we can have him right away. Can you check with the sheriff's office and see how they want to handle the transport? I can probably bring him back myself."

"I'll call the sheriff himself and tell him what we have. See what he thinks. So, are you done for the day?"

"No, I'm heading back to his house. BCI is digging up his basement where they found two bodies," replied Boyett, "I think it's going to be a long night."

"Hang in there, Three B. Sounds like a career-making case," said Palmer. "I'll let you know what I hear from the sheriff."

"Thanks, J.T. I'll let you know if anything else happens," said Boyett, and he ended the call.

As Boyett pulled onto Russo's street, he was met with the sight of several news vans and as well as the crime scene van and several police vehicles. As he parked his rental car and entered the house, he did not attract much attention from the media. Once inside, he went down into the basement where the crime scene was in full swing. The remains were being excavated from the hole on the basement floor. Crime scene technicians were busy photographing the bones and putting them in body bags.

Boyett saw Massarelli and walked over. "Well, any more news at this location?" he asked.

"Some. I spoke with Dunlap; the media has been calling him too. He basically stopped answering his phone. My boss, the director, also has gotten calls," said Massarelli. "So, after consulting with Dunlap, and with you here, I'm going to hold a very short press conference. I'm going to tell the media that Franco Russo, the resident here, was arrested after being indicted in Mobile, Alabama for a 2006 murder. That as part of that investigation, we executed a search warrant and that we're in the house gathering evidence. I'll also tell them we anticipate a hearing at the courthouse on Monday and that there will be a further press conference on Monday."

"I understand," said Boyett, "but I'm not saying anything. I'm no good at speaking to the media."

"That's fine. Now, I'm just wondering whether we should include Pappas in the press conference."

"Why would we want to include him?" Boyett barely refrained from scoffing at the thought.

"Well, the way I see it, if he'd done his job back in 2006, there might be two girls still alive in Steelton. So, I think we should invite him, let him take some of the credit in the press and then when it gets out exactly what he did, maybe he'll be forced to retire. At least he won't get promoted again," said Massarelli.

"Jim, this is your turf, I'm just here for the ride along."

"I'll call Steelton P.D. and see if I can get him over here."

As Massarelli went off to make the call, Boyett continued to watch the excavation of the bodies, which were now just bones and some tattered and decaying clothing, presumably from Janet Crowe, who was murdered while she slept.

Massarelli returned and told Boyett, "Steelton P.D. says Pappas will be here in about ten minutes. I'll send Baker out to alert the press that I'm going to make a statement. When Pappas gets here, we're going to tell him that we found evidence of Russo's participation in other murders. We're not going to mention the bodies or the Steelton girls. We're going to just talk about Mobile to the press now and tell them we'll have more forthcoming on Monday. I'm going to lay a trap that hopefully will come back to haunt his incompetent ass."

Baker left the house and told the reporters that Massarelli would be making a brief comment about the activity, if they wanted to set up their cameras and lights.

Within minutes, Captain Pappas arrived. As he approached, Massarelli and Boyett exited the house and caught him. They pulled him aside.

Massarelli started the conversation. "Captain, this looks to be a bit bigger than we even thought. Russo was apparently involved in numerous murders. We're working to gather as much evidence as we can. He has also admitted to murders in Alabama, Florida, Louisiana, and even Texas. I'm going to make a short statement to get the press out of here. Hopefully, we'll be done in a couple hours and then when we get all the details together, we'll let you know more."

"That's fine. So, he went to all those places and killed people, huh?" asked Pappas.

"Yeah, that's where the evidence is pointing," said Massarelli.

"Kind of hard to believe, and we never even heard of him. You'd have thought someone would've called if he was a suspect," said Pappas.

"Well, let's get these media people out of here," said Massarelli, and he led Boyett and Pappas toward the microphones.

Massarelli approached the microphones with Boyett and Pappas alongside. "My name is James Massarelli, and I am the special agent in charge of the Ohio Bureau of Investigation for northern Ohio. This is Detective William Boyett from the Mobile Police Department, in Mobile, Alabama and Captain Jonas Pappas of the Steelton Police Department. Back in 2006, Detective Boyett became the lead investigator on the murder of a young woman named July Marcial. Although the investigation took twelve years to come to fruition, the result was the indictment of Franco Russo, the owner and resident of this house, for first-degree murder. The crime scene team has been here since yesterday We have found evidence that Russo was also involved in several other murders in the last fifteen years. We have been working to ensure that we undercover as much evidence as possible to help gather evidence in the Mobile murder and any other murders Russo may have been involved in.

We expect Russo to appear in Mahoning County Court on Monday to answer the indictment from Alabama. We anticipate holding another press briefing after that hearing and we may have some additional information at that time. Thank you."

As Massarelli turned away from the cameras, several reporters began shouting questions.

"Did he commit any murders in Ohio?"

"How many murders do you think he was involved in?"

"Will he be charged in Ohio?" and so on.

Massarelli ignored them and walked away with Boyett and Pappas following.

Away from the microphone, Pappas asked, "Do you think he committed any murders in Ohio?"

Massarelli looked at him and said, "I'm sure he did, but at this point we haven't got enough evidence to charge him. I'll keep your department informed on what we come up with."

As Pappas left, Boyett asked, "So, how are you going to leak the fact that Pappas is a do-nothing?"

"That's easy! I'm going to get your reports entered into evidence in the hearing. They'll become public record and the press will find them. Then, when it comes out that the two Steelton girls were murdered, the press will go to Steelton searching for answers. Pappas won't weather this."

"That's good for Steelton, I've seen my share of do-nothing cops," said Boyett, thinking of Billy Zindell.

"Unfortunately, the replacement will most likely be a clone of Pappas," said Massarelli. "Places like Steelton often hire good people, but they rarely stay. They usually find a better department and leave. What stays are the drones that no one else wants."

After the press conference, Massarelli suggested to Boyett that they clear the scene, leave it up to the crime scene team to finish their work, and go get a good dinner.

It was now almost 8:00 p.m. and the Popeyes fried chicken was wearing off.

Massarelli took Boyett to the Springfield Grill located between Steelton and Boyett's hotel. As they ate, he told Boyett that they needed to meet at the BCI office in Youngstown about 7:00 a.m. on Monday and that he was going to assign an analyst to go over the interview tape and try to confirm more facts about the incidents that Russo had confessed to. Additionally, he said they wouldn't know the time of the hearing until Monday morning, but that it could be any time that day. He told Boyett that if he had extra time on Sunday, he might want to visit Mill Creek Park, which was just a few miles from Boyett's hotel, and gave Boyett directions.

As they ended dinner, Massarelli told Boyett to call if he needed anything. By 9:30 p.m., both men were in their cars and making phone calls to their respective bosses and homes.

On Sunday, Boyett sat down with his file to organize his reports, pictures, and copies of the indictment. He also listened to the digital recording of Russo's confession about the July Marcial murder, making notes, in case questions were posed during the hearing the next day. By early afternoon, he was free and decided to follow Massarelli's advice and find the Mill Creek Park. After a couple-mile drive, he saw a sign directing him into a parking area off Route 224, which was the main street from the hotel in Boardman. He got out of his car and decided to take a walk, having spent the last three days traveling and sitting as the case developed.

He began his walk along paths that ran north. He expected a park like Mobile's Municipal Park, which encompassed an area that might total one square mile. Instead, as he walked, the park just seemed to get bigger and bigger. During the walk, which must have been between three and four miles in one direction, he observed everything from an old mill to a lake with canoes and kayaks to a golf course. He stopped several people who were also walking to ask for directions, as the paths and roads seemed to go in many directions. The more Boyett walked through the park, the more he thought how it was so much better than any park he'd ever visited and what a gem of a place it was in the otherwise dreary Youngstown area.

He finished his walk and estimated that he must have walked between six and seven miles. The sun was starting to go down behind the trees and he was getting hungry. He found his car in the parking lot and headed back toward the Holiday Inn. Dinner was back at Aladdin's where he'd eaten with Gomez on his first trip to Youngstown. The evening ended with packing his bag in case he could fly out the next day, a phone call to check in at home, and watching some TV.

CHAPTER 12 – THE
OHIO HEARING

Boyett grabbed an early breakfast in the hotel restaurant. He checked out and headed to the BCI office at 6:45 a.m. As usual, Massarelli was already at the office when Boyett arrived. Within a few minutes, Bob Dunlap arrived. Dunlap told Massarelli and Boyett that he'd emailed Judge Vicki Newman over the weekend and informed her of the arrest. He'd requested that Judge Newman set an arraignment for that morning and have an attorney available to be appointed, should Russo qualify for a court-appointed attorney. Dunlap said he'd also contacted the sheriff's office and arranged for Russo to be transported to the courthouse lock-up in anticipation of the hearing.

At that point, Dunlap sat down and wanted to hear all about the evidence found at the crime scene, as well as the confession.

Massarelli related everything about the search and the evidence that had been found. He then turned the conversation over to Boyett, who talked about his initial interview with Russo at Russo's house. He explained that Russo had told him about the murders of July Marcial as well as the two girls in Steelton.

Massarelli jumped back in and explained the search the next day and the recovery of skeletal remains believed to be Tina Watson and Janet Crowe. Boyett then stepped back in and related the interview on Saturday during which Russo admitted to a dozen murders overall.

Dunlap looked at both Massarelli and Boyett for a second and said, "Well, the evidence is overwhelming for a governors' warrant hearing. Today, at the arraignment, we'll see who represents him. I'll try to convince whoever that is, that the evidence is overwhelming and maybe he'll waive and voluntarily return to Alabama. Jim, what are your intentions about filing charges here?"

"Well, we're going to be months with forensics and interviews before we have an air-tight case. I think Alabama gets him first. We get him second and all the other jurisdictions can line up to get him after that," said Massarelli.

"OK." Dunlap gave a satisfied nod. "Let's wait on a call from Judge Newman and a time for our arraignment."

The call from Judge Newman's office came at about 8:45 a.m. She wanted to set the arraignment for 11:00 a.m. and inquired whether Russo had an attorney. Bob Dunlap told the judge that to his knowledge, Russo was not represented. Judge Newman said they would hold the arraignment and if Russo was not represented, she would ensure that counsel was appointed before the governors' warrant hearing was held.

At 10:45 a.m., Dunlap, Massarelli, and Boyett arrived at the courthouse and proceeded to Judge Newman's courtroom. Ten minutes later, Russo was escorted in by the sheriff's deputies. He smiled and tilted his head at Boyett and Massarelli.

Massarelli walked over and asked him if he'd been informed of what the proceedings were about.

Russo responded that Boyett had told him about them.

"Have you contacted an attorney to represent you?"

Russo responded, "Why do I need an attorney? I plan on going back to Alabama with Detective Boyett."

"Well, when the judge takes the bench, she'll explain it to you." As if on cue, the bailiff stood up and shouted, "Hear ye, hear ye, hear ye, the Common Pleas Court of Mahoning County is now in session, the Honorable Victoria Newman presiding." As he uttered those words, Judge Newman appeared from a door behind the bench and stood, before being seated. The bailiff then called the case, "State of Ohio versus Franco Russo," at which time Franco Russo was escorted from the prisoner area to the defense table. Bob Dunlap and everyone in the courtroom, who were already standing, sat down at the prosecutor's table.

Judge Newman began the proceedings. "Mr. Dunlap, I have certified copies of the Alabama indictment and the appropriate paperwork. Is the state ready to proceed?"

"Yes, Your Honor," replied Dunbar.

"Mr. Russo, do you have counsel?"

"No, ma'am," said Russo.

"No counsel. All right. Are you aware of why you are in court today?" asked Judge Newman.

"Yes, ma'am," replied Russo, as casually as if she'd asked if he'd eaten breakfast.

"You realize that you have been charged with murder in Alabama? This is a very, very serious charge," said Judge Newman.

"Yes, ma'am. I understand that you'll decide whether I go back to Alabama."

"Yes, I will, but not at this hearing. The hearing today is solely to inform you of the charges and allow you to decide if you wish to have a hearing to decide whether you will need to go to Alabama and face those charges," explained the judge.

"Judge, I'm aware of the charges in Alabama. I want to go to Alabama," said Russo.

"Mr. Russo, do you have a family attorney or some attorney you can call?" asked Judge Newman.

"Your Honor, I don't think I need an attorney to make this decision. I know what I want to do."

"Mr. Russo, for the record, I want to make sure you understand that you are being charged with first-degree murder based on an indictment in Mobile, Alabama. The State of Ohio has an obligation to present evidence and testimony to sustain a prima facia case on those charges and to provide a prima facia case that you are in fact the Franco Russo named in the indictment. Do you understand what I'm saying?" asked Judge Newman.

"Yes, Your Honor. I still want to return to Alabama with Detective Boyett," insisted Russo.

"All right. Let the record reflect that Mr. Russo is aware of the charges against him in Alabama. At this time, I am going to continue this hearing until 2:00 p.m. and have counsel appointed for Mr. Russo in order for him to consider legal advice," said Judge Newman.

As the hearing ended, Massarelli walked over to the Mahoning County deputy. "What are you going to feed him for lunch?" he asked.

"We have a bagged lunch from the jail. Why?" asked the deputy.

"What's in a bagged lunch from the jail?"

"Probably a baloney sandwich."

"I'm going to get him something decent. I'll bring it to the lock-up," said Massarelli.

"Whatever," replied the deputy with a disinterested shrug.

As Massarelli walked back to the prosecution table, he said to Boyett, "Come on, I've got to get Russo something to eat." He looked at Dunlap and said, "We'll meet you back here about 1:45."

"OK," said Dunlap. "See you then."

As they exited the courtroom, Massarelli asked Boyett, "Whatcha feel like eating?"

"Your town. Your call," said Boyett.

"I'm sure you like Southern BBQ," Massarelli guessed.

"Southern Ohio BBQ?" asked Boyett, laughing.

"We have Southern BBQ here. Just that it's a bit limited. Come on."

They exited the courthouse, walked to the BCI office, and got into Massarelli's Mercedes. They left the downtown area and headed up the hill toward Youngstown State University. A few blocks away from downtown was Charlie Staples BBQ.

Massarelli led Boyett inside. "This is about the best we've got. Hopefully, you'll like it."

When Massarelli and Boyett ordered, Massarelli also ordered a pulled pork plate to go.

"You're treating him pretty good, aren't you?" observed Boyett.

"You get more flies with honey than you do with vinegar," replied Massarelli. "I think he's going to do the right thing if he thinks we like him. This is well worth the cost." After a moment, he asked, "Have you talked to your captain about getting him back to Mobile?"

"Yeah, he was going to talk to the sheriff's office. Maybe I should call him and see what the sheriff said," said Boyett He pulled out his phone and called J.T. Palmer.

Palmer answered the phone knowing the call was from Boyett from caller ID. "Hey Three B, I just got off the phone with the sheriff. Does it look like Russo's going to waive?"

"What did the sheriff say?" asked Boyett.

"He said if you can get him down here by air, car, or whatever, his office will foot the bill. He doesn't really want to send people up there as he's shorthanded right now. But whatever we can do, he'll pick up the tab," said Palmer.

"Perfect. At the hearing this morning, he said he wanted to come back with me. The judge put the hearing off until this afternoon so she could appoint a lawyer. We're going back to the courthouse in a few," said Boyett. "I'll call and let you know what happens."

"OK. Give me a plan and I'll make sure the sheriff has it and pays for it," said Palmer.

"Thanks, J.T. I'll call you in a couple hours."

As Boyett ended the call, their orders were served. He was pretty impressed with the BBQ, not at all what he expected, and he immediately dug in.

"So, what's your captain saying?" Massarelli asked as they ate.

"He said the sheriff's office is shorthanded, but the sheriff will pick up the tab for whatever we want to do, drive him, fly him, whatever. Why? Do you want to scam a trip to Alabama?"

"Around here, we usually don't get too much cooperation from the sheriff's offices, especially if involves spending their money. As to the trip, I wouldn't mind, especially if we can get some more information and or publicity. In our state, good publicity usually helps with budgets," Massarelli admitted.

"Well, our sheriff is the former chief of police, and he has a pretty good relationship with the city," said Boyett.

"Let's see how the hearing goes and figure out what we can do," said Massarelli.

As they finished lunch, Massarelli picked up the "to go" order and they headed back to the courthouse. He parked the Mercedes in the "Police Only" spot and threw a placard on the dash, so it could be seen through the windshield. They entered the courthouse and proceeded to the sheriff's lock-up. There, Massarelli asked to be see Russo.

Upon being taken back to the holding cell, Massarelli handed the BBQ plate over to Russo.

Russo thanked him.

Massarelli just said, "See you back in court in a few," and left.

When Massarelli exited the lock-up, he and Boyett departed the courthouse again and drove the few blocks back to the BCI office. They had just over an hour to go before the hearing. Massarelli went into an office and began making phone calls. Boyett decided to do the same and called home to report in.

As the clock rolled past 1:30 p.m., Massarelli came to Boyett and said that if Russo waived, he would be available to accompany Boyett back to Mobile. He also mentioned that there was a press conference set for the courthouse steps at 3:00 p.m.

They left the BCI office at about 1:40 and walked back the few blocks to the courthouse. When they arrived, Massarelli was approached by a local defense lawyer named Tom Chance.

Chance had defended several defendants of Massarelli's over the years.

"Jimmy, I got a call from Judge Newman appointing me to handle a hearing for Franco Russo," Chance began. "I see your name prominently displayed all over the paperwork. I'm going in to talk to Russo now. I'm kind of leaning toward asking for the governors' hearing so I can force this Mobile detective to come up and present a case."

"Well, Tom, you don't really need to ask for the governors' hearing. This is Detective Boyett." He gestured toward Boyett, and the two men shook hands. "He can probably answer all your questions in court today—unless you just want to delay the inevitable by a few days," replied Massarelli.

"Oh, great. Let me go talk to Russo. I'll see you in the courtroom," said Chance.

As Chance headed toward the sheriff's lock-up, Massarelli and Boyett proceeded to the courtroom, where Dunlap was waiting.

"Looks like the press got a tip about the hearing," said Dunlap.

"Yeah, I put the word out about the hearing and then called a press conference for 3:00 p.m. I think we need to unload on the Steelton P.D. today," said Massarelli.

"How you going to do that?" asked Dunlap.

"When we filed all our reports with the court, they detailed the entire investigation, including the lack of cooperation from Steelton P.D., specifically Detective Pappas, back in 2006. It also details the missing girls in from Steelton in 2009. I'm sure at least one reporter will pick up on the fact that if Pappas had done his job, those girls might not be dead," explained Massarelli.

"We'll see how it goes. Good luck," said Dunlap.

As they entered the courtroom, numerous reporters approached Massarelli and began asking questions concerning the case. They all had papers in their hands, obviously copies of reports filed with the court.

Massarelli stopped them. "I'm not answering any questions until the press conference after the hearing. Save them for outside, please."

Grumbling, the reporters backed off.

As Dunlap, Massarelli, and Boyett were talking at the prosecution table, Attorney Tom Chance entered the room and walked up to them.

"Gentlemen, I spoke to Russo. He says he wants to waive the hearing, but to err on the side of justice, I'm going to ask the judge for permission to question Detective Boyett so that the facts are on the record, and I can't be accused of not putting up some defense."

"Did he tell you about the confession, Tom?" asked Dunlap.

"Yeah. He said he'd confessed," said Chance.

"OK, I just don't want you to be blindsided when it comes out."

"Thanks."

As this conversation was ending, the deputies brought Russo out wearing handcuffs and shackles. The deputies placed Russo at the defense table and unhandcuffed him, but left his leg shackles in place.

Russo looked over to Massarelli and mouthed, "Thanks for lunch," and smiled.

Judge Vicki Newman appeared from behind the bench and everyone in the courtroom rose. The bailiff repeated his spiel.

Judge Newman spoke. "Gentlemen, we're back in session. Is everyone ready to proceed?"

"Yes, Your Honor," said Dunlap.

"Yes, Your Honor," said Chance.

"All right. Before your appointment, Mr. Chance, the defendant stated he wished to waive the governors' hearing and return to Alabama to face charges," said Judge Newman. "Have you had time to consult with Mr. Russo?"

'Yes, Your Honor, he has indicated the same thing to me," replied Attorney Chance. "However, out of an abundance of caution, I would request we take testimony and enter it on the record."

"So, you want to proceed with a governors' hearing now? asked Judge Newman.

"Your Honor, I would just like to have some facts and testimony on the record, and then presuming they are sufficient, we will waive," said Chance.

"Very well," said Judge Newman. "Mr. Dunlap, call your first witness."

"Your Honor, we would call Detective William Boyett," said Dunlap.

Boyett rose, approached the witness stand, and was sworn in.

Dunlap started the questions. "Detective Boyett, are you the lead detective in the murder of July Marcial?"

"Yes," answered Boyett.

"Can you tell the court briefly about the investigation and what evidence there is linking the defendant, Franco Russo, to that murder?"

"Certainly," said Boyett. "On February 28, 2006, I was called to the scene of a body found in downtown Mobile.

At the time there was no identification, cell phone, or any other items that could be used to identify the body. The body was semi-nude and rolled into a piece of carpet. The autopsy revealed that Ms Marcial had been strangled. DNA was found both in her body as well as on the carpet remnant her body was rolled into. Telephone records retrieved after the murder showed that Ms. Marcial and Mr. Russo had communications and it appeared that Mr. Russo was the last person seen with Ms. Marcial alive. On Labor Day of this year, we obtained DNA samples from Mr. Russo that matched the DNA from the crime scene. Based on that, we obtained an indictment for Mr. Russo, charging him with murder. When we executed the arrest warrant last Friday, we also executed a search warrant on Mr. Russo's house. During that search, we found numerous items that belonged to Ms. Marcial including her driver's license, her cell phone, and a toe ring. Subsequently, Mr. Russo admitted to the murder."

After waiting a few seconds for effect, Dunlap said, "No further questions, Your Honor."

Tom Chance rose from the defense table. "Detective Boyett, do I understand it took you from February 2006 until this week to find and charge the defendant?"

"Well, sir, I wasn't assigned to the case the whole time. In the spring of 2006, I was promoted out of the detective division and the case was re-assigned. This last summer, I was assigned to a cold case squad and this investigation was one of the unsolved cases. I actually only worked on it about five to six months total in all those years," explained Boyett.

"OK, Detective, so let's speed up to the confession that my client supposedly gave you. Was it just the words, 'Yeah, I did it,' or was it more detailed?" asked Chance.

"Oh, it was very detailed. The interview lasted about ten to twelve hours total."

"Ten to twelve hours? What did you discuss for ten to twelve hours?"

"Sir, your client confessed to the Marcial murder and another eleven murders all over the country," replied Boyett.

Chance's eyes widened and his face actually paled with horror as several of the reporters in the courtroom gasped. He asked the judge for a minute and huddled with Russo, whispering in his ear, and vice-versa. The attorney then addressed the court. "Your Honor, we are done with this witness. We wish to waive any further hearings in this matter."

Judge Newman addressed the court. "In the matter of Ohio versus Franco Russo. It is the order of this court that Franco Russo be returned to Alabama. Good luck, Mr. Russo. Court is adjourned."

As the people in the courtroom began to disperse, Attorney Chance came over to the prosecution table. "I wasn't expecting that."

"Sorry, I thought you knew. But obviously not," said Dunlap.

Chance then addressed Boyett. "I don't know why, but Russo likes you. I tried to explain to him that you're the enemy, but he wouldn't listen."

Boyett replied, "I think he likes me because I'm probably the first guy who's ever really figured him out, and I'm making him take responsibility for his actions. But I also think he knows I'm honest and fair with him."

As Dunlap, Massarelli, and Boyett walked downstairs, they could see the TV cameras setting up on the courthouse steps.

Dunlap looked at the Massarelli and said, "I'm leaving this to you. How are you going to slam Steelton?"

"Well, I guarantee one of the questions is going to be about any possible murders he committed here. I'm going to tell them he confessed to two and we have recovered two bodies. I'm sure that someone is going to put together the fact that Pappas hindered the investigation, thus keeping this guy out on the street an extra ten years. But I'll let them ask. I'm just going to answer truthfully," replied Massarelli.

As they exited the building, Massarelli walked up to the cluster of microphones and started speaking. "We've just finished a hearing where Franco Russo of Steelton has waived his rights to hearings and voluntarily agreed to return to Alabama to face murder charges. This investigation shows the quality of cases that can be worked if law enforcement agencies work together. Other than that, I'll take questions."

Questions were shouted at Massarelli from the crowd.

"Were any of the murders committed in Mahoning County?" asked a TV reporter.

"Yes, during the search warrant, we found evidence that at least two murders were committed in Mahoning County in 2009. We have located the skeletal remains of two females. We are performing forensic exams in an effort to positively identify those remains," replied Massarelli.

"Did Russo confess to those murders?" shouted another reporter.

"Yes," replied Massarelli.

"Can you tell us, were these dozen murders committed in a certain time period?" asked another reporter.

"It appears that with the exception of the two Mahoning County victims, Russo killed approximately one victim a year, although there were a couple years where he did not commit a murder," said Massarelli.

"I have a question for Detective Boyett. Detective, what are your impressions of law enforcement in Ohio versus Alabama?" shouted a reporter in the back of the group.

Boyett took a deep breath and slowly let it out. He hated speaking in public. "Well, I usually don't do press conferences. But I'd like to say that working with Ohio BCI has been great. They're one of the most professional law enforcement organizations I've ever worked with. They went out of their way to assist in every way possible.

Without BCI, this case probably would have never come to fruition."

"How did you end up going to Ohio BCI as opposed to Steelton P.D.?" asked another reporter.

Massarelli stepped up to the microphones, saving Boyett from having to answer. "When the investigation was in its infancy, Detective Boyett did contact Steelton P.D. During that stage, Steelton was unable to assist Detective Boyett. It was then that Detective Boyett was referred to Ohio BCI through some federal law enforcement partners."

"So, BCI has been working on this since 2006?" asked yet another reporter.

"We opened a case to assist Mobile P.D. in 2006. Their case eventually went cold, so the case here was also closed. Last summer, when Detective Boyett was assigned to the cold case squad and reopened the case, he made contact with us again and the case was reopened here too," said Massarelli.

"It would seem that Steelton P.D. should've been more involved than they obviously were, considering that Russo was living there," said the same reporter.

"Was that a question? If it was statement, I would agree with you," said Massarelli.

With that, he told the reporters he would keep them apprised of any further activities in Ohio, but that they might want to contact affiliates in Mobile as that would be the next venue in this investigation.

As Boyett, Dunlap, and Massarelli walked back to the BCI office, Dunlap said, "You know you're going to hear about the Steelton remark."

"Yeah. I figure it'll take till about tomorrow morning. I'm not sure whether I'll get a call from the chief of Steelton, the mayor of Steelton, or someone above me in Columbus," said Massarelli.

"So, what are you going to do when the shit hits the fan?" asked Boyett.

"I'm going to make sure the shit sprays everywhere and I'm not in front of the fan." Massarelli chuckled. "Think about this: If someone calls from Steelton, I'm going to tell them to take the grievances to Captain Pappas. He's the issue here. If they put pressure on Columbus, which I doubt they have any stroke with, I'm going to tell Columbus if they think I'm the problem, just ask for my retirement papers. I'm eligible. But when I leave, I'll be holding another press conference and the shit will fly—and they will be in front of the fan too."

When the trio returned to the BCI office, there were numerous messages for Massarelli.

Boyett stepped into one of the conference rooms and called J.T. Palmer. "How'd it go?" asked Palmer.

"It went fine. Russo waived. Now, we've just got to figure out how to get him back," said Boyett.

"I could probably dispatch someone up there to meet with you and either fly him back or drive him back. What do you think?" asked Palmer.

"Well, Massarelli said he might even accompany us down, if the sheriff is paying."

"I don't think that will be a problem, if he wants to do that,

Let me get with him and see what it would entail. I'll try and get back to you in an hour or so," said Boyett. "Oh, J.T., you'd better alert the chief. The press was all over the courtroom and it came out about Russo confessing to the murder of twelve women. Massarelli held a press conference afterward, but they smell a story. So, expect phone calls."

"Thanks for the heads-up, Three B. I'll get that information to the chief right away. Call me later," said Palmer.

When Boyett re-entered Massarelli's office, he was fielding questions about the Russo case. Boyett waited till he was between phone calls. "Looks like that trip might be just the thing to get you out of Ohio for a couple days."

"Yeah, I think that sounds good. What did your sheriff say?" asked Massarelli.

"My captain said if you want to come on, he'll make it work."

"Book it, then. Just make sure I get at least two nights in Mobile," said Massarelli.

"I'll handle it," replied Boyett.

As Boyett called Palmer back with the request, Massarelli continued fielding phone calls from news outlets throughout the state. The word was spreading that Russo might be the biggest serial killer in Ohio history. It wasn't going to be long before that shit hit the fan, and Massarelli knew it. No matter how big the cases were or even how well they were investigated, when they hit the news, there was usually someone who questioned something about them.

Meanwhile, Boyett and Palmer talked again. Palmer told Boyett that he would handle everything for Massarelli, including getting him in one of the premier downtown hotels. He knew how to treat cops who went out of their way to help.

By the end of the day, Massarelli and Boyett were booked on a flight from Cleveland leaving at 10:15 a.m. for Mobile with a stop in Atlanta. Massarelli arranged for Gomez to pick up Russo at the Mahoning County Jail and get him to the Cleveland Airport. That would free up Boyett to return his rental car and meet Gomez and Massarelli at the airport. Massarelli would take care of all the airport notifications.

Everything was going great. Boyett cut out of the BCI office at about 5:15 p.m. to return to the hotel and check back in. As the evening news came on the local Youngstown TV stations, the Russo story was the lead. Most of them had parts of the news conference and all had pictures of Russo's mugshot from the Mahoning County Jail.

After four days in Ohio, Boyett was physically and mentally exhausted, but he was also pleased with how events had gone down.

Tuesday morning, he was up early, eating breakfast, checking out of the Holiday Inn, and heading to the Cleveland Airport while Gomez was at the Mahoning jail where he retrieved Russo. At the airport, Boyett checked in his rental car and called Massarelli.

Massarelli told Boyett to come to Bill Rankin's office, and that Gomez was almost at the airport with Russo. In Rankin's office, Massarelli finished up the paperwork needed for both Boyett and himself, as well as for Russo.

Rankin suggested they remain in his office until the flight was ready to board and then the TSA would shuttle them to the plane so they could board in advance of other passengers, which was a rule. Boyett had never escorted a prisoner via airplane, but Massarelli had, and he assured him it was no problem as long as you enjoyed sitting three people together in the very rear row of the airplane. Rankin also said that when the plane departed, he would make a phone call to the TSA director in Atlanta in order to have a shuttle available and to give Boyett and Massarelli time to use the bathroom.

At about 9:40 a.m., Gomez pulled into the parking lot and Rankin sent a shuttle to bring him and Russo to the office. Upon his arrival at Rankin's office, Gomez handed Russo over to Massarelli and Boyett.

Boyett stepped out in the hall and called J.T. Palmer. "We're at the Cleveland airport and everything is good. We should arrive at 2:30."

"Good. When you get in, I'll have a couple guys meet you and take Russo to the county jail. I need you and Massarelli to come downtown and meet with the chief and the D.A. The media has been calling since last night and all through this morning. The chief and the D.A. want to hold a press conference this afternoon. Call me when you're leaving Atlanta and I'll have it set up for about an hour after you arrive. That way, you can brief them on details so they sound like they know what's going on," said Palmer.

"Sure, J.T., I'll also let Massarelli know," said Boyett.

Back in the TSA office, Massarelli was fielding phone calls and text messages.

Boyett motioned him to the door. "It looks like everyone's phones are blowing up in Mobile too. We have a press conference scheduled as soon as we land and get to the police station," he said.

"Partner, this is going to be easy," said Massarelli. As those words were uttered, Rankins received a radio call. The Delta flight was at the gate. Russo, who was in his original street clothes, was led out and put on a shuttle along with Massarelli and Boyett.

At the gate, Massarelli presented paperwork to the gate attendant. Within a minute, Massarelli, Boyett, and Russo were hustled onto the airplane, where they were introduced to the captain. The captain asked if they'd transported prisoners on an aircraft before.

Massarelli replied, "Many times."

The captain just said, "Go do your thing."

They proceeded to the last row of the aircraft. At that point, Massarelli told Russo to use the bathroom as it wasn't going to happen again until they reached Atlanta. Boyett stood outside the bathroom while Russo went inside and shut the door. When Russo came out, Boyett placed him in the window seat of the last row and took the middle seat, followed by Massarelli. As passengers began boarding the plane, the trio looked like any other passengers. Guns and handcuffs were not visible.

The plane took off on time and the flight was uneventful. Massarelli and Boyett were quiet, lost in their respective thoughts about the coming hours and days. Russo actually dozed off for a while, probably because he once again had not slept well in jail. Upon landing, the trio let everyone else vacate the plane before standing and walking forward, with Boyett leading the three and Massarelli behind. Upon their entering the concourse, they found two TSA agents with a shuttle awaiting them. The shuttle transported them to the new gate, where the connecting plane had yet to land.

Boyett asked Russo if he was hungry.

Russo replied that he was.

Massarelli and the TSA agents stayed with the shuttle as Boyett went down the concourse and bought some Subway sandwiches and drinks. He figured this was going to be their only meal until after the press conference. Back at the gate, the three of them ate their lunches as the Delta flight pulled into the gate and passengers filed off. About fifteen minutes after the last passengers had departed, the ticket agent called them over for their pre-boarding.

As before, they were introduced to the captain, who welcomed them onboard. They again proceeded to the last row and Massarelli again told Russo to use the rest room while he could. The seating arrangement was the same.

Boyett texted Palmer after they were seated on the plane and were getting ready to depart Atlanta. The second leg of the flight was also uneventful, landing in Mobile on time. After all the passengers had departed, Boyett, Russo, and Massarelli exited the plane in single file. On the concourse, two Mobile County deputies were waiting for the trio. Boyett recognized both from some prior dealings. As they took possession of Russo, Boyett asked them to make sure he was treated well and, if possible, be isolated from other prisoners. One deputy said he would pass the word on to the warden, but that Boyett might want to make a call to ensure it happened.

As Boyett and Massarelli left the airport, Boyett called J.T. Palmer.

Palmer told him he needed to go to the district attorney's office, where the D.A. and chief would meet Massarelli and him. Palmer would meet them there.

Upon their arrival at Government Plaza, Boyett and Massarelli proceeded to the district attorney's office, where they were ushered into a conference room. Gloria Wood and Barry Mueller were there, busy scribbling notes along with Mueller's administrative assistant, who also served as his speech writer.

Boyett introduced Massarelli to Wood and Mueller and Mueller congratulated both for a job well done. J.T. Palmer arrived with Chief of Police Herman Boyd. He went over, slapped Boyett on the back, and shook Massarelli's hand. Chief Boyd was distant from everyone else in the room, and it was obvious that he was only there because they wanted him there.

Mueller asked about the confession and what information had been confirmed concerning the other victims and murders.

Boyett explained that Russo had confessed to the murders and that some physical evidence had been found at Russo's residence indicating the identification of his victims.

Massarelli interjected that his analysts had begun doing backgrounds on the various IDs found at Russo's residence and confirmed the bodies of many of those whose IDs were found. He cautioned that each of the incidents would have to be independently investigated by the police agency with authority in that particular jurisdiction.

Mueller piped in with, "So, is it safe to say that we'll be going for the death penalty? He sure—"

Boyett interrupted, "Sir, while I'm confident that a judge in one or more of the jurisdictions will probably sentence Russo to death, I'm not sure I would even mention it right now. Over the next few months, investigators from these jurisdictions are going to come to Mobile to question Russo. Right now, he's being 100 percent cooperative. He can continue to cooperate or, if you scare him, he can stop cooperating and it might make clearing those other cases a bit harder."

"So, what do we say when that question comes up?" asked Mueller.

"Maybe we can just dodge the question and say we haven't come to a determination of what penalty we might seek. This is still an ongoing investigation," said Palmer. "And I'd like to make another suggestion. I think we should also talk about the successes of the new cold case squad. So far, we've only got Three B assigned, and in less than two months, he's cleared the Gerard case, although the defendant is deceased, and he's cleared the Marcial case, and it looks like eleven other murders along with it."

"I like that angle," said Mueller, nodding. "So, who's going to speak for the P.D.?"

Chief Boyd looked up. It seemed he'd been listening after all. "J.T., you can handle it. I'll just stand in the background and smile."

With that, Mueller's administrative assistant began taking notes and talking to each person involved to ensure that the news conference would go like a well-produced commercial. As this was going on, Mueller told his assistant to contact the media outlets and set up the news conference for 5:00 p.m., so they could go "Live at 5" on the local news channels.

By 4:45 p.m., the D.A.'s conference room had been converted into a press briefing room with a podium, several chairs lined up behind it, and the seal of the district attorney's office placed on the wall behind the podium. News crews from the four local TV stations set up their cameras and the seats began filling with reporters from TV stations as well as several radio stations and newspapers. At 5:00 p.m., Mueller and the others were in a conference room down the hall from the room being utilized for the press conference. Mueller had the TV on in the conference room and told everyone they did not want to enter the press briefing until the main news stories had played out and the news anchors had had time to mention to the audience that they were going to be going to live at the D.A.'s office with reports on the breaking of a major case.

At about 5:07 p.m., after the lead stories had been played out on the local news and as the first set of commercials were being aired, Mueller led the group down the hall and had them sit in the chairs behind the podium. The room was filled with over a dozen reporters when Mueller went to the podium.

"I am Barry Mueller, the district attorney here in Mobile County. I'd like to introduce the folks behind me. From my right to left, this is Chief Boyd of the Mobile Police Department, Captain J.T. Palmer of the Mobile Police Department, Sergeant William Boyett of the Mobile Police Department, James Massarelli, Special Agent in Charge of the Ohio Bureau of Investigation, and Assistant District Attorney Gloria Wood. This afternoon, we want to report the results of a cooperative effort between the district attorney's office and the Mobile Police Department. Several months ago, the Mobile Police Department and the district attorney's office met to discuss the formation of a cold case squad to reinvestigate the many unsolved major crimes we have had over the years. While this cold case squad is just getting off the ground, it has already been more successful than ever imagined. In less than two months, this squad, which is not even fully operational yet, has solved two murders, including one that occurred in 2006.

"Some of you may remember the murder on Mardi Gras day in 2006, when the body of a young woman was found. That case was not solved at the time. The cold case squad picked it up and ran with it, going over the old records and narrowing possible suspects to one. His name is Franco Russo and he lived in Steelton, Ohio. With the help of the Ohio Bureau of Investigation, DNA from a suspect was retrieved and matched to the DNA found at the scene of the crime. Based on that, Russo was indicted for murder. During the arrest of Russo, a search of his residence uncovered numerous pieces of evidence confirming that Russo committed that murder. Subsequently, Russo confessed to the murder. Just as important, Russo also confessed to the murders of eleven other women in numerous states including Florida, Mississippi, Louisiana, and Ohio.

"Russo was brought back from Ohio this afternoon and has been booked in the Mobile County Jail. I'd like to take a minute to turn the microphone over to Captain J.T. Palmer to say a few words. Then we'll take questions."

Palmer began his spiel. "Good afternoon. I'd just like to add a bit to what the district attorney has said. After being promoted to captain and put in charge of investigations, I realized that there are certain people in every occupation who have special qualities, and in police work, it's the same. I also knew that there were too many unsolved major crimes, especially murders. With those two things in mind, I approached Chief Boyd and suggested we form a cold case squad, choosing investigators who are known to have the tenacity and doggedness to follow up cases that others have given up on. So far, only two cases have been opened and both have been solved. In one case, unfortunately, the suspect had committed suicide before being arrested. In the second case, Mr. Russo has confessed to eleven other murders. By effecting the arrest of Russo, we may have in fact saved the lives of others. At this time, I'd like to mention the investigator who deserves kudos on these cases is Sergeant William Boyett. I'd also like to extend thanks to Special Agent in Charge James Massarelli of the Ohio Bureau of Investigation. Without the assistance of the Ohio BCI, this case may have languished for many more years. With that, I'd like to turn the microphone back to D.A. Mueller."

Mueller went back up to the microphone and began taking questions. They ranged from "Why did Mobile get to prosecute first?" to "Are you seeking the death penalty?"

Mueller was totally in his element, enjoying the spotlight. The questions only lasted about fifteen minutes and the show was over. Although he was clearly trying to contain his smile, it was apparent to all that he was very satisfied with the outcome.

J.T. Palmer thought it had easily been productive enough to ensure some additional funding for the cold case squad from the Mobile City Council.

Massarelli was impressed with Mueller and figured he might have to become friends with him as he, Massarelli, was eligible to retire and he believed Mueller may have the need for a chief investigator sometime in the future.

Chief Boyd was glad the dog and pony show was over and just wanted to get out of there, so he could go watch his grandson's football practice.

Boyett knew he was going to be stuck for a few more hours, getting Massarelli back to the airport to get a rental car, getting him checked in to his hotel, and at least stopping to have a beer with him before heading home.

Gloria Wood just wondered who would be appointed to represent Russo, whether the cooperation would continue, or whether there would be a ton of motions filed to try to suppress evidence and the confession.

Only time would tell.

CHAPTER 13 – THE LEGAL PROCEEDINGS AND TRIAL

On Wednesday morning, October 3, 2018, the day after the press conference, Boyett and Massarelli attended an initial appearance for Russo in Mobile County Circuit Court.

Gloria Wood represented the district attorney's office and local defense attorney Jack Jacobs was appointed to represent Russo. Jacobs had a reputation in Mobile as being competent, but also as never letting an opportunity for free press go unused. He often took high profile cases on appointment, even if the money was not close to what he charged his paying clients. Jacobs saw these cases as opportunities to get free advertising by holding press conferences of his own. During the hearing, Jacobs told the court that Russo should be released on bail, since the charges were only an accusation, and because he had no history of flight or violence.

Judge William Wellborn, who presided, disagreed about Russo's propensity for violence, since the charge was murder. Judge Wellborn set bail at one million dollars cash, well beyond Russo's means. Also, during the hearing, Jacobs put it on record that Boyett or other members of law enforcement were not to speak to Russo without first clearing it through him. He intended to use every potential interview as a bargaining chip for a plea bargain or reduced sentence. Meanwhile, Russo looked completely lost and continually glanced over at Boyett and Massarelli.

As the hearing ended, Gloria Wood and Jacobs talked in private. Wood told Jacobs that it might be in Russo's best interest to continue to cooperate.

Jacobs replied, "Why? So you can give him a life sentence, only for him to be sent to some other state where they'll execute him?" With that attitude, it seemed it was going to be a long, drawn-out process for everyone.

Over the next months, Jacobs filed numerous motions in court, making outrageous allegations that Russo had been denied his rights to counsel, that he'd been coerced into giving the confession, that he'd been promised things in return for his confession, and that the obtaining of his DNA was illegal, as was the search of his house.

While all of this was ongoing, investigators from each of the jurisdictions were calling Boyett, requesting to speak to Russo, demanding copies of the interview tapes as well as his notes and reports. Boyett referred many of them to Massarelli, who had taken the Saturday interview and made copies via DVDs. Numerous investigators came to Mobile to speak with Boyett.

As the case wound through the court system, the motion hearings were denied, although some of them required several days of preparation and preparing for responses to the alleged allegations made by Jacobs. It seemed each hearing was attended by members of the press. Additionally, copies of warrants and indictments along with copies of detainers began arriving from the various jurisdictions where Russo had committed murder. By February 2019, indictments and detainers had been filed by Ohio, Florida, Louisiana, and Texas. Several jurisdictions were on the fence about filing charges and getting in line for a shot at Russo.

In February 2019, with all the motions disposed of, the judge entered an order setting the trial for February 28th. That was the thirteenth anniversary of the murder of July Marcial. Boyett spent weeks contacting the many witnesses and working with Gloria Wood to determine which witnesses would be used and to determine what documentary evidence would be introduced.

Witnesses ranged from the various police officers and forensic people who had been involved in the case to the various custodians of records from the hotels and telephone companies needed to introduce the business records that would confirm that Russo had been in Mobile and had had communication with Marcial.

Wood and Boyett decided to bring in John Hood, whom the prosecution wanted to use to talk about the person July Marcial had been, as well as to identify the toe ring and cell phone found at Russo's house.

Jack Jacobs continued his barrage of press conferences after each hearing, claiming that evidence would come out about the "corrupt" Mobile Police Department. Each boast was crazier than the last and offered no evidence or documentation for the allegations.

As the trial drew within a week, Barry Mueller decided to take part in the press barrage. On February 25, he called a press conference to announce that the district attorney's office was seeking the death penalty in the case. This obviously elevated the situation as the trial drew closer.

During the days immediately prior to the trial, Attorney Jacobs made several overtures to Gloria Wood about potential plea bargains. His initial offer was to plead to an involuntary manslaughter charge with no more than ten years in prison.

Gloria Wood thought, *Has this guy not listened to Russo's confession? Has he not reviewed the evidence?*

Jacobs' next offer was to plea to voluntary manslaughter with the same sentence. Again, Gloria Wood just smirked. As the trial was set for the next day, Jacobs again came with another offer. This time, he offered to plea to a murder charge, provided that Russo wouldn't be sentenced to more than fifteen years. Again, Wood told Jacob that his antics had driven the price of a plea up. The only plea offer now on the table was a blind plea to murder, first degree, and that the State could still seek the death penalty, but would allow the defense to utilize any government witnesses to try to mitigate the sentence.

***

On February 28, 2019, both sides assembled in the courtroom of Judge William Wellborn, where the proceedings got under way with jury selection. As the process started, Boyett looked at Russo numerous times. He appeared to have lost some weight and any personality seemed to have deteriorated. Months of sitting in the Mobile County Jail without visitors and facing a stark future could easily play on someone. As Boyett glanced at Russo, Russo stared straight ahead. By noon, the jury had been chosen and sworn in and Judge Wellborn recessed for lunch.

Boyett, who was sitting inside the courtroom at the prosecution table, went to lunch with Wood, Massarelli, and John Hood. During lunch, Hood was concerned about whether Russo might actually be found not guilty. Massarelli and Wood tried to calm him down and explain that it appeared to be a slam dunk, and that he just needed to make July into a person the jurors could sympathize with. His other job was to go into detail about the toe ring and how she wouldn't take it off.

Massarelli kept saying that Russo wouldn't or couldn't take the stand.

Wood said she doubted that Jacobs would put Russo on the stand, but that anything was possible. That what was most important was for the case to be presented in an organized and methodical way.

Boyett mostly remained quiet during these discussions, listening but not actively participating.

As lunch was ending, Massarelli received a phone call. After a short conversation, he ended the call, looked at

Boyett, and said, "Well, what do you know? Captain Jonas Pappas has retired."

"Really?" asked Boyett.

"Yeah, my source tells me he's been under fire for weeks as this trial got closer and our indictment was handed down. All the information is now in the open. The Youngstown media has been all over it. Apparently, he was told to retire or there was going to be an investigation, so he retired."

When the trial reconvened after lunch, District Attorney Barry Mueller was at the prosecution table. He was there to make the opening statement for the prosecution. This was what he was good at. Wood, of course, had to defer to the boss.

Mueller got up and addressed the jury. "Ladies and gentlemen of the jury. Today is February 28. On this date in 2006, it was Mardi Gras day. The city was filled with revelers, parades, and people having a good time. One young woman who came to Mobile to celebrate Mardi Gras was July Marcial, a graduate student from the University of Southern Mississippi. Ms. Marcial came to have fun, just like tens of thousands of people do every Mardi Gras. That day, it was sunny, and the temperature reached the low seventies. Like many revelers, July Marcial was watching the parades. Sometime during her stay in Mobile, she met the defendant, Franco Russo.

"Sometime in the afternoon on Mardi Gras day, the two of them met and walked from her hotel over toward the parade route. That was the last time anyone saw July Marcial alive. After the parades were over, the Mobile police would receive a call from Steve Brown, the owner of a parking lot. Mr. Brown had returned to his lot to clean it up after renting it to people during the day's festivities. Upon arrival at the lot, Mr. Brown saw a piece of carpet rolled up. He attempted to drag the carpet and found it contained a semi-nude female body. There was no identification or cell phone with or near the body. That body was later identified as July Marcial.

"Detective William Boyett was the duty detective on the major crimes squad and responded. During the next weeks, Detective Boyett and other police officers identified July Marcial and began a long process to find her killer. That process included an autopsy and forensic exam that identified DNA found in and on the body of Ms. Marcial as well as that piece of carpet. Interviews with various witnesses indicated that Ms. Marcial was last seen leaving her hotel with a white male who resembled the defendant. The autopsy also indicated that there was an abrasion on Ms. Marcial's middle right toe, which was made after she was deceased. The testimony will detail how Detective Boyett issued subpoenas for records of various hotels as well as telephone companies in an effort to determine who Ms. Marcial was in contact with during her last days. Eventually, Detective Boyett got promoted and reassigned and this case went cold, meaning it did not get the attention it deserved.

"In 2018, last summer, Detective Sergeant Boyett was assigned to the new cold case squad. He immediately began taking a look back at the Marcial case with fresh eyes. This time, it became pretty clear that the prime suspect was the defendant, Franco Russo. Over the next months, Boyett worked with the Ohio Bureau of Investigation to obtain DNA from Russo. That DNA was submitted to the Alabama Department of Forensic Sciences and matched the DNA found at the crime scene. Detective Boyett, working with my office, presented the case to a grand jury, which issued a true bill of indictment charging Franco Russo with the murder of July Marcial, thirteen years ago today. You are going to hear testimony about the arrest of Russo, how police found evidence, including a toe ring that July Marcial had been wearing, at Russo's house, and you will hear a tape where Russo admitted to the murder. At the end of this trial, we are going to ask you to weigh all the evidence and to find the defendant guilty of the murder of July Marcial. Thank you for your time."

When Mueller sat down, Jacobs stood and addressed the jury. He explained to the jury that the job of the jury was to be the decider of facts in the case. That the jury should listen to the prosecution, but not decide on guilt or innocence until everyone had testified and all the evidence was in. At one point, he walked over in front of the jury and held up his hand, with the palm facing the jury.

"See my hand?" asked Jacobs. "If I asked you to describe it, how would you do that? You'd probably say it appears to be soft, with four fingers and a thumb running away from the palm. You might describe the lines on the palm, some of which we sometimes refer to as lifelines. This one here"—he pointed with the other hand—"runs from about one-half inch above the thumb down to my wrist. There are two additional lines running across the palm. How many joints are there in my fingers? Let's count: one, two, three. So, I know some of you are wondering why I'm talking about my hand. Well, now that we've described my hand, I want you to see the entire hand." And with that, he flipped the back of his hand toward the jury.

"Now describe my hand," he continued. "There is no palm or soft tissue. Instead, we have knuckles. The joints are there, but the middle joint is the most pronounced and we have fingernails on this side. It's quite different from the other side. So, as we go through this trial, be aware that the prosecution will only show you one side. Thank you." And with that, Jacobs returned to the defense table looking rather pleased with himself.

As the case began, Boyett took the witness stand and gave his recollection of the crime scene as well as the many pieces of evidence he'd located and processed. He brought the case up to the time of his promotion and transfer back into patrol. He continued with his transfer to the cold case squad and the events that led to obtaining Russo's DNA and the subsequent search warrant. Boyett testified about the search locating the envelopes in Russo's house and how upon examining the one marked "July," he knew that the toe ring was the one John Hood had described. He further testified about Russo's confession and his admission to strangling Marcial.

As the prosecution wrapped up the direct examination of Boyett, Defense Attorney Jacobs began cross examination. Boyett and Wood had discussed the potential attacks that Jacobs may attempt. Instead, Jacobs asked Boyett how he and Russo got along.

"Well, we got along fairly well, although it was only a couple days that we talked," said Boyett, wondering where this line of questioning was heading.

"You found Mr. Russo to be a fairly personable guy. A likable fellow. Isn't that right, Detective Boyett?" asked Jacobs.

"I'd say during the times we spoke, we had no animosity, no conflicts. He was cooperative and we got along."

"Thank you, Detective," said Jacobs. "I have no further questions," he told the court.

Boyett left the stand stunned at Jacob's approach. If this was going to be Russo's defense, he might as well have just pled guilty.

Over the next two days, Gloria Wood put on witness after witness, including J.T. Palmer, the forensic team, the medical examiner, and the custodian of records from the various hotels and telephone companies, and laid a foundation that left little doubt that Russo was in Mobile on February 28, 2006, that he was in communication with July Marcial, and that his DNA was left both in and on Marcial's body as well as on the carpet her body was found in.

The jury also heard and saw Marcial's cell phone, driver's license, and toe ring. They heard from John Hood, who explained his relationship with Marcial and related how she was a talented musician with lots of potential. During his testimony, Hood teared up several times.

Finally, Jim Massarelli took the stand. Wood asked him about how the investigation had ended up in northeast Ohio and about the search warrant that had been executed. Wood, as previously planned, only questioned Massarelli about the items found at Russo's home related to July Marcial, including the toe ring, her cell phone, and driver license. She asked about the taping of the confession.

Massarelli explained how the Ohio BCI's interview room was wired and how the interview of Russo had been recorded. The jury only heard an edited version of the confession that involved Marcial's murder. During each of the prosecution witnesses, Jacobs asked few questions and with some witnesses, he did not ask a single question.

By the afternoon of March 4, the prosecution had presented everything they wished to present. One thing they had not presented was Russo's confession to or evidence of his indictments for the eleven other murders. Gloria Wood thought that while it might have strengthened the case, it might prejudice the jury and give cause for an appeal. Besides, if he beat this case, he had a bunch more to face.

It was time for Jacobs to give his statement and present his defense. He started off by telling the jury that instead of presenting evidence, he was going to argue his closing and not present any witnesses.

Boyett was in disbelief. Three days ago, Jacobs had promised to show the jury the other side of the hand and now he came with nothing.

Closing arguments resembled the trial itself, with Gloria Wood hammering home the witness testimony and evidence, each one pointing to Russo. Meanwhile, when it was Jacob's turn to present his closing statement, he said little. He mentioned how nice it was that the district attorney's office had tied everything up in a tidy package with a big bow on top—if one believed the government—

but that there was no reason people should automatically believe the government. For that reason, the jury should give Russo the benefit of the doubt and find him not guilty.

As Jacobs finished his closing arguments, Judge Wellborn called the two attorneys to a side bar. After a brief conversation, the judge announced he was going to recess until Wednesday March 6, as the next day was Mardi Gras Day and the courthouse would be closed. The judge told the attorneys he would begin his charge on Wednesday at 9:00 a.m.

As court closed for the day, several members of the prosecution team agreed to meet for drinks. Boyett told them he had some things to do and would try to catch up with them. With the streets being closed for the evening parades, Boyett walked the few blocks down to Royal Street and entered the very bar where Russo had described first seeing July Marcial. When he entered, there was a band playing 70's rock. The lead singer was a female about twenty-three, who appeared to be far better than the band she fronted. Boyett drank a beer, reflecting on how precious life was and how many different people's paths converged to determine everyone's future, especially July Marcial's.

On Wednesday morning, after everyone had assembled in the courtroom, Judge Wellborn began his charge. "Members of the jury, in any jury trial there are, in effect, two judges. I am one of the judges; the other is the jury. It is my duty to preside over the trial and to decide what evidence is proper for your consideration. It is also my duty at the end of the trial to explain to you the rules of law that you must follow and apply in arriving at your verdict."

Boyett caught his mind wandering instead of paying attention and looking alert. As the jury charge continued, he forced himself back to the here and now. As Judge Wellborn finished his jury charge and the jury filed out to the jury room, Boyett caught Russo glancing over at him.

The judge recessed the court pending the return of the jury.

Boyett asked Jacobs, now that the trial was over, whether the no contact order with Russo still applied.

Jacobs replied, "Absolutely. This case isn't over until all appeals have been exhausted, Detective," he added.

Boyett looked at Russo, who gazed down at the floor—whether from defeat or regret, Boyett had no idea.

The jury did not deliberate for very long, which was the expectation considering the absence of a real defense. After only one hour and fifteen minutes, the jury notified Judge Wellborn that they had a verdict. At that time, most of the people involved in the case, including Massarelli and John Hood, entered the courtroom and took seats in the row behind the prosecution table. Several members of the media were also present, although cameras were not allowed in the actual courtroom. As the jury filed into the courtroom, Boyett could tell by the glances and smiles that the verdict had gone the right way.

When Judge Wellborn asked the jury if they'd reached a verdict, the foreman, an older African-American man, replied, "Yes, Your Honor." He handed a verdict slip to the bailiff, who walked it over to the judge.

The judge ordered the defendant to stand. "In the matter of the State of Alabama versus Franco Russo, charging you with first-degree murder, the jury has reached a decision." Judge Wellborn was holding and began to read for the jury form. "In the matter of Alabama versus Franco Russo, we, the jury, find the defendant guilty of murder in the first degree."

With that, the defense made a motion to poll the jury. Judge Wellborn agreed and one by one asked each juror if the verdict was in fact the verdict that they'd agreed upon. In all cases, it was. When this was completed, Judge Wellborn thanked the jury and before dismissing them, told them they were not required to explain their actions to anyone, including the media that might confront them outside the courthouse.

After the jury was dismissed, Judge Wellborn asked both sides if there were any other motions before he set the sentencing date and adjourned for the day. Neither side made a motion and Judge Wellborn set sentencing for April 16, 2019.

The media was waiting in the hall outside the courtroom as well as outside the building. Barry Mueller was giving interviews.

Boyett was approached by numerous reporters. He told each one that the department's PIO should be contacted. Meanwhile, Massarelli was free to speak to whoever he wished. His comments were mostly limited to talking about the great cooperative effort of the Mobile Police Department and the Ohio BCI, as well as what the process was for Russo being transferred back to Ohio for a trial there.

The day ended, and Boyett headed home to his family. He felt exhausted. Although it was a clear win for the good guys and Franco Russo was off the streets for good, it seemed somewhat bittersweet. Russo was obviously a guy with some sort of mental issues that were beyond Boyett's pay grade to figure out. Maybe he would get some help in prison. Whether he did or not, the deaths of twelve women and the pain to those families would not be rectified by the guilty verdict. Boyett could tell that John Hood still blamed himself in some way for Marcial's death. He, himself, had suffered many sleepless nights and too much time away from his family and friends because of this case. In the end, justice had been served, but as was often the case, there really were no winners.

For More News About Doug Lamplugh,
Signup For Our Newsletter:

http://wbp.bz/newsletter

Word-of-mouth is critical to an author's long-term success. If you appreciated this book please leave a review on the Amazon sales page:

http://wbp.bz/mardigrasa

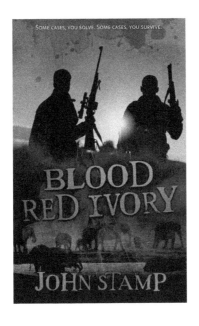

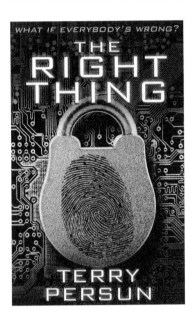

AVAILABLE FROM THOMAS O'CALLAGHAN
AND WILDBLUE PRESS!

NO ONE WILL HEAR YOUR SCREAMS
by THOMAS O'CALLAGHAN

http://wbp.bz/nowhysa

CPSIA information can be obtained
at www.ICGtesting.com
Printed in the USA
LVHW081425010422
715071LV00020B/340

9 781952 225901